Sarah

MY DIRTY LITTLE SECRET

Enjoy

CJ Foster x

MY DIRTY LITTLE SECRET

PART 2

G.S. FOSTER

The contents of this book are sexually explicit.

This book contains violent scenes which some readers may find distressing

Matador
Unit E2 Airfield Business Park,
Harrison Road, Market Harborough,
Leicestershire. LE16 7UL
Tel: 0116 2792299
Email: books@troubador.co.uk
Web: www.troubador.co.uk/matador
Twitter: @matadorbooks

ISBN 978 1805143 291

British Library Cataloguing in Publication Data.
A catalogue record for this book is available from the British Library.

Printed and bound by CPI Group (UK) Ltd, Croydon, CR0 4YY
Typeset in 11pt Minion Pro by Troubador Publishing Ltd, Leicester, UK

Matador is an imprint of Troubador Publishing Ltd

B.B. King once said 'The beautiful thing about learning, is nobody can take it away from you'.

This is very true of my author journey, I am learning to be a better writer all the time and again, with the full support of my family, friends and of course the readers, I couldn't do this without you.

THE GETAWAY

As Paul and Alice race clear in the car, from the devastation they left behind in Barnwood, they glance at each other, with a smile, almost in a sinister way.

"What are we going to do Paul, and where are we going to go?"

"Don't worry, I've brought a little something to keep us going," "let's see where the road takes us."

Alice shows a little worry on her face, whilst still looking at him.

"No regrets?" he asks, as he laughed, turning to her.

"No regrets," she replies, as they join each other's fingers, Alice raising a little grin in Paul's direction, whilst putting their little finger digits together like a chicken wishbone.

The road is dark and lonely, with just the two of them driving down the empty, narrow lanes, surrounded by churchyards and empty fields, grassland blowing, and trees swirling around them, giving an autumnal feel.

"What did you mean Paul, when you said you had something to keep us going?"

"Never mind, it's something that I've sorted, it'll give us plenty to live on, while we work out our next move."

"I didn't think we had any secrets though?" she said, with a little concern.

"We haven't and it's not something that you need to worry yourself about." "Let's just say that it's enough to tide us over for quite a while," "just sit, relax, and look beautiful, let me do the worrying."

Alice gave him a wry smile, as he put his hand on her thigh, and slowly up the dress she was wearing when they left the house.

Paul glanced again at Alice and started looking at her bulging cleavage.

"You're not wearing any panties," he smiled at her, as her hand slid across to his hardening cock.

As he continued to drive, he spotted a lay-by, and pulled over, undoing his seatbelt, whilst Alice too undid her seatbelt, and slid across towards him, straddling him in the process.

He wanted her so much, kissing her heavily like he'd not kissed anyone for years.

"God, I want to fuck you," he groaned, as Alice started to ride him, even though his jeans were still very firmly on, despite the stiffness she was starting to feel, she wanted him inside her, as quick as she could.

They both began to kiss each other frantically, Paul trying to unzip the back of her dress at the same time, to reveal her ample chest, as well as undoing the belt on his jeans, and pulling them down, almost in the same movement, like two lusty teenagers having sex for the first time.

Suddenly he was penetrating her, sucking on her heaving chest as he did so.

Alice was loving his attention, she had not felt his hands on her body for so long, not felt the thrusting from him, and he had not felt the yearning for her for what seemed like an eternity.

Harder and harder he thrust into her, pushing deeper and deeper into the moistness of her pussy.

"Oh god baby, fuck me hard," she cried, pulling his sweaty head into her chest, which had beads of sweat dripping down it, they both rode each other faster, however awkward it was on the car seat.

They suddenly both let a gasp of sexual release, as he thrust every last ounce of energy from his body, sweat continuing to drip down his forehead, beads of sweat still rolling down her neck to her hard cherry red nipples.

They had both cum, she put her arms around his neck to relax, collapsing, and laying herself into him, whilst still staying straddled on his lap.

They stayed motionless for a few moments, still filled with unrivalled lust for each other, having not had any contact with each other during their plan in Barnwood.

"So, what did you mean when you said you had something that would keep us going for a while?" she asked again.

"Doesn't matter, let's just say we've got plenty to live on," "come on, we need to go."

Alice got off Paul's lap, and adjusted her dress, before pulling herself over to the passenger's side and putting her seatbelt back on.

Paul managed to pull his jeans back up, adjusting his belt, putting his seat belt on, before pulling out of the layby and continuing to drive.

"Where are we going to go?" asked a worried Alice, "we need to go where we won't be found don't we, the police will be out looking for us."

"I've got a plan," "I know a town, it's very remote but, it's a few hours away so, you get your head down, get some rest, and I'll just drive." "I'll wake you once we're there, we'll be fine, you'll see."

She looked worryingly in his direction, after all, they'd left a scene of devastation behind them, and she was sure that they would be hunted.

She spotted a jacket in the backseat, grabbed it, and put it over her shoulders, as she was starting to feel a little cold, with them deep into the night, before slowly closing her eyes, drifting off, relaxed by the motion of the car.

"We're here," Paul nudging her, to open her eyes.

It was seven in the morning, the birds were chirping outside, and it was a warm, bright, and sunny day.

She stretched and yawned, shielding her eyes from the bright sun, having been used to the darkness, before pulling her arms out from underneath the coat, where she had felt so warm and snug during the journey, though now a little uncomfortable on the car seat.

"Where is HERE?" she said in her half-awake voice, her eyes still trying to adjust to the daylight.

"This my darling wife, is Chammerley."

"Why here?"

"I know a few people here that could hide us for a while, contacts, that sort of thing." "You'll love it here, trust me."

"You have been here before then I take it?"

Many times, yes." "Come on, let's go and get some breakfast, I'm famished, I don't know about you," he smiled, almost having a spring in his step, like the world had been lifted from his shoulders, as he raced around to the passenger's side door, to open it for Alice, before grabbing her by the hand, and elegantly leading her out into their new hideaway.

Chammerley was a busy little town, with lots of people going about their daily business; going in and out of shops with their partners and small children, it seemed like any other little town.

Alice got a few stares from some of the locals, mainly because of how she was dressed, having still been in the same clothes that she left Barnwood in.

"Come on, there's a café over there, let's go and eat," he smiled, as he led his wife by the hand, and across the street to Chammerley's Family café.

It was bright and airy, and Paul couldn't wait to order some food.

Alice paused by the café door, unsure if she could sit inside.

Paul glanced across at her as he was ordering.

"What's wrong?" he asked.

"The last time I was in a café, I was in Barnwood, and …" she paused.

Paul wandered over to her, grabbing her hand to reassure her.

"It's ok, it's all over now, remember our plan."

"I know but …" "I'll be ok in a minute."

He glanced in her direction before returning to the counter to carry on ordering.

Alice slowly wandered over to a table near the far corner of the cafe before gingerly sitting down.

"Is she ok?" said the owner, she looks like she's seen a ghost or something."

"She's ok, we've just been partying too hard, taken its toll on her, some people just can't handle it anymore, can they?" Paul chuckled, trying to make light of the situation with the café owner, so as not to raise any suspicion.

The owner of the café, Giorgio Rodrigues, was a tall, well-dressed, curly-haired man, with a dark, thick moustache, that glistened on his olive-skinned face. He had blue eyes and a beaming smile.

"What can I get for you both?"

Paul was scanning the menu above Giorgio's head, undecided about what he wanted to get for him and Alice, but wasn't too bothered anyway, he just wanted something rustled up fairly quick.

"Just rustle us up something hot, and two coffees please." "Can you make it quick, as we don't have long."

"Sure, I can do that," the café owner was a chatty man with his customers and wanted to be that way with Paul.

"Not seen you in here before, are you new to the area, or just passing through?" "Either way, you're very welcome."

"If it's all the same to you, we'd just like to eat and then just go," Paul was not in a chatty mood, he knew that they could be made known very quickly, through social media and television.

Paul was reluctant to show his face for too long, worried that they'd be recognised, and police informed as to their whereabouts.

"I'll prepare you something then sir, I was only trying to be sociable."

Paul, with his head bowed, quickly walked back to the table where Alice sat, and waited for their food and coffee.

"Are we going to be here long?" Alice sighed, "I'm getting hungry and tired."

"We've got food coming, we'll get that down us, then we'll go and find somewhere to stay for the night ok."

A waitress was soon approaching them, holding a tray of food, and two coffees.

The tall, dark-haired waitress looked in Alices' direction, smiling at her.

Alice stared back at the waitress, with a smile of her own, looking the waitress up and down, and provocatively biting her bottom lip.

Alice glanced at the waitress's breasts that were bulging out of her blouse, with the waitress bending down, putting the plates of hot food and drinks on the table, and Alice couldn't help but feel a little turned on.

Both the waitress and Alice continued to gaze at each other as if they knew each other, and Paul quickly noticed this.

"That'll be all thank you," he said.

"I was only having a bit of fun," Alice huffed, "where's your sense of humour?"

"Darling, we can't be noticed here for too long, people will wonder who we are, and when the police get to Barnwood, they'll be on the look-out for us so, we need to be as inconspicuous as possible," eat your food, drink your coffee, then we really need to go," Paul was trying to make Alice see sense, that they were not in the clear, that people might start to recognise them, from the devastation of what they had just left behind.

Paul and Alice tucked into a fried breakfast; sausages, eggs, bacon, beans, toast, and their coffees, and were soon finished and good to go.

They got up from their table, and Paul wandered over to the counter to pay, his head still as bowed as possible.

"Here's a twenty, keep the change," Paul left the note on the counter with Giorgio, before grabbing his wife's hand and leading her out of the door.

"Thank you for your … custom, hope to see you again …soon," came the reply from the café owner, with a half wave, but he was too late with his gratitude, the couple had already left his shop.

They hurriedly walked down the road, and came across a Guest House, which had rooms available to let.

"This'll do, let's check in here, maybe the odd night or two but, we may soon need to move on, we might have to keep moving around," Paul could see that his wife was still feeling a bit weary from the travelling they had been doing, fleeing Barnwood.

They walked up the steps, and into the Greendale Guest House, where they were met by a middle-aged lady; plump, frumpily dressed in a pink one-piece flowery dress, that looked like had been bought in the sixties, with bushy, greying hair.

"Hello, I'm Mrs Bloombury, are you looking for a room?"

"A double if you have one, maybe a few nights," Paul had been left to do all the talking, Alice was feeling too tired to do anything.

Mrs Bloombury checked her guest book and saw that a double was indeed available for them.

"Ah, yes we have, follow me, and I'll show you to your room."

The couple walked behind Mrs Bloombury as she led up the stairs.

"Here we are, room two-zero-nine," "there are tea and coffee making facilities, room service, and we offer a full English breakfast, which starts at seven in the morning, until ten-thirty." "We also offer lunch and an evening meal, if you'd like that too?"

Paul glanced at the guest-house owner, with a cold stare that spoke a thousand words, she didn't have to say anything else.

"Well, erm, you know where we are, make yourselves comfortable, and welcome," before Mrs Bloombury abruptly left the room.

"We can bed down here for now, until we work out our next move," Alice sat on the bed, and looked forlornly in his direction.

"Are we constantly going to be on the run Paul?"

"Just for now, until things start to settle down," "besides, it'll probably be a while before they find her body anyway."

"How can you say that?" "they'll soon notice her missing at work, her girls aren't stupid."

Paul walked over to her, from where he had been standing, and got down on his knees to talk to her, to put her mind at rest.

"Look, don't worry, it's all under control." "You know how Sarah went on her business trips, they'll just think that she's gone on another one, at least for a while." "When someone starts to notice that something is up, we'll be long gone, don't worry, I've got all bases covered."

"... and how are we going to live? How are we going to pay for staying here?"

"As I say, I've got it all under control." "Go and grab yourself a shower, I'm just going to pop out for a while, and speak to a few people, I shouldn't be too long." "Get yourself a bite to eat."

Paul went over to kiss her, but her reaction was very unresponsive, like she didn't enjoy the situation they were in, and maybe wished that things were different but, she had gone along with the plan, she just had to trust him.

Alice jumped up from the bed to head for a shower, just as he was heading out of the door.

She pondered on how things were going to turn out, but she had faith in her husband, whatever plans he had, and what the future held for them.

As she got undressed to get in the shower, which was sparkly clean, and looked very inviting, her dress fell seductively to the floor.

She also remembered the times she had showered with Sarah, and how sexy they were. She turned the large shower head on, and the water started to spray down her perfectly formed body. Alice started to fantasise about how Sarah used to touch her, she was feeling very turned on and started to touch her pussy, in a way that Sarah used to. She paused, as she found a sponge, and lathered some shower cream into it, soaping up her ample breasts and hardening nipples, slowly working the suds down to her pussy, again, fantasising that Sarah was doing it instead.

Alice worked the sponge harder onto her waiting lips,

grinding against it, as the spray from the shower lashed down onto her head, her hair now soaked with water, spraying onto her toned skin, down her arms and onto her pussy.

Harder and harder she ground onto the sponge between her legs, her breathing becoming faster and heavier, her hand clasped to the wall of the shower, as she could feel her juices flowing inside her, she knew that she wanted to cum.

Caressing her breasts as she did so, she pushed hard onto the sponge, grabbing it tighter, before letting out an emotional burst of energy, her legs quivering, as she exploded all she had.

Her breathing started to slow, feeling like she had run a race, she needed to cum so much, she missed Sarah because she knew how good she was at making her cum as hard as she had just done.

Her breathing had just about returned to normal after her sexual excitement, she carried on with her shower, washing her hair, and continuing to wash her body with the shower gel provided.

She was soon done, and turned the shower head off, before stepping out and wrapping the towel around her.

She also grabbed a smaller towel to dry her hair with and found a purple hairdryer in the room.

She pulled a brush out from her bag, that she had taken to Sarah's the night before, and partially dried her hair, before brushing her damp, blonde curls with it.

She unravelled the hairdryer cord, plugged it into the wall, and turned it on.

'He's been gone ages; I wonder what he's doing?' she thought to herself.

'Hmmm now, what to eat,' she thought.

She picked up a menu resting on the side table and started looking through it.

There was an array of food and snacks to choose from; sandwiches, hot food, alcohol, but she had her eye on something hot, she hadn't eaten since the café, and that was only something light.

'That looks nice, I'll have that I think, maybe with a glass of wine'.

She picked up the phone and pressed zero for room service.

"Yes hello, room two zero nine here, could I order some food please to be brought up to the room?"

The phone on reception was answered by a softly spoken woman, definitely not Mrs Bloomsbury, and sounded younger.

Alice liked the sound of this woman and hoped it would be her who would bring it up.

"Yes, what would you like?" said the woman.

'You' thought Alice.

"Erm, I'll have the toasted ham and cheese sandwich please, and maybe a bottle of your finest white wine, sweet preferably."

"Will it be you who will bring it?" she continued.

"Yes," "we've got quite a lot of staff on today so, I'll bring it up to you."

"Twenty to thirty minutes," the waitress replied.

"Can't wait," Alice purred before she put the phone down.

Alice was relaxing on the bed, looking forward to her food, but also contemplating what life was going to be like in the future.

Suddenly, there was a knock on the door.

"Room service" came the voice.

"Come in," replied Alice, and in walked a stunning, tall, dark-haired woman, her hair shoulder length, piercing green eyes, leggy, and wearing a black and white maid's outfit, and carrying her food and bottle of wine that she requested.

"Oh, just pop it on the table over there will you honey, thank you," Alice had taken an immediate shine to the attractive girl, and wanted to admire her just a bit more before she had to leave the room.

The woman did as she was asked, and put Alice's food on the table, near the window in the room, which was situated close to the en-suite bathroom, which was a large bathroom, with a plush walk-in shower, and roll-top bath.

"… and what's your name?" Alice was curious as to who this beautiful, sexy lady was.

"It's Isobelle," said the shy maid, with an awkward smile in Alice's direction.

"Well Isobelle, thank you, I will be ordering more in a while, especially if it's YOU who's going to bring it up to me," Alice provocatively putting her index finger to her opening full red lips, the tip of her tongue also coming to the front of her mouth, whilst looking the maid up and down at the same time.

"Is there anything else I can help you with?" asked Isobelle.

"Hmm, not just now but, if I think of something, I'll be sure to give you a call," Alice was feeling in need of some female attention, and was missing Sarah, who she knew would have given it to her.

The maid smiled and blushed, her cheeks going bright red, slightly nervous at the attention she was being given, knowing that Alice was making a pass at her, before turning around and leaving the room, closing the door gently behind her, giving Alice a final smile as she left.

She walked over to the table where her food and bottle of wine had been left, picked her tray up, and took it back over to the bed, she was far too comfy on it to want to move anywhere else.

'What is taking him so long?' she thought but was also too hungry and thirsty to think of that at the minute.

Alice poured herself a glass of wine, in a tall-stemmed wine glass, thinking that the glass would easily hold half of the bottle, and reminiscing how she would meet Sarah for a drink at the bar during lunch at work.

She soon scoffed down her ham and cheese toasted sandwich and was thinking of ordering some more, as she was still feeling a little peckish.

She got up from the bed, and walked over to the window, glancing outside, to see if she could see Paul anywhere.

Chammerley was a hive of activity, with lots of men walking around, some women, and a few children. She suddenly caught sight of him, talking to a rather well-built balding middle-aged man, puffing on a cigarette, looking like his grey suit had seen better days. She also noticed that Paul was holding a rather large brown bag, stuffed with god knows what inside.

She stood staring out of the window at the men, as the large man whom Paul was talking to, suddenly glanced up at her, giving her a stare that she found very uncomfortable, his gaze almost piercing through her eyes.

She suddenly pulled herself away from the window, out of sight of the man's stare, and went and laid back on the bed, sitting upright.

A few minutes had passed, and she could hear footsteps coming towards the door.

Paul then hurried inside, closing the door, like he didn't want to be seen, still holding the rather large, brown bag, a bag that looked worn and tired.

"Who were you talking to out there, and what is in that bag you're holding?"

"He's just an acquaintance of mine, we go way back, and erm, this is our escape out of here," he was sounding very guarded about what the contents of the bag were.

"Escape route? "What is that supposed to mean?"

Paul went and sat down on the edge of the bed where she was sitting and decided to explain to her in more detail what he meant.

"While I was away from you in Barnwood, I got involved with drugs, well, Dean got me involved," Paul was making very little sense to her.

"Wait… what?" Alice wanted a clearer picture of what was going on.

"I basically got involved with a drugs baron, and he threatened to hurt my family if I didn't do his shit for him."

"Why didn't you just report him to the police?"

"Darling, they're as crooked as he is, he has friends in VERY HIGH PLACES, I was being watched all the time." "One word to the police, it would have got back to him, then mine or my family's lives would not have been worth living." "I had to go along with it, it just seemed like the easier option to me."

"So, what's in the bag?" "What's your plan?"

He smiled at her, a smile as wide as the Grand Canyon, as he reached down to the scruffy bag that he had brought in with him.

"THIS, MY DARLING WIFE, is our escape route."

He pulled the bag up from the floor and put it on his lap.

He opened the zip of the bag, itself, looking like it could fall off at any minute, and pulled it sharply open.

"Now THIS is what I mean by our escape route."

Alice looked inside and saw what on appearance, looked like a hell of a lot of money.

"Where the HELL did you get all this, or shouldn't I ask?" "I take it this money is dirty?"

"As I said, I was pushing some stuff around, I was given a haul to distribute, but don't worry, I've been able to sell the stuff I had, that's what I've been doing since I've been out," Paul was doing his best to reassure Alice that the drugs were gone, and they had enough money to survive, at least for the time being.

"They're going to catch up with us, are you CRAZY not to realise that?" "Then there's the police to think about too", Alice was concerned that they were in a lot of trouble.

Paul got up from the bed and started to pace the floor, before joining Alice back on the bed.

"Don't worry, I've got it all figured out." "We'll be ok here for tonight, maybe tomorrow too, but then we must head off again, change our names, get false documents, we'll be well hidden, away from everything, no one will know who we are." "There's a quarter of a million in that bag, it'll get us somewhere to live, but we both may need to find some work, to keep us going." "Hey, maybe you could go back and do some more modelling," Paul joked, trying to make light of the situation, as he could see that Alice was far from amused.

"Oh yeah, I'll go modelling again, why didn't I think of that!" she said, in a sarcastic tone.

"It'll only be for a short while, just while we work out our next steps, just let things settle down." "Let's change the subject, shall we?" "Let's order some food, I'm famished," he laid on the bed next to Alice, and went to put his arm around her, but she was still in a mood with him, and shot off the bed, practically as soon as he got on it.

"Where are you going?"

"I'm heading for a shower, ALONE." "You order yourself something, I'm not hungry."

Alice walked briskly towards the bathroom, before slamming the door shut to go for her shower.

Paul lay on the bed to contemplate their next move, as he heard the shower turn on.

"You sure I can't get you something?" he shouted, not knowing if she could hear him or not.

"NO, I've already eaten!" came the reply, as he picked up the menu that was next to the bed.

'Hmm, it all looks so good, I might have a steak sandwich, then take my beautiful wife out for dinner tonight, that might cheer her up a little' he muttered to himself.

He picked up the phone, pressed zero, and was greeted by an attractive voice.

"Hello reception, how can I help?"

"Hi yes, Room two zero nine here, I was wondering if I could order some food?"

"Of course sir, what would you like?"

Paul was liking the sound of the woman on the phone, so softly spoken.

"Yes, can you bring me up a steak sandwich please, English mustard on it too, if you have any, and maybe some of your local bottled beer too?"

"How would you like your steak cooked sir?"

"Rare to medium please," how long are we looking?"

"Be about 30 minutes sir if that's ok?"

"That's fine," replied Paul, "just add it to the room tab please."

"Anything else I can get you sir?" said the girl on reception.

"That'll be all for now thank you," before putting the phone back down on the receiver.

He pondered what the girl looked like who he'd just spoken to, just as Alice had probably also done earlier.

He could still hear the shower going but knew that Alice enjoyed long showers.

"You ok in there?" he shouted.

Just then, the shower turned off, and a short few moments later, Paul saw his stunning wife come out with a towel wrapped around her toned body, and another towel wrapped around her head.

She still looked in a mood with him, so he was unsure whether he should talk to her or not.

"I've ordered myself something to eat, should be here in a bit, but thought I'd take you out tonight, better than constantly being stuck in here."

Alice came and laid back on top of the bed, the towels still wrapped around her.

"Maybe," she grinned at him, starting to feel a little less annoyed, coming to terms with their situation.

"Then, maybe, we could erm, come back here, and have a little fun," he teased, as his hand was slowly starting to slide up the white fluffy towel clasping her olive skin, and up between her legs.

Alice started to part her legs for him, so he could touch her easier, as he teased her moist pussy, still wet from the shower, but also feeling wet for him too.

"Mmmmm, that feels nice," she purred, as his fingers started to go deeper inside her.

"Ah baby, that feels so good, mmmmm, don't stop," but Paul got off the bed, hurriedly taking his jeans and shirt off, just as Alice was pulling the towel off her drying body, and putting it in a heap on the floor.

He jumped back on the bed, and went down between her legs, swirling his tongue around her clit, sucking it every so often, and sliding two or three fingers in and out of her.

"OH MY GOD, I want you inside me now," she purred.

Paul kissed his way up her curvy body, kissing her ample breasts and sucking on her nipples, before sliding his erect cock deep inside her, thrusting hard, and getting as deep as he could.

The bed was banging hard on the wall, she was clasping his arse cheeks, feeling the motion of him passionately thrusting inside her, her hands all over his muscly chest.

Their breathing became faster and harder, he wanted her so much.

Just then, there was a knock on the door.

"Erm, room service," came the voice.

"Ok, erm, we'll be right there," Paul was quickly trying to find something to put on.

Alice recognised the voice as being the same girl who brought her food up earlier.

"No, do come in," teased Alice with a smile at Paul, as the door was gently opened.

"Oh, erm, I am sorry, I'll come back," said the waitress, feeling slightly embarrassed that the pair were still naked.

"Don't be silly," Alice smiled at her, "close the door and put the food on the table."

Alice noticed that Isobelle was peaking around at her, every so often, as Paul watched on, his erection still in clear view.

"Now, you brought me some lovely food earlier, and I was rude, and didn't leave you a tip did I," she teased. "Now, what tip can we give her Paul?"

Alice got off the bed and slowly wandered over to Isobelle, who didn't quite know what to do but was seemingly in no real hurry to leave either.

Alice slowly and seductively walked around her, brushing her hand over her body as she did so, around her breasts and waist, before coming round to face her.

She pulled herself in close to the waitress, and gently ran her fingers through her hair, looking Isobelle up and down.

Alice pulled her lips closer to Isobelle's, to see if she would react, or even struggle to break free, but she didn't, and it seemed that Isobelle was getting quite turned on by the idea, whatever Alice had planned for her.

Their lips gently touched, and Isobelle responded by nervously kissing her back, wrapping her hands around Alice's naked waist.

Alice started to unbutton Isobelle's dress from the back, as they kissed, before the dress fell to the floor, revealing dark stockings and red lacy underwear.

Alice pulled away, taking her by the hand, and leading her to the bed, before laying her down, Alice climbing on top of her.

Paul was starting to get very aroused, seeing the two of them having fun with each other, and he wanted a piece of the action.

"I can't be long," Isobelle whispered, "I'll be sacked otherwise."

Alice was too busy pulling Isobelle's knickers off, kissing her way around her body, kissing between her legs, exploring her pussy with her tongue, just as Paul had been doing on her moments before, Isobelle was starting to pant with pleasure.

"Oh GOD, hmmm, that feels so good, please keep doing that, hmmm, right there, ah baby," Isobelle was in the height of ecstasy, tightly grabbing the back of the bed, passion running through her body.

Alice pulled herself up, so she could kiss her, both girls' bodies meeting as one.

"I want some too," chuckled Paul, as he also clambered onto the bed, first kissing his wife's bare back, before kissing between Isobelle's thighs, then sucking her pussy.

Alice lay beside her, Paul getting between her legs, and sliding his still-erect cock deep into Isobelle's pussy.

Harder and harder he thrust, Alice sucking her nipples, Isobelle also caressing and kissing Alice's breasts and erect nipples.

The girls continued to kiss, as the force of Paul having sex with Isobelle, was banging the headboard against the room wall, and he knew that he was soon going to cum.

Isobelle's breath quickened, as she too felt that she was going to explode with ecstasy, while Alice fingered herself watching them.

Suddenly, the three of them all slowed their pace, they had all cum, Isobelle's and Paul's legs both quivering, Alice still feeling like she'd still had fun too.

Paul climbed off her and laid beside her, Alice going to sit at the bottom of the bed, as they all started to try and catch their breaths.

"I really must go," they'll wonder where I've got to."

Isobelle clambered off the bed, smiling across at them both as she did, grabbing her dress from the floor, before hurriedly putting it back on.

"Let me help you," smiled Alice, walking over to the waitress, and helped do her dress up at the back.

Isobelle was now dressed and made sure her hair was looking as nice as it was when she got to the room.

"Your sandwich will be cold now sir," smiling to Paul, would you like me to go and warm it back up for you?"

"Don't worry about that," he laughed, "you both more than satisfied me for now."

Isobelle glanced over at them both, smiled, and left the room.

Alice, still catching her breath after the sex session, was still worried about what their future held.

"Paul, don't you think we should get out of here tonight, maybe take Isobelle with us to keep us warm, so to speak."

"One more night isn't going to do any harm, I'm sure we'll be ok here tonight, but then, yes, we must plan our move away from here," "I don't think carrying an extra passenger would be such a good idea, do you?"

"I know but… yeah, you're probably right."

Though she longed for a female companion, missing Sarah as much as she did.

"We're going to need to change our identities too, maybe disguises, we've got to try and avoid the police as much as we can." I've got a contact who can get us some fake passports, maybe get away for a bit."

"Where did you have in mind?" she asked.

"Anywhere, just away from here, just while things settle down, it wouldn't be for long." "Why don't you get dressed, and I'll take us to dinner," Paul was trying to keep things as normal as possible.

"I've got nothing to wear though have I, apart from this dress?"

"That's ok, you look sexy in it, just wear that tonight, and we'll go shopping tomorrow when we get away from here."

"Where are we going anyway, you've still not told me?" Alice was intrigued as to what he had planned.

"There's a city I know, it's about 100 miles from here, maybe a bit more, it's called Lansburton, and you're just going to love it there."

"Sounds posh," "ok, let's roll," Alice was starting to come to terms with their position, and if it bided them some time, she'd go with it.

She got off the bed, grabbing the dress she had been wearing, seeing that she didn't really have anything else to wear, before going to the bathroom, swiping up the large towel from the floor that she used to wrap around herself earlier. She also decided to get back into the shower, after the frolic she'd had with Paul and Isobelle, wanting to smell fresher and more alive.

She closed the door behind her, and got back in, turning the shower head on full blast.

She contemplated where this new life was going to lead them both, as the water sprayed down on her, she lathered up her toned, bronzed body, using the sponge that was provided to wash with, first her face, before slowly circling her neck and down to her ample breasts, before she worked on her flat stomach, her thighs, her bum and to make sure that she covered herself all over, going down to her knees and lower legs, before washing herself further up her body.

She momentarily paused, remembering how Sarah used to do this for her, making love in the shower, as well as on her bed, it was something she missed.

Alice loved Paul, but she also missed the touch of another woman, especially being with Stacey all the time she had, and of course, the time she had spent with Sarah.

Alice gently touched herself, thinking about her times with the girls, and started to feel a little turned on by the images in her head, as the spray from the shower head, continued to pour down onto her, like being in a heavy rainfall, but, warmer.

She began to touch herself once more, slowly fingering herself, circling her clit with her middle finger, as her breath quickened.

She was becoming more and more aroused, touching her pussy and caressing her right breast as she did, her nipples hardening.

'Maybe we can smuggle Isobelle along somehow' she fantasised.

"Are you ok in there?" came the cry from the bedroom. "Didn't want to leave it too long before we went out.

"Nearly done," she called, turning the shower head off, being interrupted by her sexual thoughts.

Alice grabbed the towel that she had taken back in with her, and wrapped it around herself, before opening the door and re-entering the bedroom.

"God I've got a sexy wife, lucky me," Paul raised a smile in Alice's direction.

She was still in her thoughts for the ladies she left behind, but this was a new chapter, and one that she was excited about, if a bit apprehensive.

She let the towel fall to the floor, her long flowing blonde locks, still dripping, even after she had given it a gentle rub with the towel.

Paul couldn't keep his eyes off her, as he got off the bed that he sat on, whilst waiting for her to finish her shower, he stood up behind her, Alice still hot from her shower, and wrapped his arms around her waist.

She could feel him starting to get aroused once again, his cock pressing against her juicy arse, as he slowly kissed his way around her neck, and nibbled her ears.

"Thought you were taking me out to dinner?" she chuckled, though still enjoying the attention he was giving her.

"I am but, can't help wanting you can I," he whispered, his breath becoming denser, clearly getting very turned on once again.

"We need to make our plan don't we, but we can do

it later I guess," Alice was still feeling a bit nervous about going out, especially after the aftermath in Barnwood, whilst trying to ease Paul off her at the same time, so she could get ready for dinner.

Paul could see that she was just wanting to get ready and realised that she was right, wanting to get out, eat, and plan their course of action later.

Alice was soon dressed, in lacy black underwear and an elegant dress, and Paul in his clothes from earlier, though not quite smelling the best, as he'd practically been in them for a few days.

He went to the bathroom to freshen up as best he could, washed, and brushed his teeth, using his finger, from some toothpaste that had been provided in the room.

"Ready?" he smiled at Alice, as he grabbed her hand, and lead her out of the room, before locking up.

They walked down the corridor, and down the stairs of the Guest House, being greeted by the owner, Mrs Bloombury, on their way down.

"Going somewhere nice?" she smiled at them, being a warm and kind lady.

"It's a surprise," Paul smiled back, as he carried on leading his wife out into Chammerley.

"Where ARE we going?" she quizzed, unsure as to her surroundings.

"I kind of know this area, and I have a few people to meet along the way too," "don't worry, no expense spared for my wife," he smiled at her, clutching her hand tighter, in an acknowledgement of security.

"People to meet?" she asked, "I thought it was just going to be me and you for dinner, and I thought all your business had been sorted?" this made her feel slightly uneasy.

"Don't worry, they're not joining us, just a little bit of business to sort out, then it is just me and you darling."

Alice still looked glamorous in the dress that she had been wearing, hardly a hair out of place, and looking every inch the model that she previously was, and Paul still looked smart in his suit, apart from looking slightly dishevelled.

"Ready?" he asked.

Alice glared at him, almost with a sense of disdain, knowing that she wasn't going to be alone with her husband for the evening.

It was around five in the afternoon, and Paul walked her confidently towards a restaurant that Chammerley was famous for, 'Chammerley's Champion Steakhouse'.

It was a popular place to eat for locals, albeit a very expensive one.

Paul opened the door for his wife to walk in, and she was impressed with the décor and the layout of the restaurant.

She glanced around, the restaurant was both very clean and airy, but also very warm, especially with the openness of the kitchen and the hot plates, where the various dishes were being prepared by the chefs.

She could see many staff busying themselves, going up to tables to clear plates, as well as tending to new customer needs.

She could also see many people with smiles on their faces, laughing and joking, and this put her at ease, it wasn't at all like she imagined it would be. She had a vision that it was going to be very dark and dingy, so she was pleasantly surprised.

They were both greeted by the front of house, the manager, Harry Longthorn.

"Good afternoon sir, madam, are you looking …" ah, dear Paul, it has been so long", Paul was then greeted with the biggest hug, like old friends.

"How long has it been?" Harry smiled, "and this is?"

"This is my wife, Alice," Paul smiled back.

"Such exquisite taste you have my dear friend," come, let me find you the best table."

Paul and Alice followed him to where they were being led, to a table almost slap bang in the middle of the restaurant.

"It's so good to see you again Paul, it really has been too long." "I will get a waiter over to see to you straight away," Harry smiled, "… and I'll be over myself a bit later to see if you're enjoying our food, and to have a quick catch-up."

Paul grinned and nodded to him, as Harry walked away, to leave them to settle in.

Harry quickly returned with menus for them both.

"Here you go, take a look at what we have to offer you this afternoon, and here's a little something from me, on the house," Harry was passed a bottle of the restaurant's finest champagne by one of the waiters, quickly followed by a bucket full of ice, for the bottle to sit in.

"You really are so welcome here again Paul, you really shouldn't leave it so long, we MUST catch up," Harry beamed, he had the widest smile anyone could have, seeing Paul again.

Harry paused momentarily, glancing briefly at them both, before turning around and walking away, leaving the couple to decide what they were going to have to eat.

"Is that who you had come to see?" Alice asked, "he seemed nice."

"No, it was, erm, it was …" Paul was scanning the room, almost forgetting that his wife was there with him.

Paul then spotted two men who he had come to meet, Charlie Grunge and Karl Mahoney.

"I'll be back in, erm …" Paul quickly stood up to walk away.

"… aren't you going to at least pour …" but, it was too late, he was up and gone, walking over to the two men that he'd gone to see, spotting them sitting at another table.

'Guess I'll have to pour my own champagne then,' she thought.

She plucked the champagne out of the silver ice bucket, the ice cubes clinking as she did, and popped the cork from the bottle, making the loudest sound, making many in the restaurant turn round to Alice's table to see what she was doing, it was so loud, it was as if shots were being fired.

She turned her large champagne flute over and began to pour the champagne in, fizzing as it went into the glass.

She was getting lots of admiring glances from both men and women from other tables, no doubt noticing how glamorous she was looking and, not to be rude, she glanced and nodded back to those who were, raising a genuine smile.

She too then scanned the room, admiration still raining down in her direction from various tables.

She sat back, to enjoy the expensive tasting champagne that she had poured herself.

She then noticed Paul, and the other two men, walking casually back to the table where she sat.

Karl and Charlie arrogantly smile at her, both men sitting side by side with her, with Paul sitting opposite his wife, with the two men giving her somewhat of a false smile.

"Hello, I'm Karl …"

" … and I'm Charlie," Alice quickly glancing in both of their directions in acknowledgement, giving them a gentle yet nervous smile, with the men sleazily eyeing her up, looking her up and down, leaving Paul to feel distinctly uneasy, but not muttering a word, almost in fear of them, not giving his wife any kind of manly husband protection at all.

"You're a pretty little thing, aren't you?" Karl arrogantly muttered; his eyes still fixed firmly on her.

He started to stroke her arm up and down, in a creepy kind of way, giving the impression of dominance.

Alice quickly pulled her arm away, she wasn't his property, and she didn't want to be treated as such.

"DON'T TOUCH WHAT YOU CAN'T AFFORD!" she angrily snapped, making sure that he knew exactly how she felt by his advances, and they weren't wanted.

"Ah, feisty, I like that," he chuckled to Paul, who tried to raise somewhat of another false yet nervous grin in his direction.

Charlie wasn't saying too much, he was still busy looking Alice up and down, yet she could sense this, turning round, and giving him as angry a scowling look as she had just given Karl, Charlie pushing himself away from her a little in the process.

"So then Arnold, have we conducted business for now?" Karl smirks, "or, is there more business to be had?" perving once again in Alice's direction as he said it.

"No, that's it for now," I'll let you know if I need to speak to you again, now, I'd like to eat with my wife if that's ok."

Both Karl and Charlie stand up at the table, glancing in both Paul's and Alices' direction.

Nice doing business with you," giving a gentle shrug of his shoulders, smouldering in his long beige Kingsman coat, that draped over him, before he pulled out a big, fat cigar from his top pocket.

"Oh, I forgot to remind you, make sure you pick up your little gift on your way out, just my little way of saying thank you for your business," giving a chilling grin, as he and Charlie turned around and walked away.

Paul stared motionless at them both, before waiting to speak to Alice.

"What did they mean by a little gift?" Alice angrily whispered, "and how have you got yourself involved with creeps like them?"

"People like that choose YOU, not the other way around," Paul was trying to reassure her that they had seen the last of them, "they won't bother us anymore, my business with them is done, now, let's eat."

Alice could feel the restaurant's eyes on her, not because of how glamorous and sexy she looked now, but more the activity at the table just now.

"I'm not sure I'm in the mood to eat now, they've put me off my food."

"Relax darling, they had just come in here for me, and I cannot see them here now, let's just enjoy our meal, then we'll head back to the room, and pack, perhaps we can leave tonight, get away a bit quicker, I'm sure we'll soon be tracked down."

He and Alice picked up the menus on the table and started to look through them, Alice still with a hint of unease at what had just happened.

A leggy waitress, with brunette hair and gleaming

white teeth and bright red lipstick, approached their table, pen and notebook in hand, and prepared to take their order.

"Are you both ready to order?" she smiled at them.

The couple both decided to have the same meal; a ten-ounce sirloin steak, medium-cooked, baby potatoes soaked in garlic sauce, and petit pois peas.

"Anything else to drink?" the waitress politely asked.

"Bring us another bottle of this champagne would you," Paul smiled, holding the bottle up that they had earlier, and that Alice had practically drunk on her own, with Paul trying to admire the attractive waitress, without being caught out by his wife.

Alice however could see that he was looking the waitress up and down, having a glint in his eye, but she too also found the waitress sexy, so she could forgive him a little, as she too was secretly looking her up and down.

"Thank you, should be twenty to thirty minutes," the waitress casually walked away, wiggling like she was on a catwalk.

As promised, their food came out, piping hot, the other bottle of champagne in the ice bucket, which had also been taken away and re-filled with fresh ice and the food was devoured in double quick time, the champagne bottle half empty.

"That was delicious, time for the bill I think," Paul smiled, as he tried to summon a waiter over.

The restaurant owner Harry came over to them and asked how their meal and service was.

"It was delicious, just need the bill now," Paul was wanting to leave as soon as possible.

"Ah, there's no need for that Paul, your meals have already been taken care of, by the two gentlemen who came over to your table earlier," Harry smiled, as if he knew what was happening, what was being discussed.

"That was very kind of them," yet he was not happy that their meal had been paid for, feeling that they were being controlled in some way.

"Well, at least let me leave a sizable tip for your waitress in that case, and your chef," Paul pulled his wallet out of his pocket, and put three fifty-pound notes on the table.

"Here's one for you too," Paul stuffing a fifty into Harry's top jacket pocket, as they departed the table, grabbing Alice by the hand to leave.

The couple left the restaurant, swiftly heading back to the room they'd booked at the guest house.

They walked back to their room for the last time, as they were prepared to leave that night.

They passed Isobelle on the corridor, the maid flashing them a little smile as the couple passed her, while Alice glanced back, and gave her a cheeky wink and a smile.

As the couple entered the room, Alice had something else in mind before they left, pinning Paul up against the wall near the door, slamming the room door shut with her leg.

She thrust her mouth onto his, her hand sliding between his legs, and caressing his cock.

She could feel him starting to get aroused, as she continued to kiss him ferociously.

She continued to caress him, he then, in turn, caressed her shapely body.

She was soon unbuttoning his shirt, not being able to

get it off quick enough, as he was frantically trying to undo her dress.

Paul was now hard, she pulled the top half of her dress down herself, and unclipped her bra, revealing her heaving chest.

He caressed her, they couldn't keep their hands off each other, they were now all over each other.

He went down and started to suck at her hardening nipples, as Alice started to gasp with the pleasure that was now running through her body.

As he was kissing around her breasts and neck, she began to undo the button on his trousers and soon felt a stiffness in him.

He pushed Alice away from the wall, as they both collapsed on the bed, Paul falling on top of her, as they continued their passionate moment.

He was soon kissing his way down her body, before he reached her curvy thighs, kissing his way around before his mouth began to explore her now very moist pussy.

His tongue was soon circling it, as she continued to let out groans of pleasure, beads of sweat appearing to drip down from her forehead, her thighs quivering the more he explored.

She wanted him inside her, and he duly obliged, coming up for air, cupping her breasts, before he slid his hard cock deep inside her, thrusting as hard as his energy would allow him, Alice running her nails down his back, and caressing his arse, feeling every inch of his toned olive-skinned body.

He too was perspiring all over, they were caught up in the moment of intense sex.

"Ah baby, I so want you," "I'm going to cum," then, in almost a split second, he climaxed inside her, she too seemed to cum almost simultaneously, as he collapsed on top of her, trying to catch his breath.

As they had been making love, the maid had been listening outside their door, looking round to make sure that no one was catching her, her hand touching herself intensely, her legs slightly parted, as she listened to the pair having sex, being as quiet as she could, so as not to be heard by the couple.

As soon as the maid had noticed no more sound, she got herself together, making sure that her knickers were back in the right place from her touching, and her maid's outfit was too as it should have been, before walking away, and back to her duties.

"Come on, we've got to think about moving," we can't stay around here too long."

"Where are we heading now?" Alice was unsure as to what plans he had for them.

"I'm going to drive us to that place called Lansburton remember?" "It's a bit of a drive, so, we've got a long journey ahead."

Alice, with little hesitation, got up from the bed, as he began to get himself together, putting his trousers back on, and buttoning his shirt back up.

As soon as they had gathered their things together, he picked up the bag stuffed with money, making their way out of the room as quickly as they could, before locking up and hurrying down the stairs of the guest house.

"Hang on, let me grab some money out quickly, and leave the keys on reception here," despite them wanting a quick getaway, he wanted to be as courteous as he could be.

He got out four fifty-pound notes, sticking another one on top as a tip.

There didn't appear to be anyone around, no sign of the owner or Isobelle, so they quickly made their way towards the car.

It was late, and Paul knew that he had a long drive ahead.

"Where is this place?" Alice muttered as she began to correct her dress from getting in the car and doing up the seatbelt.

"It's out in the sticks, we shouldn't be recognised there, it's pretty remote." "Now, sit back and relax, I need to concentrate.

Paul had thrown the bag in the back of the car, so it was concealed.

He had been driving for around an hour but recognised that there was still some way to go.

"I'm cold," Alice shivering in the cooler night air.

There's a jacket in the back, grab that."

Alice leaned her arm back, without looking, and felt the jacket.

There appeared to be something under the jacket, something hard.

A tired-eyed Alice looked back, to grab the coat, and, as soon as she pulled it up, noticed a certain maid, cowering underneath.

It was Isobelle!

The maid had somehow found an unlocked back door to the car and made her way inside.

The maid, in silence, looked at Alice, and put her finger

to her lips, to ask if Alice would not let him know that she was there, but, he was going to notice eventually, looking in his rear-view mirror.

Alice pulled the coat over herself, glancing occasionally back at the maid on the backseat, and kept as quiet as she could.

Paul could sense something was amiss with Alice.

"What is it?"

"Nothing, I'm erm, just starting to warm up now, this jacket is so comfy," Alice smiled at him, in the hope that it would be a while before he spotted the maid.

Alice was smiling to herself though; she had some company.

Paul glanced over to Alice, noticing that there was something on his wife's mind.

He too began to smile.

"Come on, what is it?"

"It's nothing darling, you just concentrate on the road ahead, I'll just close my eyes for a while."

Suddenly, he noticed some movement in the back of the car, just a slight movement, in his rear-view mirror. As he looked into his mirror closer, he noticed the maid in the back seat and found a place to pull over.

"What the HELL are you doing in here, get the FUCK OUT OF MY CAR!"

"Aww, leave her alone Paul, she could come in useful," Alice knew that she had more than just him now, and she did miss Sarah.

"She'll only get in the way, easier just the two of us."

"Nonsense darling, besides, whatever the plans are, I'm sure she'll come in handy."

Paul glanced angrily in Alice's direction.

"If she messes things up…"

"She won't, I'll keep an eye on her."

Alice glanced back at Isobelle, giving her a smile and a wink, as the maid sat up on the backseat, now she had been spotted, but continued to stay as quiet as she could, as to not antagonise Paul any more than she already had by being there.

Meanwhile, back in Chammerley, a familiar face had appeared…

It was Neil, the detective from Barnwood.

He had been showing photos of Paul Arnold around, but no one was saying much, as not knowing anything about him.

He also called into the café, where Paul and Alice had been the day or so before.

"Yes, they have been in here, a lovely couple," said Georgio.

"Any idea where they might be now?" Neil quizzed.

"Err, I'm sorry sir, no I don't but, you are welcome to stay for a coffee, I make the best coffee here, and maybe a bite to eat for you sir too," the café owner smiled.

"No thanks, I'm not hungry, thank you for your help."

Neil hurriedly made his way to the door and soon exited.

He had been walking around Chammerley, but no one seemed to know anything.

The detective found his way to Greendale's Guest House and was greeted by Mrs Bloombury, the owner.

"Yes, they've been here, stayed in room 209, you're welcome to go and have a look around if you wish, I have a key."

Mrs Bloombury took Neil up to the room where the couple had been staying.

She unlocked the door, and they both walked in.

"Such a lovely couple," she declared, "even left me a bit extra for the room, hardly heard a peep out of them," she glowed.

"Not in any trouble, are they?"

"No no, just making a few enquiries, that's all," Neil didn't want to give anything away to the guest house owner, as he continued to look around the room, into the en-suite bathroom, looking in the cupboards, drawers and even under the bed.

"Huh, don't know of any good maids I could hire do you, think mine has done a runner," Mrs Bloombury sighed.

"Any idea where they were heading?"

"No, like I say, didn't hear from them, weren't here long."

"Did you say your maid had done a runner?" "Might she have gone with them do you know?"

"I'm not sure if I'm being honest, seemed such a sweet girl when I took her on but, she did do some strange things sometimes."

"Can I take her details Mrs Bloombury?"

"Sure, I'll take you back downstairs, unless err… are you done here, or do you need another look around?"

"No, don't need to look around here anymore," "yes, as much detail about your maid as you can please."

"Also, can you remember what the couple may have been wearing when they left?"

Mrs Bloombury gave Neil as much detail as she could, about Paul and Alice, as well as her maid, as Neil wrote everything down in his detectives' notebook.

Neil thanked Mrs Bloombury, before heading out of the Guest House.

He stood outside Greendale's, pondering his next move, to try and find them, but he knew that they could be anywhere, but he was determined to catch up with them, whatever the cost.

OH NO, NOT AGAIN

Paul, Alice and Isobelle had been travelling for quite a few hours, with all of them starting to feel rather tired.

"I need to use the toilet," muttered Isobelle.

"You can shut the FUCK UP and wait," Paul shouted angrily, glancing briefly back at her, with a wave of anger on his face, clearly in no mood to stop for his unwanted passenger.

"Paul… really?" said Alice, "there's no need to speak to her like that".

"She was YOUR IDEA, I didn't want her with us, too much of a distraction, so keep her fucking quiet."

There were lots of twisty, windy and lonely roads as they travelled, before seeing signs saying, 'Welcome To Lansburton'.

Paul drives on a little further into the sleepy town, a lot different to the places that Alice had become accustomed to.

He turns into one street, then another, then another, and finally ground to a halt.

"This is where we're going to be staying, at least for the time being," he knew that they were going to have to move on again eventually.

The street where they had parked up was very narrow, with lots of rubbish strewn across the road, didn't look to be the nicest of places, and it was eerily quiet.

The buildings on the street, named Concorn Street, were old-looking buildings, had a very worn look about them, graffiti on the walls, and what appeared to be bullet holes too but, maybe that was because of the age of them.

Alice and Isobelle looked out of the car windows, with trepidation and a touch of fear, wondering where they were staying.

Both girls gingerly got out of the car and looked up at the building where they were parked outside, number ten.

Paul could see that the two girls were fearful of the unknown, what their new surroundings had in store for them.

"A lick of paint here and there, and some tender loving care, it'll soon feel like home," he was trying to reassure them that this would be home for them for the considerable future.

Both girls once again glanced at each other, more so with acceptance this time, as opposed to fear, Paul locked the car, opened the front door of the house, and all three of them stepped inside, with various neighbours' curtains twitching, and staring nosily across at the new residents.

Upon entering the house, it felt somewhat cold and a bit unloved, like it hadn't been lived in for years.

The walls had slightly ripped white woodchip wallpaper, that looked as if it hadn't been decorated for years.

Alice turned the light on in the hallway, and the lightbulb gave out a dim light, covered over by a dirty brown light fitting, which wasn't helping the bulb give out its maximum amount of light.

They carried on walking through the narrow hallway towards another dingy-looking room on the left, a large sitting room that again, felt very unloved, with floral wallpaper this time, old-smelling furniture.

Paul was under no illusions that there was plenty of work to be done to make it look somewhere near liveable, but he knew that he would do just that.

The girls, both looking at each other, appeared totally unimpressed.

"We won't be here for long, don't you worry," Paul grinned, trying to put a positive slant on their new surroundings, it was somewhere that they weren't used to, with it being a tired-looking house.

They venture their way upstairs and, lo and behold, the house appeared to be just as dark and tired looking as downstairs, a musty smell coming from each of the three bedrooms, like it had been lived in by squatters.

"How long do we have to live here then Paul, I hate it, and I don't think Isobelle is that keen either."

"Well, it was your idea to drag her along so, she's your responsibility now, not mine," he was not very amused by his wife's comments.

"Come on Izzy, let's get out of here, leave him to it," Alice giving her husband a look of disdain, "let's check this area out, got to be better than hanging around in this hell hole," and, as quick as a flash, they were down the stairs, and out the house.

The girls wandered aimlessly for a little while, what seemed like hours, but had only taken them around half that time, before coming into the sleepy-looking town of Lansburton. There were, as you'd expect, lots of quaint-looking shops, restaurants and cafes, and there seemed to be quite a few people around.

They headed over the road, to browse more shops, but not coming across anything they fancied, before standing outside of a bar named 'Coco's'.

With their bright dresses flapping in the gentle breeze, they stood and smiled at each other with anticipation.

"Fancy a drink"? Alice was quick to get the question in first, with what she thought Isobelle might also have been thinking.

"You read my mind Alice."

Coco's was a swanky-looking wine bar, the smell of fresh paint, a delightful shade of turquoise, with shades of off-white mixed in.

It looked as if it had not long been renovated, both girls liked the feel of the place after stepping inside.

There were lots of murals on the walls, bright colours that matched the colours of the bar, and it made it feel very plush, somewhere the girls felt they could come and hang out when they needed to get away.

They wandered up to the bar and looked at the drinks menu in front of them.

"Anything particular you fancy to drink Izzy?"

Alice had found a nice little shortcut to Isobelle's name, and she didn't seem to mind it.

"I like you calling me Izzy, it's what most of my friends have called me down the years, and I prefer it in truth,"

Isobelle was trying to work out what to drink, whilst chatting away to Alice, "erm, I'll have sex on the beach please," she smiled to Alice, with a slight chuckle.

Alice smiled back at Isobelle sexily, slightly biting her lower lip.

"I might have sex on the beach with you," she teased, both girls being in a playful mood.

"What can I get you girls?" came the question from the tall, strapping and very handsome bartender.

"Yes," Alice smiled at him, "I want sex on the beach, as does Izzy," she teased again, biting her bottom lip, giving the bartender a sexy little grin and wink.

"Coming right up," smiled the hunky man, with a slight chuckle in the girl's direction, though it was a comment that he'd heard a million times before, upon ordering the cocktail.

Sitting at the other end of the bar, was a well-dressed man, gazing in the girl's direction.

He was sitting on a bar stool, wearing what appeared to be a designer suit.

A dark-haired and olive-skinned man, beaming bright white smile, piercing green eyes, and slinked back hair, almost touching his shoulders, and very clean-shaven.

It was as if he'd just come from a film set.

The girls took their drinks, Alice paying the bartender, as she again glanced briefly across at the well-groomed man, who had been staring at them, and who was still flashing a shiny white gleaming smile in their direction.

The girls wandered over to a table for two that they spotted near the far window of the wine bar and sat themselves down.

"Don't turn round Izzy but, did you spot that guy looking at us, sitting at the bar?"

"What man?" Izzy quickly turns around to look, as she was intrigued as to who Alice was talking about.

"DON'T LOOK!" Alice whispered sharply to her, leaning in quickly towards her friend, like a naughty schoolgirl, not wanting to give the man any signals or encouragement.

Alice quickly glanced across to see if he was still looking at them, as she could feel his eyes staring intently at them.

Lo and behold, he was still gazing in their direction, more fixed on them than before.

Alice thought the best course of action, would be to find out more about her sexy new friend.

"Tell me a bit about you then Izzy, because I don't really know you" she quizzed, leaning forward in Isobelle's direction.

"What do you want to know?" Isobelle was a slightly shy girl, despite her having sex with Alice and Paul back at the guest house.

"Well, tell me where you're from, do you have a boyfriend or girlfriend, what you've been doing workwise?"

"Well, believe it or not, I'm not normally into girls, men mostly but, I was just a bit curious about you, and I guess when we were all about to have sex, you were making me feel horny, so, I just went with it," she chuckled, holding her hand to her mouth in slight embarrassment.

"Where are you from originally?" Alice continued, whilst chuckling at Isobelle's response.

"Do you know the Chadley Islands in Canada?"

"Canada?" Alice sat back, slightly surprised, "but you don't sound Canadian at all."

"I left Canada some years ago now, my parents split, and my mother decided to move to England," I've moved around a bit, town-to-town, you know how it is."

"I've also had my fair share of boyfriends, messed around with some friends, shall we say but, nothing really special to tell you really," Isobelle continued.

Alice was intrigued to know more about her companion, despite the eyes from the bar in the back of their heads.

Isobelle was sitting side-on at the wine bar window, where she had a full view of the bar.

"He appears to have gone," "he's not there now Alice."

Alice quickly pulls her head around, also seeing no sign of the handsome stranger, who had been staring at them from the moment they had walked in.

The two girls chatted for a few more minutes and were looking out the window when they could suddenly smell the gorgeous scent of a man standing over them.

It was the handsome, well-groomed man from the bar.

He stood over the girls, well dressed in a dark navy casual blazer, and light-blue shirt, with a few buttons undone at the top, showing off a thick gold chained necklace, and what appeared to be a very expensive looking watch, blue designer brogue shoes, faded blue jeans, with slight tears at the knees, and expensive smelling aftershave, whilst giving them a gleaming smile, every inch the model type.

The girls stared at him momentarily, giving the dashing man a stare and a brief smile.

"I couldn't help but notice two beautiful girls in here, not seen you in here before," he said.

"Let me introduce myself; my name is Valentino, and I am originally from Milano in Italy," "and you are?"

The girls were a little reluctant to give their names, yet were also feeling a little flirtatious.

"I am Alice, and I am Isobelle," their collective voices came, as he glanced at them one at a time.

Valentino went and grabbed himself a chair, putting the back of it up against the table, and proceeded to chat with them.

"Erm, did we say you could join us?" Alice remarked, "we were enjoying our own company thanks."

The girls glanced at each other, with a slight smile to each other, while giving the suave Italian a flirty smile at the same time.

"Siete due belle ragazze" he muttered to them in Italian, holding his thumb and finger to his lips, as he had just cooked the perfect Bolognese.

The girls glanced at each other, feeling slightly bewildered by what he had just said but, going by his expression, they thought that it might have been complimentary.

"Err, excuse me," he mumbled," "I just said that you are two beautiful girls, I admire beauty," he exclaimed.

"I am sorry to interrupt your day, but I own a modelling company, and I think you girls would be perfect, here's my card," speaking in slightly broken English, but enough for the girls to understand.

He stretched across and passed his business card over to Isobelle, who then, in turn, showed it to Alice.

"So, what makes you think we are even remotely interested in anything you have to offer?" Alice smirked at Isobelle, in a slightly mischievous way, trying to almost play hard to get.

"Erm, I'm so sorry ladies, I will interrupt your day

no longer," said the suave Italian, yet hoping that the girls would want to know more.

Alice was feeling in a playful mood and wanted to let Isobelle know what was on her mind, tapping her foot on Isobelle's leg under the table, and giving her a cheeky grin in the process.

Valentino was just getting off his chair, and about to leave the two girls in peace.

"Hang on, hang on, who said anything about you leaving?" said a curious Alice, wanting to know more about what the classy Italian had to offer.

The Italian wanders back over to his chair and sat back down, having been halfway across the bar.

"Sorry, I thought you wanted to be alone," he felt better, knowing that the girls might have been interested after all in what he had to say.

"So, tell us about this agency of yours," Isobelle smiled towards Alice, and the three of them chatted into the night.

The drinks flowed, there was lots of laughter, and as the night came to an end, Valentino was the first to get up to leave.

"Girls, it has been a lovely night, think over what I have told you, and give me a call if you are interested," talking in his broken English.

He looked back at them, as he started to finally walk away from the table that they had shared for most of the evening.

"Bit cheeky he was, wasn't he Alice?"

"Hmmm, maybe but, I'm a bit intrigued by what he has in mind," "and is it just me, or the both of us do you think?"

"I guess until we contact him and see, then we'll never know, are you seriously considering it?"

Alice pondered for a few moments.

"All we know about him is that he runs a modelling agency, so, won't hurt to take a look will it, unless you'd rather not, and we can just throw this card away, we don't have to do we."

"No, let's hang onto it, and see what he has in mind, as you say, can't hurt can it."

It was late into the night, they were in a place that they were not familiar with, and they were feeling a little drunk, so they decided to head back to the dingy house that they shared with Paul.

"You do look sexy tonight, Isobelle, I've got to say."

"I was just thinking the same about you if I'm honest Alice."

The pair stumbled out into the clear yet dark night, stars shining above them, the full moon lighting up the sky.

There were other revellers out and about, but they soon disbursed, as the girls drunkenly stumbled further away from the town. They had their arms linked together, helping keep each other up, just as Alice unlinked her arm, and put it around Isobelle's waist, laughing and giggling like naughty children, who had just been up to no good.

Alice then ran her fingers up and down Isobelle's back, and down to her peachy bum, Isobelle then proceeded to do likewise, they were starting to feel quite turned on.

Alice looked at her, with a wanting in her eyes, giving Isobelle the biggest smile in doing so.

She then grabbed her by the hand, and seeing a dark gap by the side of a doorway, and with no one else around, pulled her across the dark lonely street, pushed her up onto the wall, and started to vigorously kiss her, her hands all over Isobelle, caressing her breasts and down her curvy body, and down between her thighs, whilst kissing her neck, as if the pair had just met in a nightclub, and were just wanting a late night grope.

Isobelle was loving the attention she was getting, and she didn't care if any drunken revellers were going to see them.

She opened her legs so Alice could touch her, and Alice pulled Isobelle's top down, so she could suck on her breasts.

Alice was touching herself too, loving the moment of passion they were both feeling.

Just then, with the pair engrossed in passion, Isobelle lost her footing, slipped, and collapsed in a heap on the floor, the pair bursting out in fits of laughter, her dress nearly tearing in the process.

"Come on, let me help you up," Alice laughed, "I've plenty of time for you, let's head back."

They pull their outfits back straight and head back, they weren't too far away.

The door was unlocked, and they stumbled inside.

They walked into the dimly lit lounge, the lightbulb looking like it was about to blow, and there stood Paul, soaked in blood, with a big burly man, about six-foot tall, stocky build, looking like he worked out regularly, sprawled out in front of him, seemingly dead, his blood-soaked shirt laying across the floor, blood seeping onto the dirty carpet.

"WHAT THE… AHHHHHH," both Alice and Isobelle let out shrieks of fear and horror.

"Hush, keep quiet, we can't let anyone find out about this, neighbours will hear," Paul scurrying over to Alice, covering her mouth with his cupped hand, whilst also putting a finger to his mouth with his other hand in Isobelle's direction, asking her to keep her noise down.

"He, he… just, barged into the house, and we fought, and…"

Next to the dead man, lay a blood-soaked kitchen knife, his blood still dripping from its tip.

The girls stood motionless in horror, Isobelle stood stunned by what she was witnessing, covering her mouth up with both hands, shaking with fear, she had not seen anyone dead before.

Alice walked over to Isobelle from behind, grabbed her shocked friend around the waist, to try and usher her out of the room, she noticed that Isobelle had begun to cry.

"We've got to keep this between us, everything will work out," Alice tried to reassure her that everything would be ok.

Isobelle continued to tremble with fear, giving a blank stare at the dead man, her eyes bulging, with tears rolling down her bright red cheeks, smudging her mascara.

She tried to calm herself, sniffling and wiping away tears with the back of one of her unsteady hands, not quite being able to process what she was witnessing.

"There are some fresh clothes upstairs for the two of you, but you need to try and help me move this body before you do anything," he wanted the girls to understand that they were now all in this together.

"WOOOOO… JUST YOU HANG ON! YOU got YOURSELF in this, YOU need to get yourself out of it, don't you go dragging us into whatever THIS IS," Alice raging with both anger and upset with her husband.

"We're going for a shower, and then we're going out, and we don't want to see HIM still here when we get back."

Alice could be quite forceful when she wanted to be, especially being a former model, she had to have a strong character, especially in her line of work.

She grabbed Isobelle by the hand, and, after giving Paul a stern look, led her upstairs to the shower, and to find something nice to wear for them both, trying to act as normal as possible, as Isobelle gently sat down on the bed, still in shock.

"I've… I've… got to get out of here," stress was strewn across her tear-soaked face, "there… there was a dea… dead man down there… aaaah, I've got to leave, shaking uncontrollably, and bursting into tears.

"Hush… listen to me, it'll all be ok, let's just calm down, take a shower, get dressed and get out of here ok," Alice trying to be the voice of reason.

"… And go where exactly?" "Your husband has just killed someone, I cannot stay around here, I should never have left the guest house, who knows what he'll do next, I mean, how do I know that I'm even safe?" Isobelle still shaken and sobbing, Alice sat on the bed next to her, putting her arms around her waist, in a show of comfort, and looked at her face-to-face, noses almost touching.

"It sounds like it was all just a terrible accident, she whispered to her, "look at how upset he seemed, let's leave him to sort it out, let's have that shower and get dressed, go out and have some fun, ok?"

Alice continued to stare into her mascara-stained eyes,

feeling Alice's calming voice and manner, had Isobelle feeling less tense.

Isobelle raised a little smile at her, Alice's finger cupping Isobelle's chin.

Alice gave her a kiss on her tear-soaked nose, tears dripping down from her eyes, giving her a big smile back as if she was trying to raise her spirits.

"Come on, let's find a nice dress each to wear, and head for that shower," Alice getting off the bed, brushing Isobelle's hand with her fingers, as Alice walked towards the dusty and tired-looking, dark brown wardrobe, before giving Isobelle a sexy smile as she did so.

Both girls were soon in the shower, lathering each other, yet not wanting to be in the same house as Paul and the dead man, they were soon out, and started to put on their dresses, Isobelle wearing a long silky purple dress, that almost reached her ankles, Alice wearing an equally off the shoulder green dress, just above the knee, looking just beautiful as Isobelle.

After both of their hair had dried, using the towels that they had used to shower with, they finished off getting ready and applied their makeup.

They looked a million dollars, looking like they could strut a catwalk, they both looked like models, even though Alice had already been one previously.

"You look amazing Izzy," she couldn't help but look proudly and lovingly at her new friend, "you've been in the wrong profession all this time," she joked, with a big smile.

Isobelle laughed.

"Really think so?"

"Oh yes," as Alice walked up to her, close enough to

breathe in each other's perfume, both wearing Chanel number five that Alice always carried around with her.

She stared lovingly into Isobelle's eyes, with a wanting of her, though just wanting to arrange her hair slightly.

As she clasped her arms with her hands, giving them a gentle squeeze, and a sexy smile, in approval of how she thought she looked, they heard the front door open downstairs, hurrying themselves over to the dark brown thick curtains, gently pulling one aside, pulling it enough to see what Paul was doing.

The street was empty, just a black cat, with a pure white front, running along the other side of the street, licking its lips, as if it had just captured a mouse or a bird, suddenly darting further down the path, upon seeing Paul, who appeared to have a large black bin bag, that clearly looked heavy, seemingly having the body of the dead man inside.

They saw him quickly open the back passenger seat door, struggling to bungle the bulky bag inside and, as he did so, shoved it as hard as he could inside, worryingly looking left and right, to make sure that no one could see what he was doing.

He could sense that he was being watched, as he glanced up to the window, where the girls were standing there, watching him.

He paused momentarily, as all their eyes met, before he jumped into his car, and screeched away.

"Think it's time we got out of here," Alice declared, "don't really want to be around when he gets back.

She grabbed Isobelle by the hand and hurriedly shuffled out of the bedroom, where they had changed, down the stairs, and out of the door, slamming it shut behind them, a slam so loud, the whole street would have heard, not before Alice had grabbed a spare key that she had spotted, just in case they needed to get back in.

The girls headed off in the direction of Coco's bar, where they had met the suave Italian Valentino previously.

They walked in, trying to act as normal as possible, in the circumstances, strolled over to the bar, ordered their drinks, and sat down, almost in the same spot that they were sat at before, the last time they were in there.

Isobelle's hand started to shake once more, almost spilling her drink over her beautiful dress, still thinking about what she had witnessed back at the house.

"Try not to worry darling," Alice whispered to her, "it will all be ok," Isobelle's eyes were starting to get teary once again, the shock of it all was again starting to hit her.

"Come on, put your drink down, I'll take you to the ladies, and get you all cleaned up."

They get up from the table, Alice grabbing her by the hand once more, and finally find signs for the lady's bathroom.

It was bringing back memories of when she had got upset back in Barnwood, and Sarah had taken her to get all cleaned up, but she was in no mood to have fun with her, however sexy she looked.

They wandered out of the bathroom, and back to the table, where their drinks still sat.

Isobelle had calmed somewhat by this point but was still not in the mood to have too much of a good time, she just couldn't switch off from the horrors of the house.

Both girls glanced across the well-lit room, and, true to form, there sat Valentino at the bar, raising his glass to them, flashing his smooth smile.

He casually got up from his seat, almost arrogantly finding his way over to the pair.

"Nice to see you both again," smiled the suave Italian.

"Have you given it any thought about calling me?"

"Calling you?" Alice smiled politely.

"Yes, er, I recall when you girls were both here before, I gave you my card," Valentino pulled up a chair, and sat down, with the back of it pressed against the table that they sat at.

He was once again smartly dressed, wearing what appeared to be a designer Italian suit, with the jacket casually undone once more, and his crisp white shirt unbuttoned at the top, displaying a smart silver cross and chain, and a sparkling wristband on his left arm.

"Is your friend all right?" he continued.

"Yes, she has just had a bit of bad news, that's all," Alice was trying not to give anything away with the events of earlier.

Valentino kept glancing over at Isobelle, who was quietly drinking her drink, hardly giving him a look, and letting Alice do all the talking.

"Sorry, remind me what you do again?" Alice enquired.

"I'm a fashion shoot photographer, take my models all over the world, and go back to my home often, where we do lots of shoots." "I am looking for a few more models if you're interested, show you the sights of Italy, it is, as you say, quaint, very romantic, give me a call, and we can discuss it more."

He looked at Isobelle once more, with emptiness, as she hadn't been involved in their conversation, busy looking down into her glass of wine.

"Ok, I'll, leave you two girls to it," as he got up, and put the chair back when he found it.

As he started to walk away, Alice called out to him.

"Wait!" "Maybe we could talk, not now, tomorrow, we'll meet you here."

The Italian stopped in his tracks, his back still turned to them, but giving himself a wry smile, before turning round to face them.

"What are you doing Alice, Isobelle whispered across, "we barely know this guy."

"Anything has got to be better than what we have right now hasn't it?"

Isobelle silently agreed, looking at Alice, yet not saying another word.

"Shall we say nine a.m.?" Alice said confidently.

"Ok, nine it is," said Valentino, "I'll take you to my studios here, show you around, see what you think, then, we can talk, how you say… shop."

"*Ti faro implorare di piu,*" "that means, I'll see you both tomorrow," he said, smiling, as he walked away, and back to his seat at the bar, raising a glass to the girls, with a smile, once again.

"We still don't know this guy though Alice," a concerned Isobelle mumbled from her glass.

"Look, we'll meet up with him in the morning, he can show us around his studio, don't worry, I've got a keen eye for people like him, he sounds ok to me so far, let's check it out, if you're not comfortable then, we'll just say no, ok?"

Isobelle was still a little uneasy at the thought but, was trusting of Alice, who had been a model in the past, and she was sure that she'd know what she was talking about.

"Besides, he could find us a way out of our current situation couldn't he, takes his models around the world, Italy, plus I imagine the pay would be good, give us a chance to go it alone for now," Alice said, to reassure her.

"Come on, let's go, maybe find another bar around here," but Isobelle was not really in any mood to carry on drinking.

"Where are we going to go after all this?" Isobelle said, nervously.

"Don't worry, I've thought about that." "I've got plenty of money on me so, we could maybe find a bed and breakfast around here until we both decide what we're going to do because we certainly cannot go back there can we!"

"Just what I was thinking, but won't he come looking for us?"

"I'll text him, tell him that we need some time by ourselves for now, maybe just for a few days, you leave him to me."

The girls wander for a while, browsing around shops, Isobelle not as relaxed as Alice appeared, even though she was as tense as her friend, just was able to hide it better.

They walk a little further, for another ten minutes, and come across a bed and breakfast, with a room-to-let sign showing outside, 'Diane's Bed & Breakfast' friendly and warm atmosphere, no pets.

"Come on Izzy, let's check this out".

They walk up the pure white, yet, slightly stained steps to the guest house door, and walk inside.

They were then greeted by a petite, middle-aged lady, with long blonde hair, and with the biggest smile.

"Good evening ladies, my name is Diane, Diane

Retford, and I am the owner of this bed and breakfast, are you looking for one room or two?"

"Nice to meet you Diane, we are looking for somewhere to stay, possibly for up to a week, and we saw that you had a sign outside, showing rooms-to-let," Alice was going to do all the talking for the girls, as Isobelle still seemed a little shaken by earlier events.

"Let me see what we have," "are you looking for two separate rooms, or a double room?" said Diane, looking at both girls in turn, while still giving them a warm glowing smile, that was as genuine as she appeared.

"A double will be fine, thank you Diane."

The girls glanced around the warm, cosy hallway of the bed and breakfast, surrounded by both old and modern art on the walls, as Diane buried her head in the guest book, elegantly putting her stylish Gucci glasses on, to see what was available.

"We have a double room, ninety pounds a night, that's for the two of you, and also includes a full English breakfast, which starts at seven-thirty, how does that sound?"

Diane patiently waited to see what the girls wanted to do.

"Yes, we'll take it."

"That's great, do you have any bags?"

"No, we're travelling light," Alice joked, trying to make light of the situation that the girls were in, also hoping it might make Isobelle raise a smile for her.

"OK well, here is your room card, room twenty-four, up the stairs, take a left, and along the corridor, hope you enjoy your stay with us." "If you need anything, just use the phone in the room." "Oh, the house is manned twenty-four hours, so, if you go out, there is always someone on the front desk so, just press the door buzzer, and you'll be let in."

Diane watched the girls walk up the stairs, still giving them her warm smile, the same one that she had for them when they came in.

They found their way to their room, and Alice opened the door easily, using the card key that had been supplied.

The fire door closed quietly behind them, as Isobelle collapsed on the comfy double bed, stretching her arms way above her head, in a way that she looked ready to fall asleep.

The room was spacious, warm and airy, if slightly dated, with bright white wallpaper and blue stripes running vertically, with a few quaint pictures hanging up around the room, depicting hunting scenes, as well as pictures of old men smoking pipes outside of old Inns.

"I need a shower," Isobelle sighed.

"Aren't you hungry, I could always call for room service, unless you'd like to venture out to eat."

"Hmmm... maybe we could request something from that lovely lady, Diane wasn't it, sorry, I wasn't paying much attention."

"OK, I will ask her to rustle something up for us, you just relax, and I will give her a call now.

Alice sat at the end of the bed, close to where the phone table was.

She lifted the receiver and pressed zero for assistance.

Diane answered the phone.

"Hello, reception," Diane answered.

"Hi Diane, could we order some food for room twenty-four please, nothing too heavy, maybe some pizza and fries too," Alice replied.

“That’s fine, anything for you girls to drink?”

“No, think that will be everything thank you,” “how long are we looking Diane, we’re ravenous!” chuckled Alice.

“Give me about half an hour if that’s ok, and I’ll have it brought up to you.”

Alice glances over to Isobelle.

“Maybe time for a quick shower,” Alice raised her eyebrows at her.

“Not in the mood for any fun though,” Isobelle was still feeling traumatised by the day’s events.

“No, that’s ok, we’d need longer before the food arrived anyway,” Alice chuckled, hoping it would raise a smile.

The girls were in the shower not long after Alice had come off the phone, both washing each other, Isobelle was still feeling down and seemed distracted as she washed Alice’s body, but they were soon out again, patiently waiting for their food to arrive.

There was soon a knock at the door, and Alice answered it.

Diane has brought their food up to them, all nicely wrapped in foil.

“Enjoy ladies,” she smiled, “how is your room, ok I hope?”

“Yes thank you, Diane, very cosy, thank you for doing some food for us.”

“You’re very welcome,” she smiled, as she walked down the corridor and back downstairs.

“Come on Izzy, let’s eat, and we’ll just chill here tonight, get some rest, and we’ll venture out tomorrow, we need more clothes anyway so, I’ll take us both shopping.

They finished their food, and were soon in bed naked

together, they had nothing else to wear, as their other clothes were at the house.

Alice put her arms around her, Isobelle having her back turned from her lover, and the girls were soon asleep.

Morning arrived, and it was six-thirty.

Isobelle had been tossing and turning pretty much all night but was wide awake and seemed more like her old self.

"Morning sexy," planting a kiss on Alice's lips.

"Hmmmm… morning," Alice stretched her arms out above her head, giving a tiny yawn, with her having slightly broken sleep with Isobelle's restlessness during the night.

"I'm sorry if I disturbed you in the night, but let's head for a shower before breakfast, let me make it up to you."

Isobelle starts to sexily kiss Alice, and slides her hand down between her thighs, touching her pussy, as Alice gives out a little groan, parting her legs.

Alice is suddenly wet, Isobelle's fingers sliding inside her wet pussy, gently sliding them in and out, pulling the sheets down, and started to suck on her ample chest.

Alice is loving her being more like her old self and is feeling very horny and very wet with her touch.

She climbs on top of Alice's naked body, as both girls start to have sex, Isobelle grinding her well-toned body on her.

They kiss passionately, Alice squeezing Isobelle's peachy bum, as she feels the muscles in her body working hard to pleasure her.

Isobelle grinds herself harder on Alice, their kisses becoming more passionate, as they feel each other about to cum.

"Ah baby I've missed this, you're going to make me cum," cried Alice.

Isobelle continued to writhe her silky body on Alice, kissing her passionately, caressing her cherry-red nipples, and going down to suck on them.

The bed starts to hit the wall, as the girls' sex gets faster.

"Oh my god I'm cumming," sighed Isobelle, both panting with the pleasure from each other.

Suddenly, they come to a halt, both girls had cum, as Isobelle rests her now sweaty body on her lover.

"Well, that was a pleasurable wake-up call," Alice laughed, giving Isobelle a few brief kisses, with her hands still on her lover's peachy bum. "Come on, let's head for that shower, and head down for breakfast, I'm hungry after that," she smiled.

She rolled Isobelle off her, took her by the hand, and led her to the big double shower, before turning it on.

The shower head was powerful, covering them both, as they washed each other down, lather covering their bodies, as the girls in turn washed each other once more, like two lovers who had been together for years, it seemed so natural.

They both got out of the shower, dried each other down, and got dressed back in the same clothes they wore the day before, but Alice knew that she was going to take Isobelle out shopping, to grab some new clothes, but more so, have some girly time.

They were ready, and were out of their door, to head down for breakfast.

There was an array of breakfast food out, cereals galore, fresh fruit, yoghurts, as well as fruit juices.

They had a designated breakfast table for their room, and they sat down at it.

The breakfast room was both bright and airy, and smelt very clean, with colourful wallpaper and bright and artistic pictures hanging on the wall.

There were a few guests in, mainly older people, and they were greeted with a good morning from most of them smiling at the girls.

"Good morning everyone, nice day for a walk isn't it," Isobelle smiled, though it not being aimed at anyone in particular in the room.

Diane and a maid walked into the room to greet them all, the maid, Amelia, a small, petite girl, only around eighteen years old, approached Alice and Isobelle's table, asking them what they'd like for breakfast.

"A full English for me please," smiled Isobelle to the maid.

"Make that two," replied Alice.

The girls also requested to have both a tea and coffee pot brought to them, as well as both white and brown toast.

"This takes me back," smiled Isobelle, "feels weird being waited on for a change."

"This shopping trip today, what if we bump into that husband of yours?" Isobelle just wanted it to be a day for just the two of them.

"Don't worry, I'm sure we'll be able to steer clear of him."

Suddenly, their breakfast arrived, this was going to keep them filled up for the day, there was so much of it.

They finished their breakfast and hot drinks, and left the table, thanking both Amelia, their waitress, and Diane, before leaving the room.

They both went back upstairs to grab whatever bits they needed for the day.

It was a warm day, the sun beating down, was going to stay that way for the day, so they knew that they probably wouldn't need too many more layers on.

They walked into the room, Alice picking her handbag up, which contained her purse, and other bits, including a small vibrator, in case of needy emergencies, as well as lipstick and spray perfume, a tiny bottle of Lady Million being one of her favourites.

"Right, are you ready sexy?" she smiled at Isobelle, "let's go shopping, but only after we've been to meet up with that Valentino at nine, but we've got time to have a quick browse before our meeting with him, maybe even treat ourselves a little first."

"I'd almost forgotten about him," she chuckled.

Isobelle walked out first, Alice pinching her bum on the way out, Isobelle turning round, giving her a broad smile, as Alice made sure that the card-controlled fire door closed behind them.

They walked down the narrow corridor, and down the flight of stairs, that they had walked up to get to their room.

There was a set of lifts that they could have used, but both preferred to walk.

They were soon out of the bed and breakfast, feeling the gentle warm sunny breeze hit their faces, neither of them had any sunglasses, so that was going to be on their agenda too.

They walked into the centre of Lansburton, a quaint yet vibrant little town, full of quaint little shops, lots of people bustling around, browsing in shop windows, children laughing, joking and messing around, many people with smiles on their faces, the sun has brought the good out of people, and it also made the girls smile too.

"It seems nice here," Isobelle said to Alice.

"Over this way, there's a cashpoint over here," Alice replied.

They wander over to the machine, and Alice draws out a handful of money.

"There now, let's go and treat ourselves."

They wander from shop to shop, trying on outfits that they like, all looking expensive, but Alice didn't care, she wanted to spoil Isobelle, and they needed new clothes anyway.

"This shopping must have cost you a fortune, and I don't have a lot of money on me," Isobelle preferred to pay her way, but it was Alices' treat.

"That's ok, I offered so, just want you to be happy."

"Oh, I've loved it so far, I will pay you back."

"Don't be silly, like I say, my treat."

They find another stylish-looking shop and wander in.

There was so much to choose from, the girls separated in the shop, so they could browse around.

Alice took out a beautiful looking lime-green dress, sequined, off the shoulder, looking like an evening dress, cut just above the knee.

She held it up, so she could take a proper look at it.

"Ah, that would suit you," came a familiar-sounding voice.

She pulled the dress down, to see who it was, it was a smiling Valentino.

"What are you doing in here?"

"I should hope I am in here, I own it," he chuckled, "anyway, were we not meeting at nine?" he continued.

"Yes we are but hang on, I thought you were a fashion photographer?"

"I am but, how you English say, I have many strings to my bow?" "Is that how you say this?"

Isobelle spots Alice, talking to a man, and wanders over.

"Ah, you have your friend with you."

"Yes, we needed to come and do some shopping." "Anyway, nice to see you," Alice smiled, getting ready to walk away.

"I thought you were going to take a look at my studio, it is just down the road here."

"Yes, we'll take a look…"

Isobelle mutters to her.

"This could be our ticket out," she whispers, directing her eyes in his direction.

"It's number one-four-five, not far, just called Valentino's, I'll be there around five this afternoon if you're both free?"

"Yes, yes, we'll be there," Isobelle interrupted.

Valentino gave the girls a confident look and smile, as he walked away, briefly glancing over to them, with a look of reassurance.

"Isobelle!" Alice whispered back.

"I know but, it's worth a look isn't it?"

The girls carried on shopping, bulked down with clothes and perfume, enough to create a shop of their own, and strolled out of Valentino's shop, and straight into a waiting taxi, almost parked outside.

The taxi driver, his badge hanging up on the rear-view

mirror, Glenn Hutton it showed, a middle-aged man, with a Midlands accent, and was very chatty.

"Wow, you're ladened with bags there girls, have you cleaned the shops out around here?" he joked.

"We're getting ready to open our own shop, Glenn is it?" Alice, leaning forward, to talk to him, and was in the mood to joke along.

"You're not from round here I'm guessing, not seen either of you before," he continued, "I think I've picked up most of Lansburton," he laughed.

"No, we're erm, just passing through really," Isobelle jumped in before Alice could reply.

The girls were soon outside of the bed and breakfast where they were staying, and Alice paid Glenn, just four pounds forty.

"Nice to see you girls, hope to see you again soon," said the cheerful driver.

The girls struggled to pull their bags out, such was the weight, but were soon back inside the B&B, as Glenn pulled off, giving them a wave.

They were met by Diane, the owner, who also mentioned how much they had.

"Might be better for you to use the lift with all those bags," she chuckled.

"Might be a good idea that," Alice smiled.

Diane called the lift for the weary pair, and it was soon opening for them.

The pair were soon at their room, plonked the bags on the bed, and started to rifle through what they had.

"Let's chill here for a bit shall we, and I'll give Valentino a call to see how long he'll be there for, if you want to that is?" Alice was just as keen to see what he had to offer, though she wasn't too keen to go back into the seedy world of modelling again, especially since she hadn't done it for so long.

The girls had found the dresses they liked the best, the light green sequined dress that Alice liked, when she saw Valentino, and Isobelle had brought a stylish navy-blue, knee-length sparkly dress, that glistened in the sun, that still shone through the clear windows in their room.

They took the dresses off, that they had worn pretty much after leaving Chammerley, and proceeded in trying their new dresses on.

"Wow Alice, that dress looks sensational on you, you look absolutely amazing," Isobelle was gawping in awe at her leggy lover.

Alice checked herself out at the full-length mirror they had in their room, just as Isobelle was trying on her equally sparkly black dress, Alice also giving admiring glances in her direction, going to check herself out in the mirror, twirling, so she could get a full view of it from different angles.

"Look at us, two glamour girls, ready to go and rock Lansburton," "this little town isn't going to know what's hit them with us are they," Alice winked to Isobelle.

"Not felt this glamorous for… probably ever I'd say, thank you so much honey but, I should pay you for this somehow," Isobelle was feeling very grateful for how much Alice had spent on her.

"Right, I've still got that card of Valentino's somewhere, let's go downstairs to the bar, grab a drink, and I'll give him a call from there, what do you think?" Alice was wanting to take charge, as she had the experience to deal with these situations, being a previous model, as well as Sarah's PA.

"Yes, that sounds like a plan, might need a few bottles downstairs, I'm parched after all that walking."

The girls left the room, looking all glamorous, almost like they were about to go onto a catwalk or a red-carpet event, and walked down the stairs, which were wide enough for them to go down side by side.

They turned around the corner and walked into the bar, where they saw a few of the other residents having a quiet drink.

"Wow, you pair look beautiful, need a chaperone for the evening?" one of the elderly resident men asked.

"Ha ha, no, we're good thank you but, maybe another time," Alice was quick to respond in a jokey manner.

Once again, Amelia was standing behind the bar, ready to serve them.

The girls both ordered a glass of wine each and sat down.

Alice proceeded in taking her phone out of her handbag, and called Valentino, after finding his card tucked away in her bag.

He answered almost immediately.

"Hello, wasn't sure if you were ever going to call, it was good seeing you girls today."

"Well I have, and we wondered if you were around in your studio at some point."

"Erm well yes actually, as I mentioned that I would be here from five this afternoon, and I have a modelling shoot up until nine tonight if you wanted to come and see what I did."

“I have modelled before so, I know what is what,” Alice replied.

They finished their drinks, and once again, bumped into Diane.

“Would you call us a taxi please Diane, we’re going into Lansburton,” Isobelle asked.

“Wow girls, you’re a sight for sore eyes, you should be on a catwalk, not going into Lansburton,” Diane joked.

She called for a taxi, gave them a card to the local taxi rank, and a car arrived within minutes, and, as the girls ventured outside, they were once again greeted by Glenn, who was glad to see them once more.

“Fancy seeing you two again,” he smiled, “where is it to?”

“We need to get to Valentino’s on Cheston Road, number one-four-five,” Alice replied.

“Ah yes, I know it, I’ve dropped a few girls off there before, seems popular.”

They were soon pulling up outside Valentino’s, Alice paying him, as they gingerly walked towards the door.

The door was swiftly pulled open, and there stood the Italian, face beaming, looking the girls up and down.

“Well, I’ve got to say, both of you girls look fantastico,” Valentino could not quite get over just how stunning they both looked.

“Please, come in, come in, take a look around, I am just doing a photo shoot right now but, make yourselves comfortable, I have taken the liberty of pouring you both a glass of wine, I hope you don’t mind.”

They look around the very clean, airy room, with bright white walls, with a very warm feel, and see portraits of naked girls scattered around the walls, every inch the professional set-up you would expect.

The sound of the camera clicking away could be heard vibrating around the room, with a screen protecting the reception area, to the modesty of the model behind it.

"That is good but, if you could just stand slightly to your side, head looking directly at me, yeah, that is good" he could be heard, talking to the model.

"I'm intrigued to go and see what is happening," smiled an excited Isobelle to Alice.

"All in good time Izzy, let him and the model do their thing."

The snapping away of the camera continued, along with the instructions directed towards the model; 'turn left, turn right, turn away from me, with your head looking at me over your shoulder, yeah, this is good yes'.

Suddenly, the clicking stopped, and Valentino appeared from behind the screen.

The girls were still sipping away at their wine, from the flue glasses that it had been poured into.

"Do you girls wish to come over, come and meet my model."

"We don't want to interrupt your work," smiled Alice, "we're happy to wait."

"No no please, I insist."

The girls put their glasses on the table near them and walked over, and to the other side of the screen, to be greeted by the sight of a naked blonde, slender model, with an almost perfect figure, tall, leggy, with small breasts, bobbed-cut hair that glistened in the light from the spotlights beaming down on her, wearing shiny red stilettoes on her perfect looking feet.

"Wow, she looks amazing," Isobelle gawped, "you look amazing, whatever your name is," in awe of the model.

The model gave her a cold stare back, as if Isobelle wasn't even there, before striking the pose she was in before.

"Please, let me introduce you," "girls, this is my model Leona, Leona Bulcock, but she just prefers Leona yes," smiled the Italian.

"Nice to meet you..." smiled Isobelle, but Leona was in no mood for idle chit-chat.

"I want to take a few photos of the three of you, standing together, you two girls on either side of Leona, but pressed in together," Valentino smiled.

Isobelle looked at Alice with a beaming smile, a smile of excitement in her eyes, she was looking forward to coming out of her comfort zone, yet also relishing putting herself in the spotlight, she had not had this kind of attention before, yet Alice was more cautious, given her modelling previously.

The girls flanked the naked model, Isobelle on the left, facing the leggy model, and Alice on the right.

They both looked slightly uncomfortable, Isobelle not knowing where to put her hands, yet Alice was more of a natural, gently putting her hands around the model's waist.

"Put your arms around her neck, as if embracing her for a kiss," Valentino smiled.

Sure enough, Isobelle did just that, and pushed her face up close to Leona, looking as if they were about to share a loving kiss.

"I like that, I like that, good," an excited Valentino smiled, his camera flashing and snapping away.

"You know girls, why don't you lose your dresses, I want to see some skin-to-skin," he smiled, wondering if the girls would agree.

Again, Isobelle had become very relaxed and excited in front of his camera, as if she was playing to it, and was more than willing to take her dress off, if it meant pictures of her being taken, and knowing that she had the comfort of Alice being there.

"Ah, you're a natural Isobelle, are you sure you have not modelled before?"

Her cheeks went bright red with embarrassment.

"No, never but, have always wanted to give something like this a go."

Alice joined her in removing her dress, and again, went back to the pose they were all previously in.

"How about pulling your bra straps down, just off your shoulders."

'Oh no, not again,' thought Alice, knowing that she was going back into a world that she vowed she would never go back into again.

Valentino's camera snapped away like never before, Alice's bra pressed into the back of the model, with Isobelle's bra pressed into the slender model.

"This is just fantastico," smiled the suave Italian, "you girls just look… every man's dream."

"Would you like us to take our bras off, but only if you pay us," smiled Isobelle, looking in Alice's direction, hoping that, a little bit of her flesh, might make Valentino pay.

Alice was a bit reluctant to take her bra off, but Isobelle was having such a good time, she would also take hers off, if Isobelle wanted to.

"Yes, I will pay you all, as I need to pay for this model also," I will give you all five hundred pounds each.

"Oh no, you know it's more than that," "a thousand each at the very least," said a stern Alice, knowing what the going rate was.

"Ok, ok, I give you all one thousand each…"

"… In CASH," Alice demanded.

"Yes, of course, I pay you cash."

The girls then removed their bras, making sure that they hadn't gone as completely naked as the other model. As carefree as Isobelle had become, she wanted to retain some dignity, however much she was enjoying the limelight.

"The girls' bodies shimmered in the lighting of the spotlights on them, their look seemed every inch worthy of a top fashion magazine's front cover.

They all had suddenly become very natural together, and Valentino was loving the look that he had in front of him.

"Hang on," this is going in a fashion magazine isn't it?" said a concerned Isobelle, "I mean, I don't want these being used for your own personal use."

"Did you not see the magazines that I use when you came in?" he smiled.

"No, I didn't but, I will before we leave," Isobelle looked at Alice for reassurance, and Alice gave her a gentle nod of approval as if to say that she had seen them herself when they walked in.

The camera continued to snap away at the three of them standing in front of him, they were a picture of beauty and looked very artistic.

After an hour, but seemed much longer, all three girls

got dressed, and waited for Valentino to bring them the money he promised them.

He wandered into a back room, and, sure enough, came out with bundles of money for them all.

"There you are girls, a thousand pounds each, as promised."

He handed the money to the girls, Leona hadn't said a word to them, since they had arrived at the studio, she put on her long brown fur coat, that sat majestically on the coat stand that was just inside the doorway, gave the other two girls the same look that she had given Isobelle earlier, and swiftly left.

"She is chatty isn't she!" Isobelle sarcastically said to him.

"Ah yes, Leona can be a little like this," he smirked.

"Listen girls, there is lots more money where this came from, plenty more, tens of thousands each, you are both so beautiful, and I would like to do another photo shoot, maybe in Italy, I will pay for you to travel but, this is up to you yes," he waited for a reaction from the girls, but Isobelle was almost in a trance.

"Italy? Are you being serious?" smiled an excited Isobelle, "I mean, do you think that we are that good?"

"Yes, yes, why not," "you're clearly good in front of the camera, and Italy would love you."

'Italy!' she thought, 'I could get to model, see Italy, and be paid well.'

"I think that is a great…"

"We need to think about it," interrupted Alice, "we will give it some thought, we cannot make any decisions right now," she continued.

"Can I offer you girls a lift home?"

Isobelle looked at Alice, but Alice had a card, and would rather get a taxi back, as she wanted to get to know Valentino a bit more first, before jumping into a car with him.

They thanked the Italian, before grabbing their bags, and leaving the studio.

Alice called for a taxi, which turned up almost straight away, and again, it was Glenn who arrived.

"Are you the only one working for this company?" Isobelle joked.

"Seems like it sometimes," he smiled, "had a good time?"

"It's been, educational!" Isobelle replied.

Alice was a little quieter in the car heading back, with plenty to ponder.

They were soon back at the B&B, it was getting quite late, and both were exhausted and just wanted to go to sleep.

They were soon out of their dresses and in bed, giving each other a kiss goodnight, like an old married couple.

Isobelle turned her back to Alice, Alice wrapping her arms around her waist.

Isobelle was soon asleep, but Alice was wide awake, wondering what the photo shoot meant for the two of them, and pondering if Italy was going to be a good move or not, they had a lot to discuss.

I'M HUNTING YOU DOWN

The next day, the girls are up, all fresh from their photo shoot the night before.

It was seven-thirty, and they were in the mood for some breakfast.

"Good morning gorgeous, shall we do breakfast then shower?" Alice asked.

"Sounds good. I'm still buzzing from yesterday, and I'm up for this trip if you are."

"Are you sure?" "It's a long way to go, especially as we hardly know him but, we can talk about it, especially if you're really keen."

"I am keen, and I also picked up my passport when I hitched a lift with you so, I'm also able to travel."

"Ok, let's do breakfast, shower, then maybe, we can sit down and discuss it."

"It's got to be better than going back to that killer of a husband of yours, isn't it?"

"Well, I know, there is that." "Let's talk more after breakfast, ok?"

The pair dressed in something a little more casual from the day before; Isobelle wore a pair of yellow trousers, an off-the-shoulder crimson blouse and a pair of blue flats, she looked divine.

Alice was looking equally as stylish, in a light blue, above-the-knee skirt and flowery blouse, that showed off her ample chest. They both looked equally stunning.

"You look… WOW," smiled Isobelle.

"You look pretty hot yourself darling," "come on, let's head for breakfast."

The girls made their way out of the room and down the flight of stairs.

'Good morning' they smiled to everyone, most of the other residents were also down, having some breakfast.

They all turned to the girls collectively and wished them a good morning.

The elderly gentleman from the previous evening, couldn't take his eyes off them, his mouth gawping open, as the pair headed towards their table, getting ready to order.

"Erm, you need to watch what you're doing there sir, you've spilt some beans down your shirt," Alice joked, pointing at his spoon slightly tilted, allowing some food to fall off it.

The man's elderly wife sat opposite, was giving him an evil stare, that he was with her, not the girls. This caused a slight chuckle from the other residents, at the elderly gentleman's expense.

After ordering their breakfast with Amelia, they sit and chat a little.

Diane entered the room, wished them all a good

morning, and asked if the girls were enjoying their stay, with the same beaming smile that she always had.

"Yes thank you Diane, we may need to be checking out soon though but, we'll let you know when."

"That's absolutely fine, Diane beamed," "you stay for as long as you need, it's nice having two glamour models around the place," she chuckled.

"Oh, not me," smiled Isobelle, "but Alice is a former model."

"Well, enjoy your day everyone, see you all later," and with that, Diane left the room, pretty much the same time as Amelia, who had finished serving.

"You're set on this Italian trip aren't you," Alice whispered, leaning in towards Isobelle, sitting opposite each other.

"I think if we can get round that monster of a husband of yours, yes," she whispered back.

The girls chatted away for a little while longer, before finishing their breakfast, and drinking their tea and coffee, thanking Diane and Amelia once again, before heading up to their room.

"Shower?" Alice winked.

The girls stood close to each other, almost in an embrace, before undressing each other.

Alice grabbed a naked Isobelle by the hand, led her towards the shower, and turned the shower on.

They slowly kissed and caressed each other's bodies with a lather of soap from the dispenser, using a soft sponge that was hanging up to be used.

They gently caressed each other's breasts, slowly kissing as they did.

Alice's hand slowly worked its way down between Isobelle's thighs, to make sure that her pussy wasn't overlooked.

Isobelle began to sigh with pleasure, as Alice started to nibble at her neck and earlobes, her fingers slowly entering Isobelle, as both girls' breathing began to quicken, Isobelle cupping the back of Alice's head, not wanting her to stop.

"Ah baby, that feels so good, don't stop... oh my god," Isobelle was clearly having fun with Alice.

Isobelle then turned Alice around and wanted her to also have some enjoyment of her own.

Isobelle's hand was quickly between Alice's thighs, her hand was slightly shaky, as she still was a little inexperienced with women, but wanted Alice just as much.

Isobelle's fingers were also penetrating Alice just as quickly as Alice's were with Isobelle, though her fingers were going deeper inside Alice, also going down to suck on Alice's hardening nipples, Alice was riding Isobelle's fingers, feeling like she wanted to cum.

Alice's fingers were back inside her lover, and both girls were riding each other, while also vigorously kissing each other's necks and licking each other's ears, in a height of passion.

"Oh my god, I'm going to cum," squealed Isobelle, their fingering got faster and more intense.

Their legs quivered, and as they both let out an almighty groan, both had reached climax.

They stopped and held each other for a few moments, the spray of the shower still beating down on them.

They slightly parted, giving each other a loving smile, and chuckled with one another at what they had just done.

They continued to shower and started to wash each other's hair.

They thought they heard a slight tap, but carried on regardless… it was Amelia, bringing fresh towels in.

"Hi, it's only Amelia, thought I'd bring…" "Oops, erm, I'm so sorry, I didn't realise you were, erm," her face going red with embarrassment, at the sight of seeing the girls in the shower, the girls quickly covering up as much as they could, "I did, erm, knock," she continued.

"I'm so sorry, I'll, erm… leave them here with you," nervously averting her eyes away from them, before quickly making a sharp exit out of the room.

"Breakfast will be interesting in the morning then," smiled Alice, and they both fell into each other's arms, chuckling.

"Right, let's get out and dressed, sit and discuss what we're going to do about Italy, and how we're going to get hold of my passport," Alice smiled to Isobelle, almost in declaration that she was going to go, besides, it would be an adventure for them both.

Meanwhile, Detective Buchanan, was still on the hunt for them, and, having left Chammerley after an extensive search, with no one knowing too much as to their whereabouts, he drove on and came into a town called Flynton-on-the-Wrye, a small quaint little town, with lots of elderly people, and not a place where he thought the couple would hide out, yet, at the same time, a place where, by past experiences, he knew that it might be a place that no-one would think of looking for them.

He found a spot to park his car, got out and locked up.

He walked around the centre of the town, bustling with elderly people, and with photos of both Paul and Alice in his hands, and he asked the locals if they had seen any of the two of them.

There were naturally lots of puzzled faces looking at the photos, as well as Neil being given no encouragement as to their possible whereabouts.

He carried on walking around, asking people who passed him, with again, no sign of anyone knowing them.

'I'll give some of these shops a try, they might know something' he thought to himself.

He went from shop to shop, again, with no information, and saw a shop called 'Anita's Fashion Footwear'.

He purposefully strode in and was greeted by the shop owner Anita Trewick.

She was a slender lady, who held herself very well, and greeted Neil with a smile.

"Hello sir, can I help you?"

"Yes, I hope you can," "I'm looking for these two individuals, sorry, I'm Detective Neil Buchanan from Barnwood police, have you seen them at all?"

Anita carefully and closely inspected the photos of the two, even pulling her thin-framed glasses up, just in case she was missing anything.

"Hmmm, no, I can't say I have I'm afraid, I'm sorry, have you tried any of the other shops?"

Neil let out a slight sigh, almost in defeat of his chase of them.

"Yes, I have, to no avail with them either."

"Can I leave you with my card, you know, just in case you see anything, or hear anything, I'd be much obliged."

He pulls a few cards out from his inside jacket pocket and proceeds to pass one to Anita.

"They're not dangerous are they?" "I mean, I need to keep me and my business safe."

Neil gave Anita a slight grin.

"Nothing for you to worry about, erm, Anita wasn't it?"

"Yes, it is."

"It's all fine, thank you for your time and, remember to give me a call if you see or hear of them would you."

He leaves the shop, and stands outside, putting his hands on his hips, not quite knowing what to do next.

'They could be anywhere but, where?'

Suddenly, he gets a call on his radio from headquarters.

"Detective Buchanan, we have some news for you, and I think you're going to like it."

"A credit card and a cashpoint have been used, in a town called Lansburton, by a user going by the name of Alice Johnson."

"That's fantastic, great job, I'm about to head there now." "Despatch all units to Lansburton, I'll meet them there, I'm not far away."

Neil trots towards his car, jumps in and screeches off, taking on-lookers by surprise, and a little shock, as Flynton-on-the-Wrye was a sleepy little town.

The girls meanwhile, decided to carefully head back towards the house, in the hope that Paul wasn't there, to look for Alices' passport.

Alice opens the door with the spare key that she had, and they crept inside.

There didn't appear to be any sign of movement, the house was both dark and eerie and felt slightly cold.

"He's not here," Alice sighed with relief.

"What makes you think he isn't?" "He might be upstairs with another dead body laying in front of him."

"No, I can normally sense that he isn't here," "Paul?" she shouted, are you here?"

There was no response, so the girls separated to look for Alices' passport.

Alice went upstairs, while Isobelle checked downstairs.

"I've found it!" Alice shouted and raced downstairs, clutching it in her hand, with a big beaming smile, which Isobelle gave back to her, perhaps even a bigger smile came from Isobelle, as she knew that Italy was now in sight for them both, a foreign adventure awaited her.

"Come on, let's go," Alice said in a quickened voice, "before he gets back here."

The girls head away from the house, and into a taxi, parked not far away, and head back to the B&B.

"If you're absolutely sure about Italy, we'll give him a call," smiled Alice, getting the reaction from Isobelle that she was expecting, another big smile, flinging her arms around Alice in the process.

They get to their room and start to pack, as there is no time like the present, Isobelle was so keen to go, and they couldn't stay at the B&B for too much longer.

"You pack, and I'll go and pay the bill," smiled Alice, "I'll be back up in a minute to pack my things."

Alice heads downstairs and is met by Diane, the owner.

"Hey Diane, come to check out I'm afraid, all good things come to an end as they say," she smiled.

"Well, it's not going to be the same without you two girls around, you come back whenever you like, and you're always welcome here, plus, I think you had an admirer in one of the residents, though I know his wife wasn't best pleased," Diane joked.

"Ha-ha I know," Alice smiled, and he lost some of his breakfast the other morning," both Alice and Diane chuckled.

Alice settled the bill with Diane and was about to walk back up.

"Don't suppose you have a couple of spare suitcases we can borrow have you, we should have got some when we went out on our shopping spree," Alice asked.

"Yes, I think I have a couple of spare ones under the stairs," "have been left there by some families over the years, they're bulky, but have pull-out handles and wheels so will both be easy to manage, you might as well keep them because they're just clogging up space under the stairs, and I'm sure we'll end up with more over time," Diane chuckled.

Diane gets the suitcases for Alice, who then thanks her, and uses the lift to take them up the stairs.

"Here, I've managed to get us some luggage, Diane has been kind enough to give them to us, put our clothes in these," she smiles at Isobelle.

"Carry on packing, and I'll call Valentino."

Isobelle grabs one of the suitcases, still smiling away to herself, excited at the thought of modelling in Italy, and starts to take all of her clothes out of the bag that she had originally put them in, and into one of the slightly dusty suitcases that Alice had brought up with her.

Alice goes to give Valentino a call.

Ring… ring…

He answers swiftly.

"Ciao," the suave Italian answers.

"Hi Valentino, it's Alice," "we've decided to take you up on your offer and come with you to Italy." "The thing is, we would like to go straight away, as we have decided to check out of the B&B today, and we'll be coming over to you now."

"Now?" "Well ok, I will put in charge people at the fashion store and, I will wait for you to arrive, same place, and we will arrange when to go."

"Can I ask what made your minds up?"

"It was Izzy… Isobelle really, she is really keen and, well, we can't stay here forever."

"… And of you?"

"Yes, I too am just as excited, but I've done all this before remember but the money will come in handy."

"So, I look forward to seeing you," as he swiftly hangs up the phone.

Alice then calls Glenn, the taxi driver, to ask for him to pick them up.

She arranges a time with him and begins to pack herself.

The girls have packed all their clothes, making sure all their make-up is also packed, checking the room one last time, in case they have missed anything, before calling the lift to take them down.

They arrive on the ground floor, where they are met by both Diane and the sheepish Amelia, going by what she witnessed when going into their room, and Alice hands them an extra one hundred pounds and asks Diane to share it amongst the staff.

They say their goodbyes one last time and pull the luggage outside and towards the waiting taxi of Glenn.

As Alice is putting hers and Isobelle's suitcases in

the boot, she notices a few police cars coming around the corner, and sure she has also spotted Neil, driving an unmarked car, puts her head down, and scurries into the taxi, hurriedly asking Isobelle to get in.

"SHIT! SHIT! SHIT!" shrieks an agitated Alice."

"Glenn, PLEASE, just DRIVE, and HURRY," Isobelle was looking concerned at Alice, she had never seen her look so frantic.

"What's happened?"

Isobelle noticed Alice looking nervously out of the back window and seeing all the police cars suddenly swarming Lansburton.

"Let's just say that Paul and I, had a bit of an 'accident' and the police may have got involved."

"OH MY GOD, has he…"

"Shhhhh," whispered Alice, in a slightly snappy tone, "I'll fill you in when I get a chance ok but, not now."

"I knew it, that husband of yours," she angrily mumbled back, worried that Glenn would overhear their conversation.

Glenn kept looking at the two girls in his rear-view mirror, whilst also keeping an eye on the road.

"You girls' ok?" he asked.

"Yes, we're fine, thanks Glenn, just something that has happened, nothing I can't handle," smiled Alice into his mirror, as Glenn continued to drive towards the studio, where Valentino was waiting.

The taxi pulls up outside Valentino's studio, the girls get out and are once again greeted by the smooth Italian.

Glenn gets the bags out of the car and passes them to the girls.

"Been lovely seeing you two again, hope to see you

again sometime," Glenn gets back into his taxi, and pulls off, Alice watches as he drives off into the distance.

The girls go inside, as Valentino gestures them inside.

"Leona isn't here today, so, if you girls just want to make yourself comfortable..."

"When were you thinking of taking us to Italy, maybe the sooner the better," Alice nervously smiles.

Valentino looks at them both with slight concern.

"You girls in any kind of trouble or..."

The girls look at each other.

"No, of course not but, we would just like to get on with the assignment as soon as possible, Isobelle has never been abroad, never done anything like this, and it would be great to see another country again," Alice once more looks at Isobelle for agreement, as Valentino stares at Isobelle for confirmation, as she smiles and nods to him.

"Well ok, we can fly..."

"No no, we can't fly, erm, Isobelle gets nervous flying you see," Alice again looking in Isobelle's direction.

Even though both had their passports, Alice was unsure if hers will have been stopped, and that she might be arrested at the airport during check-in, so she thought it might be safer to go by road.

"Ok, it can be by road, I will get one of my drivers to come but, it will be a long journey, I warn you."

"That's fine but, when can we leave?" Alice asks.

"Well, er, we can leave tonight but, let me get a few things together, I will call my driver, and he will take us," "rest assured, you will have an experience, I will show you the sights, you may see some other girls there too," "help yourselves to the drinks bar, it is over there," Valentino pointed over in the direction of the room where there was a bar, as he walked off, taking his smartphone out of his pocket, to make a call.

Alice walked over to the bar, grabbed two glasses, and proceeded in pouring wine for them both.

Valentino didn't seem to have gone for long.

He was holding a black sports holdall, bulked down with something inside, and smelling like he had just come from an Italian fragrance store.

"Ok so, I call my driver, he will be here in about thirty minutes ok!" "You girls just sit and relax and look forward to your adventure."

The car soon pulls up, and out steps a strapping man, six-foot-tall, very muscular, and broad-shouldered, bald head, dark glasses, wearing a bomber jacket, chewing some gum, someone you'd see in a gangster movie, and is greeted by Valentino.

Valentino hugs and plants a kiss on each of his drivers' cheeks.

"*Ah, Ciao Bruno, bello vederti qui (Hello Bruno, good to see you here).*"

The girls step out of the studio to come and greet Valentino's chauffeur.

"This is my driver ladies, meet Bruno, Bruno Lucetti" smiles Valentino.

"It's nice to meet… you," smiled Isobelle nervously, holding out her hand to greet him, but Bruno was both motionless and expressionless, looking down at Isobelle, as if she was almost inferior to him.

"Ah, excuse Bruno," smiled Valentino, "he doesn't say much."

The burly driver opened the back door of the car for the girls, both tentatively getting in, both looking at the stone-faced driver, wondering if they were doing the right thing.

Bruno drives off for the long journey, and now all of them are safely inside the car.

Meanwhile, back in Lansburton, the police are swarming all over the town, also doing house-to-house calls.

After going to catch up with nearby friends, Paul drives back into the town, just in case he needed to pull in a favour, and starts to head back to the house.

Along the way, he sees several police in the area, and he suddenly starts to get very nervous.

He stops a few hundred yards away from them and pulls his car into a vacant parking spot.

He gets out, puts his head down, and hides behind a wall, to see what was going on.

His breath quickens.

He decides to call one of his friends, who he had just been to see, Scott Connelly, to help him out of his current situation.

"Scott, I need your help," I've driven back to Lansburton, and the place is swarming with police, I need you to come and get me, drive me back to the house, so I can grab my stuff, and disappear."

"Where abouts are you now?"

"I'm on a street called, hang on, Tadbury Avenue," Paul, stretching his neck back to see where he was.

"Ok, I know it, hang on there, I'll come and get you, stay low."

Scott was one of Paul's oldest friends, along with John and the others.

He didn't always see eye-to-eye with him and had lost touch after Scott had moved away, but he knew that he lived near Lansburton, and just looked him up.

Scott is a mild-mannered man, beefy, around five foot eight, stocky build with a bald head, he also likes his beer.

"Hurry Scott, they're closing in," Paul whispered, sounding slightly breathless.

He peers around the side of the wall and thinks a police officer has spotted him, as Paul sees him gradually walking towards the wall that Paul is hiding behind.

Paul's breath quickens, faster and faster, he closes his eyes at the inevitable, he's sure they've caught him, as the officer raises his gun, pointing towards the wall, where he thinks he's spotted the fugitive.

'Hey, everyone, over here, I think I've found something,' Neil calls out, and the officer who was heading in Paul's direction stops, still paused, holding his gun towards the wall, before turning around, and heading back over to where Neil had called out.

Paul heard the call, opens his eyes, and peered around the wall, to see the officer had gone.

Suddenly, Scott's car pulls over to where Paul is standing.

He immediately darts into the car and slams the car door shut.

"You got here just in time, I thought they had me there."

"I told you that I wouldn't be long, and I drove as quick as I could, even did some red lights I think."

"Ok, let's go," Paul defiantly said, and, as Scott's car once again screeched off in the opposite direction from where the police were situated, Paul scrunched himself down as far as he could in the back seat of the car just in case he was noticed by any police who may have been looking back.

Meanwhile, Neil thought he had noticed a gun in some overgrowth of grass nearby, but it just so happened to be an old black bin liner, that was in the shape of a gun, having blown around in the wind.

"Never mind, just keep doing ground searches, and carry on making house-to-house calls," said the bullish detective, "someone around here must know something, though, by the looks of some of them here, it doesn't look like we'll get much out of anyone."

Neil was feeling very frustrated at not making any breakthroughs, but he felt that it was just going to be a matter of time before he did.

'I'm closing in on you, just you wait until I catch up with you, you fucking bastard, you won't know what's hit you,' he thought to himself.

"I'm going to take you back to my place, well, mine and Julz, stay with us for a while, keep your head down, he won't come looking here, you'll be ok here for a while," smiled Scott, as he kept on driving, as fast as he could, not wanting to break any speed limits, in case it was detected.

Scott was driving back to his four-bedroomed house, in a village called Jeromesley, a tiny village set back in the middle of nowhere, and was a hundred miles from where Paul and Sarah lived, but about fifty miles from Lansburton.

"So, where were you when I called, for you to get to me so quick I mean, not that I'm complaining," chuckled Paul, hardly hearing himself speak, with Scott driving so fast down the motorway, with his window wound down slightly.

"I was kind of nearby, Julz asked me to pick a few bits up for her, you know, sanitary towels, bits for her hair, you know what women are like mate, can't get them where we are."

"Anyway, what of you, how's that woman of yours, been ages since I saw her," Scott continued, glancing across to Paul, whilst also trying to keep his eyes on the road.

"Not sure, not seen her myself for a few days."

"What do you mean, you've not seen her, not had a falling out have you?"

"No, nothing like that." "She's… she's brought a friend along with her, and she's kinda getting in the way a bit, wish she hadn't joined us, long story, tell you another time perhaps."

"Oh yeah," smiled Scott, "you fucking lucky fella, get in there, threesomes are always fun," he chuckled.

"No, nothing like that, well, we have, but this girl is more of a hindrance mate, she needs to be gone."

"So, where are they now?"

"No idea, swanning about somewhere but, at the minute, I don't really care, I just need to get back to yours."

The two men are soon back and walk in the door.

Julie is in the kitchen prepping some food, made aware in advance that they were going to have company.

Scott met Julie Adley during a wedding that he had attended with some friends, she was the photographer, and a successful one at that, going all over the country, such was her popularity.

She had also worked for some of the country's top fashion magazines, where she had been asked to take many pictures, some pictures she had taken were of some very famous people, so she was glad for some rest, so she could spend a bit of time at home.

Julie was petite, standing around five foot three, with wavy auburn hair and bright brown eyes, and Scott had become instantly attracted to her, they had been dating for around two years, they didn't have any children though, Scott was never really a fan of having his own kids.

"Hi Julz, look who I have with me?"

"Hi Paul, good to see you, Scott has filled me in, you must be in need of some food, come on, sit down, I've just prepared a stew."

Paul looked towards Scott, as both men sat at the table, Julie bringing the big pot over, it smelt so good.

"So Paul, what's your next plan of action, and don't you think you should try and get hold of Alice, just to check that she's ok?" muttered Scott, with a munching on a mouthful of stew.

"Scott! Talk after you've eaten, couldn't you?" snapped Julie.

Scott glanced towards Paul, waiting for him to answer.

"I'm not sure yet," "like you say, think I'm just going to lay low here for a while, if it's ok with you guys, let the dust settle a bit, maybe I could help you both around the house, got to earn my food somehow," he smiled, in both Scott's and Julie's direction.

"You stay here as long as you need, you know there is always a place for you here," smiled Scott, though Julie didn't look as pleased as Scott with his statement.

"Well, maybe not too long hey Paul, we are used to each other's company and well, it's a bit awkward but yes, for now, of course, you can stay," Julie was a little hesitant with the duration of his stay, and, knowing that he was probably in trouble with the police, Scott had not told her too much, only that he needed to get his head down somewhere for a while, as he was having a few issues with the police, but that it wasn't anything too serious, even though Scott knew better.

"Got to say Julz, this stew is delicious, you're a very lucky guy Scott to have someone who can cook as good as this," grins Paul, his head almost buried in his bowl of food, before glancing at both of them in turn, but Julie was in no mood to smile back, but to just give both him and her boyfriend a slight look of disdain, the table falls silent, you could cut the atmosphere with a knife.

Food was all finished, and Paul sensed that Julie felt uneasy about him being there.

"Erm, thank you again, that was delicious, I'll wash..."

"No you won't, sit down, I've got this, besides, there isn't much, I'm sure you boys have a lot of catching up to do," Julie collected up the plates and cutlery and frostily headed out towards the kitchen area.

It was a large open-plan house, with a conservatory and very large garden, where they entertained throughout the summer, Scott was equally a good cook and they entertained regularly.

The house felt very warm and homely, all year round.

There were arty paintings spread out around the house, some looked expensive, which Paul was looking around at.

"So Paul, what's going on, how deep a trouble are you in?"

"I've had some trouble with some drug dealers, and I've

had some heavies come round and try and sort me out, let's just say that I was ready and waiting for them."

"DRU… DRUGS?" whispered Scott, leaning across to him, hoping that Julie hadn't heard the conversation, Scott was slightly angered and exasperated at what Paul had just told him, and thumping the table, but not too much so Julie had heard.

"Yes," he whispered, "it's a long story, too much to go into, another time but, needless to say, I feel like public enemy number one right now."

"I'll speak to Julz, maybe you need to keep your head down longer than I thought."

"I've killed a few people along the way too."

"God mate, you are in a mess," "why don't you try calling that wife of yours, let her know you're here, especially since she'll probably be wondering where you are."

"No, she's off with her new floozie, she'll call me if she needs me," Paul was in a defiant mood, and wasn't at all worried about what was happening with Alice and Isobelle at that moment, besides, what if his phone had been tapped by the police.

"I'm going to need a burner phone, I'm sure this one will be tracked by the police."

"Wait there, I have an old phone stashed away somewhere, and an old sim card that I got that I didn't end up using," Scott got up from the table, and practically ran upstairs, so he could find what he was looking for as fast as he could, almost not wanting to leave Julie with him for too long.

She had finished washing up, and was busy drying, giving Paul glances over her shoulder every so often, with an almost fake grin, one of almost disgust, like she had overheard the conversation.

"Nice house," Paul trying to lighten the mood between the two of them, as he heard drawers being pulled out above him upstairs.

"Yes, we like it, been here a few years now, and wouldn't want to be anywhere else."

You could still cut the atmosphere with a knife between the two of them, it was still very frosty.

"Listen, I know you don't like me very much, but I will be as helpful as I can be around the house, as much as you need me to be anyway." "Scott has always been a good friend of mine, we lost touch for a while, but I managed to find his number again," Paul had got up from the table, gone into the kitchen area, where Julie was still drying up, and had leaned on the breakfast bar to talk to her, but not too loud, so it didn't embarrass Scott if he was suddenly to appear from the stairs.

"I don't dislike you Paul, just think it's dangerous for all of us, the longer you stay here but, while you are here, you can start by putting these plates and pots away for me," Julie raised a brief smile to him, in the hope that it might ease the tension a little.

"There, found it, I knew it was about somewhere, I just had to rummage around a bit," Scott smiled, having raced down the stairs in double-quick time.

Scott passes both the phone and the sim card to Paul and tells him to take the sim card out of the phone he has, so he's not tracked.

He looked at both his girlfriend and his friend, as he could sense there was still a bit of tension in the room.

"It's all good, we've had a bit of a chat," Julie smiled at

Scott and then looked at Paul in turn.

"Maybe we should get you a bit of a disguise Paul, how does a short dress, glasses and an old woman's wig sound to you?" Scott joked, he always had a sense of humour, and Paul wondered why they had lost touch but, realised that it was just life, plus he had met Julie in the meantime.

"Oh yes, and a tutu to go with it," Paul chuckled, with even Julie raising a smile and a chuckle to their wit.

"I'm going to go out and grab some food and bits, is there anything you need Paul?" "Will you be ok with Julie for a while, I should only be a few hours but, whatever you do, keep your head down."

"I could do with some wash stuff, deodorant, aftershave, here, here's some money."

"It's ok, I'll cover it, you've looked after me in the past, I'm sure I can sort you out."

"I shouldn't be too long."

Scott grabbed his keys, kissed Julie on the cheek, and made his way out of the door.

"Right, just going to go and give my wife a call," Paul looking in Julie's direction.

He walks up the stairs, and into the bedroom that he was going to be staying in, at least for the time being.

He tries calling Alice…

(Ring… ring)

'Sorry, I can't come to the phone right now, so, you know what you do.'

'She's probably out fucking some randomer," he thought to himself.

He heads back down the stairs, where Julie is sitting having a coffee and watching some tv.

"Anything interesting?" he says to her, nodding his head in the direction of the television.

"Not really, but I'm just wanting to chill for a bit, help yourself to a coffee if you want one."

"What's it like living with Scott then, he's a great guy, don't know why or how we lost touch really."

"Yeah, I love him, and he has spoken about you a lot since we've been together."

Paul sits next to her, and they carry on chatting.

"So, what next for you, long-term I mean?" "You can't keep running forever!" Julie was curious to know what he was going to do with himself, with his current situation.

"Scott hasn't really told me too much, and, I'll be honest, I don't particularly want to know but, whatever it is, it doesn't sound great for you."

"Maybe you shouldn't know," "let's change the subject."

"How's your photography business?"

"It's going well thank you," both were happy to shift the focus away from what was going on in Paul's life.

"How are things between you and your wife?"

"They're ok, but she's brought this chambermaid with her, a bit of a long story really, and she's a bit in the way," an angry Paul snapped.

"Oh, kind of two's company?"

"Yeah, something like that, just wish she wasn't around."

"She's nice enough but, you know..."

"Scott was saying that you have brothers, and your mum and dad?"

"Yeah, I have brothers but..." Paul started to well up a bit, when thinking of his parents, "I've not long lost both parents and, if it's all the same, I'd rather not talk about it."

"Of course not, I'm sorry."

There was a sudden silence between them, Julie not quite knowing what to say, after talking about his past.

"Anyway, I need a shower, I won't be long," Julie getting up from the sofa, leaving the television on, "carry on watching this if you like."

Paul glanced at Julie with a half-hearted grin, as she headed towards the stairs, giving him a little glance and a grin of her own, before going up.

He could hear the shower being turned on, and a slight running of the water.

He stared into space a little, not quite knowing what his plans were himself, let alone what he was going to tell the couple, who were good enough to put him up until he sorted himself out, he just knew that he couldn't go back to the rented house, with the police swarming all over the place.

'I need to go up to my room, organise it a bit if I'm going to be here a while,' he thought to himself.

As he walked up the stairs, he could see that the bathroom door was ajar, enough to see in, and this aroused him slightly, as he had not had sex for what seemed like ages.

Julie was showering, and the shower door was completely see-through.

Paul tried to avert his eyes but, knowing what an attractive woman Julie was, he couldn't resist anymore, and paused slightly to watch her.

Julie turned around and saw that he was watching her, but she didn't seem to mind, she just smiled at him, almost beckoning him to join her.

Although she had a tiny frame, her breasts and figure were almost perfect.

She continued to shower, not taking her eyes off his glazed look, he tried not to look, though he couldn't resist, as the water sprayed off her beautiful body.

"Like what you see?" she muttered to him through the glass shower door.

Paul carried on watching her, as she continued to rub body wash into her shiny body, using her finger and biting her bottom lip, to try and entice him in with her.

He pondered momentarily, really wanting the feel of a woman's touch again, the feel of being wanted once more, as it had felt so long, and he was a highly sexed man.

He carried on watching for a few more moments, before deciding against the invite to join her, besides, Scott could return at any time, and he didn't want to put himself in the situation of cheating on his friend, so he decided to carry on walking towards his bedroom instead, to do what he had initially come up the stairs for.

He went and sat on the bed, and wondered what it might have been like, and he still had an erection, which slowly went down but, he did admit to himself that it was a close call, and maybe staying with the couple might not have been the best idea but, at that moment in time, he didn't really have much choice but, how long could he resist temptation, but knew that he would be ok, as long as Scott was in the house.

He heard the shower turn off, so he got off the bed and started to look as if he was straightening his bed sheets, as well as looking out of his bedroom window.

He felt the presence of Julie, standing at the doorway,

a lime green towel wrapped around her dripping body, covering her breasts, her hair swept back over the back of her neck, droplets of water dripping on the laminated floor.

“What stopped you?” Julie felt a little disappointed that he hadn’t joined her, “I’ve heard you’re a bit of a stallion, and wanted to see for myself how good you were.”

“I’m not doing that to my friend,” “he’s bailed me out by allowing me to get my head down here, and you want me to re-pay him by fucking his girlfriend?” he snapped.

“Let’s just say, we have a bit of an understanding,” “do you think he doesn’t go out fucking other women, he does, but, that’s ok with me, and us,” she smiled at him, giving him a little wink, “besides, I could see that you were, shall we say, tempted, I could see that by the look of your jeans,” licking her lips, and loosening her towel a little, so he could see a bit of her cleavage.

“That may be so, but, right now, it’s not the right time, I need to sort myself out.”

“Mmmm… maybe another time then,” as she turned round in a sultry manner, licking her lips and smiling in a sexy way, looking back at him, giving him a teasing wink, before walking away to go and dry herself, and put some clothes on.

“They’ll be another time, I will have you,” she said as she turned the corner and into the hallway, and into the bedroom that she and Scott slept in.

The door downstairs went, startling Paul initially, darting towards the window, and cowering down, just in case it was the police.

He needn’t have worried, it was just Scott returning, armed with big white bags, almost weighing him down, even though he was a fit man, but he looked like he was struggling a bit with them.

"I'm back, where are you both?"

"Just upstairs honey, just jumped out the shower, down in a sec."

Paul came out of his room, giving Julie a slight stern stare, before heading down the stairs.

"God, have you left anything else for others to buy?" Paul smiled.

"I need a beer, this stuff weighed a ton."

Both men sat down, Julie also coming down the stairs shortly after, giving Paul a little look, but he was more interested in what Scott had brought.

"Couldn't find you a tutu in your size," Scott chuckled, "but I hope you'll be happy with what I got."

Scott opened the bags and pulled out what appeared to be lots of different clothing, as well as various disguises, a baseball cap, moustache and beard set, sunglasses and various pieces of clothing.

"This is just perfect Scott, thank you," "I can't stay cooped up in here all the time, I'll need to get out at some point, maybe even get back to the house to grab some bits."

"That might be a bit risky at the minute mate don't you think?"

"Yeah, it might be, I didn't mean right now, I meant when the dust has settled a bit."

"Maybe I could possibly act as the landlord of the property, they wouldn't suspect me would they."

"That's a good plan but, for now, I'll just sit tight and keep my head down here, as you said, if that's ok," giving Julie a look in the process.

"I'll go and fix us some lunch," Julie got up, after momentarily looking at Paul with a brief smile, and headed into the kitchen.

Scott pulled the rest of the bits out of the bag, including some deodorant and some aftershave for him, even some underwear.

"Hope you don't mind me getting you some boxers and stuff, thought you might need it until I can get to the house."

"No, it's really good of you Scott, thank you, it is appreciated."

Paul sifted through all the stuff that Scott had brought back, put his bits back in one of the bags that were now empty, took it all upstairs, and laid it all out on the bed, so he could try it on when he got the chance.

"Lunch is up Paul," Julie shouted up to him.

They all sat down to lunch and had idle chit-chat before Scott asked about Alice.

"Did you manage to get through to that gorgeous wife of yours?"

"No, I wasn't able to get hold of her but, she's a survivor, she'll be ok."

"Don't you think you should try her again, especially if she's unaware of the police swarming around?"

"She's a bright woman, she'll work it out, I'll try and give her a call a bit later."

The rest of the day, they sat inside, watching some tv, and generally just chatted, before it was time for them to go up to bed.

"You coming up darling?" smiled Julie to her fella.

"I'll be up in a minute darling, just going to chill with Paul for a bit, have a chat, I won't be too long."

She goes upstairs and leaves the men to carry on chatting and drinking the whisky that Scott had poured them both.

"Goodnight Paul."

"Goodnight, see you in the morning," he calls up to her, as she's walking up.

"So, where do you think your wife is mate, you don't think they have her do you?"

"No, if they had, they'd have found my number wouldn't they, I'm sure they'd have traced me here somehow."

"Not if you now have that burner phone they won't."

"That's true but, I'm sure they won't have her, she's probably fucking someone mate, I've got to think about myself for now haven't I."

"No, you're right, we must keep you safe here," "I'll take a drive round to your house tomorrow, maybe wear one of those disguises I brought back, they won't suspect anything, that's if it's not cordoned off but, I will go and check."

"Right mate, I'm heading up, won't hear the last of it from the missus if I don't go up, night."

"I'm heading up myself in truth, I'm whacked."

Scott paused on the stairs and looked across at him.

"It'll all work out ok in the end, you just see if it doesn't."

Paul sat and pondered his next move, whenever that was going to be, finished his drink, and headed up to bed himself.

He closed the door, got undressed, and climbed into bed, to try and get some sleep.

Suddenly, he could hear Julie and Scott's bed banging against a wall, and hearing lots of groaning and moaning, she was very noisy.

Paul's bedroom was adjoined to the bathroom, and the main bedroom was at the far end of the house, so the sex was loud enough for him to hear, but it didn't bother him this turned him on, and he suddenly got another erection, and decided to masturbate to the sound of their love-making.

He pushed the bedsheets back so he didn't get them too messy.

He cupped his balls whilst gripping his shaft tightly, as the sex down the hall got more intense, the bed hitting the wall faster, and the groans becoming louder, mainly from Julie, almost as if she wanted Paul to hear, though he could hear them clearly.

His cock was hard, and he knew that he was going to cum at some point, and wondered if he should have had sex with her in the shower, but he was also thinking about what Alice might be doing with Isobelle if they might be fucking each other too, and this turned him on even more, and he masturbated harder and faster, and before he knew it, he was cumming all over his stomach, he spurted that hard, that he almost got some in his eye, he also didn't think he was going to stop cumming, just as Scott's and Julie's bed had stopped hitting the wall, and the groaning had stopped.

He missed a woman's touch and wasn't sure if he could carry on resisting Julie if the situation arose again.

He laid still momentarily, taking stock of what had been happening to him recently, and wondering how he was going to get out of his situation, but the disguises were certainly going to help.

He pulled the covers back over him, as he started to feel a little cold, and wanted to sleep.

He woke the next morning and checked his watch, it was seven-thirty, it was time he got up, though he didn't have much to do, though he could wear a disguise, and go out with Scott somewhere.

He walked naked towards the shower, yawning, not remembering that he was in Scott and Julie's house, and went to walk into the bathroom, to find Julie once again in the shower, soap suds dribbling down her body.

Julie turned around and motioned for him to join her, looking down at his manhood and muscular body, and licking her lips.

"Hush, Scott has gone out to take a look around the area of your house, he'll be gone a while so, in the meantime, you're mine."

He knew that it was wrong, but he needed to feel the love of a woman once again and decided he was going to get in with her.

She opened the door, and he climbed in, slowly starting to kiss her, feeling her breasts as he did so.

He began to passionately kiss her lips before he muzzled on her neck, Julie caressing his balls as he once again started to get an erection.

He carried on kissing her around her neck, before working his way down to her hardening nipples, flicking them with his tongue, and sucking each breast hard in his mouth.

He also slowly moved his hands between her legs to feel her pussy, sliding his finger in, as she started to pant.

She turned him around, pushed him against the wall, kissing him around his neck, and also sucked on his nipples, before going down and sucking his erect manhood.

He watched her put most of him deep into her throat, moving her head slowly backwards and forwards.

He pulled her up, turned her back around, pulling her tiny frame up, as she wrapped her thighs around his waist, pushing his manhood inside her, thrusting her up against the wall.

They continue to kiss, before he starts to nibble on her neck once again.

The feeling of having sex once again felt so good, however bad he felt, and Scott mustn't know.

Julie was loving the attention she was getting from Paul, and she finally got her wish of having him.

Paul's legs were shaking, as he felt himself about to cum inside her.

He thrust harder and harder, and as she pulled his neck harder with her hands, she too felt she was going to cum, tilting her head back as much as she could, and groaning as loud as she did the previous night.

He suddenly stopped, as he had cum, pressing her petite body up against the shower wall, both stopping to catch their breaths.

Julie started to laugh, and Paul looked at her with disdain once again, for teasing him enough to do what he did.

He stepped out and grabbed a towel to dry himself off.

"Don't worry," she smiled, "Scott won't find out, like I say, it's an agreement we have, he fucks others too, and I know he's a good friend of yours."

"... and that's supposed to make me feel better is it, with what I've just done?" he snapped.

She carried on washing in the shower, while he walked

towards his bedroom, to get dressed, in some of the clothes that Scott had kindly brought him, albeit it was minimal.

He put on some dark grey trousers, and a thick woollen cream-speckled jumper, that made him feel very warm and comfortable, almost a little too warm, just after the shower with Julie, which he was starting to regret.

He was all dry, and walked down the stairs, without even giving her a second look, who was just stepping out of the shower herself, drying her body with the other big green bath towel.

As he was walking down the stairs, Scott was coming in through the front door.

He could see that Paul had used the shower, as his hair was still slightly wet.

Paul looked at Scott slightly sheepish.

"Sleep well?" smiled Scott.

"Erm yes, I did, thanks mate, I was almost out for the count.

"Sorry if you could hear us last night," Scott smirked, giving his mate a wink as he did.

"Oh that, yes, no…that's ok, you're a couple, and it is your house so…"

Suddenly, Julie appeared, walking down the stairs, again, looking as if she had showered herself, as she had grabbed a smaller towel, and was still rubbing the back of her head, to dry her hair.

Scott paused, looking at them both individually.

"You two ok?" he asked, showing no expression on his face.

"Yes, Paul went for a shower, so I waited for him to get out before I had mine."

Paul continued to look a little sheepish, not quite being able to look his friend directly in the eye, as Scott continued to look at him, expressionless still.

"Oh, ok. Anyway, I've been to take a look around the area around the house, "there is still some police activity, but not as much as there was before, but it looks as if they've got your car so, that's gone mate, sorry."

"I'm going to go back later, put a disguise on, and tell them that I am the landlord if I'm questioned or stopped," Scott continued.

"Do you really think that's such a good idea, you don't want them dragging you in, or you're both screwed," a worried Julie replied.

'You can say that again' Paul muttered to himself.

"What was that?" Scott asked.

"Nothing, just thinking that we will both be in deep shit if you get caught, and it leads them back here."

"Look at it this way, I'll have your keys, I'll have a great disguise on so, they won't know me, and I will have worked out what to say if I am challenged. I'm the master of talking my way out of stuff, been doing it all my life."

"I'll grab some bits for you; clothes, smellies, and anything else you need."

"Passport?" asks Paul.

"No, that'll be marked now, you won't be able to leave the country unless we go somewhere by car perhaps, your passport will be the end for you." "Why, are you planning on going somewhere?"

"Just thought maybe a change of scenery."

"Listen, you've just got here ok, we'll be able to get out and about, especially now you have that disguise, plus, you have no chance of leaving the country, not now, maybe never."

"As I say, just keep your head down here for a little while, let the dust settle, and we'll soon be going out, maybe see if we can track that missus of yours down, make sure she's ok."

"Yeah, I'm going to give her another call now."

He went upstairs to grab his burner phone and made the call, which he knew off by heart.

He dialled the number once more.

Ring… ring…

Ring… ring…

'Hi, sorry I cannot come to the phone but, you know what to…'

'Where the hell can she be, I know she's off galivanting with that pain in the arse Isobelle but, why isn't she picking up?' he thought to himself.

He was slightly worried yet, again, he had to think of himself for the time being.

He put the burner phone away in his pocket and walked back downstairs.

"She's still not picking up, but she'll be off fucking that chamber-maid Isobelle so, I need to think of me right now, but, I'm confused as to why she isn't answering."

Paul sat back down, Scott looking at his friend, with slight concern.

Paul also had other pressing matters to be worried about because, as well as the detective chasing him, he also had another sinister character tracking him down…

TRAPPED

The girls and the men had finally made it to Italy, which took around a day, seeing the beautiful sights and countryside along the way, making many stops, to eat and sleep, mainly in the car.

They finally arrived in a beautiful town called Tropea, which has a population of around six-thousand people and is surrounded by the clear Azure Sea, with golden sand coves, caves, lagoons and thousands of fish.

They got out, Bruno going and grabbing their bags from the boot.

He was a beefy, muscular man, and the weight of the bags didn't bother him at all.

Isobelle turned full circle several times, gawping in awe at the beauty of the place, and immediately fell in love with it.

"This is just amazing," she excitedly shrieked to Alice, while Alice herself was also looking around in awe, she had never seen this part of Italy before during her modelling days and stared at the beauty surrounding her.

"Maybe we could go snorkelling or something honey," smiled Isobelle, "never done that before, and what better place to do it than here."

"All in good time girls," smiled Valentino, over-hearing their conversation, flanking Isobelle on her left, while the driver Bruno flanked Alice, "there is plenty of time to go exploring," speaking in his broken English, "but first, we need to take you back to where you'll be staying, then maybe, you could do some exploring, come please, we are just up here," smiled the suave Italian, pointing up to an old looking castle, that looked fit for a king.

They walked up to the castle, an old-looking building, dating back centuries.

Isobelle could see that one of the four towers of the beautiful building had been destroyed, due to damage centuries ago, but this was now just old rock.

The castle overlooked the town of Tropea and was high up by some other ruins.

They walked up the bright white steps, to be greeted by another hunky Italian man, standing in the big white marble-like doors, looking like he was a doorman from a nightclub, wearing an expensive looking light-blue designer Italian suit, big dark sunglasses, a bald head, no expression on his face, just like Valentino's driver.

"This place is incredible," smiled Isobelle to Valentino.

"Yes, this castle has been in my family for centuries, passed down from my ancestors, and now it is mine," he smiled back.

"*Vai e metti a tuo agio le ragazze*" (go and make the girls comfortable) mutters Valentino to the doorman, as he nears the top of the steps, looking sternly at him.

"Come, my compatriot Luca will take your bags and take you to your room."

Covering the walls of the castle were very old huge paintings, depicting battles of centuries gone by, but also paintings of true beauty, artistic paintings of naked men and women again, from many centuries ago, and the girls could not get over just how beautiful and incredible the castle looked.

They followed Luca to the long winding white marble stairs, which were pristine and clean, and wondered how long it would take them to reach the top, they seemed to go on forever.

"This way," pointed Luca to their room, as they reached the top, again showing next to no emotion in his face, yet very authoritarian in his voice.

"We eat in one hour," Valentino shouted up to the girls, "then tomorrow, I show you the sights, and we go exploring, before the photo shoots begin, after all, this is why you are here yes?"

Isobelle turned to Alice, with pure excitement in her face.

She felt that she was needing to pinch herself, as she never thought she would not only be in beautiful Italy, but also having never modelled before, that in itself was a new experience, she didn't think that she was beautiful enough to do it, but she felt in great company with Alice, and she knew that she would guide her but, not only that, but she was going to do it in an amazing foreign country, she felt in dreamland, the excitement she felt and showed, was a sight to behold for Alice.

Despite the castle being old, the whole building was very warm, cosily warm as opposed to too warm, and there was a log fire on as they entered the castle, even though the weather outside was comfortably warm, as were the days in Tropea generally.

Luca dropped the girls' bags inside the doorway of their room and casually walked away.

They looked around and again, there were many old paintings, it was a very large grand room, with a huge king-size four-poster bed for the two of them.

Isobelle came over to Alice, after taking in the size of the room, and planted a kiss on her lips.

"This is all down to you," "I cannot thank you enough," Isobelle shrieked once again, dancing around the room like a young teenager, she couldn't get over the situation she had found herself in, falling back onto the bed in pure excitement, stretching out and shaking her body, such was the thrill of the moment.

"Well, let's make the most of it, this kind of thing doesn't come around very often, but we've also got to be a bit wary, we still hardly know this guy, we're in a country, miles from home so, we still need to be on our guard."

"I'm sure it's all ok, just a sexy Italian man, who just wants to photograph beautiful girls, and why wouldn't he want to do it in his homeland, it is beautiful after all?"

Alice didn't want to dampen Isobelle's excitement and enthusiasm but, she had dealt with men like this before, and she knew that she needed to get out of England, she was sure she was being chased.

The girls decided to dress for the occasion of dinner, putting stylish dresses on, from their shopping trip in England, before their new adventure to Italy, and the girls were excited at the thought of shopping during their time in Tropea.

Alice wore a beautiful lime-green strapless gown, looking every inch the model that she was previously, despite her slight reservations about being in Tropea, she wanted to enjoy the experience herself.

Isobelle wore an equally elegant gown, dark brown, almost black looking, with a silky cream rose at the top of the strap on her left shoulder, slightly different in design to Alices' but just she looked just as beautiful.

Both girls had also put their hair up in a bun, and they looked just divine.

It was approaching seven-thirty in the evening, around the time that Valentino had planned for the meal.

He had also dressed for the occasion, in a maroon-coloured jacket and black trousers, looking every inch the host of the evening.

"You look.just…wow," smiled Isobelle to Alice, looking her up and down, with the biggest smile on her face, "If we had time," she chuckled.

Alice smiled at her and returned the compliment.

"You look pretty special yourself, now, shall we head down to dinner?"

They linked arms, and left the room, standing at the top of the stairs, Valentino standing at the bottom, glancing up at them, with a smile as wide as the sea, his eyes bulging at the sight of their beauty.

"*Solo magnifiche signore*" (just magnificent ladies), putting his two fingers to his lips and pulling them away, like blowing them a kiss, in appreciation.

"It is an honour to have you in my home, come, let us eat."

Valentino linked arms with Alice, and Isobelle linked

Alice's other arm, and they went to sit down at the large king-size table in the centre of the open-plan castle hall, that seemed to adjoin every other room, apart from the kitchen, where the aroma of the food that was about to be served to them, drifted through.

"Oh my god, that smells amazing, what is it?" asked Isobelle inquisitively.

"It is Bistecca Fiorentina," he smiled, leaning back in his chair, that looked throne-like, "how you say, good old-fashioned ribeye steak, we eat this mainly, hope you girls are hungry after all that travelling?"

"Ah, excuse my rudeness to my guests," and like a proper gentleman, he got up from his chair, and strode over to each girl in turn, to pull their chairs out for them to sit next to each other, Valentino sitting at the head of the table.

"It's ok, I'll get my chair," Isobelle smiled at him.

"Please, I insist," he smiled back, as he gently pulled out her chair, as she sat elegantly down.

Valentino clicked his fingers, the man was in charge, and out came dinner, carried by Luca, who wasn't just a doorman, and steam was coming from the very large tray containing the three plates, with metal covers over each plate, to keep them warm, and the aromas were unmistakable.

Luca put the tray on the table and carried the plates to each of the girls first, before carrying Valentino's to him.

He then went back over to the girls, to lift the covers off the plates, first he uncovered Alice's, then Isobelle's, before finally Valentino's.

Luca went back to the kitchen and brought out salad, Italian tomatoes, red onions and the best lettuce, crispy and fresh.

He also brought a bowl full of small, boiled potatoes, more than enough for all of them.

"Wine?" asked the host to the girls.

"We have a cellar downstairs, where we have an array of wines, Luca has brought up a few bottles of red, two hundred years old so, very mature wines, I hope this is satisfactory to you both," he smiled, leaning back in his chair, with a slight arrogance.

Luca soon arrived at the table with the uncorked wine and poured Valentino's wine first into his large crystal glass, followed by the girls' wines, before he walked back towards the kitchen area.

"*Un toast*!" (A toast) "*essere pronto per il duro lavoro*" (be ready for hard work), "this means ladies that we are here to work, not just to sightsee."

He raised his glass with a slightly sinister look, and a smirk in their direction, Isobelle smiles, slightly nervously clinks glasses with Alice, and gestured her glass in his direction.

Both girls' eyes meet, looking slightly nervous at each other.

"Let's eat," he smiled, gesturing his knife down at the food in front of them.

"Tonight we rest, then tomorrow, I will take you on a boat trip, a company that my good friend Giovanni Tello runs, he will look after you, and you will see the sights of the Tyrrhenian sea, a sight to behold" he smiles, "Tropea is also famed for its delicious red tomatoes here," he said smugly, again, sitting back in his chair.

"How is your food, to your satisfaction?"

Isobelle again looked nervously up to Alice, looking for reassurance.

"Yes, mine is delicious thank you, is yours Izzy?"

"Yes, yes, it's very nice thank you," she nervously smiled, not being able to look Valentino in the eyes, looking more down at the table, sipping her wine.

"More wine?" Valentino, leaning forward in his chair, to grab the bottle, and offer to the girls.

"No, we're fine thank you," Alice speaking for the two of them.

"How long do you think we'll be here; we won't be able to stay here forever will we?" Alice wanted some assurances of how long their assignment was going to be.

Valentino sat arrogantly back in his chair, looking at both girls in turn.

"You have just got here, and already you are wanting to leave?"

"No, we just want to know what the assignment arrangements are, so we can make plans, and where we will go," Alice was in no mood to be messed about.

"It will take as long as it takes, you will both be paid well, and I want to show you more of my country."

They had all eaten their food, and it was time to leave the table.

"Come, let us sit by the fire, talk business."

They all used the napkins to wipe their mouths, before leaving them on their plates, again Valentino almost arrogantly throwing his onto his plate.

They all sat by the roaring log fire, which had been burning brightly for a few hours, but logs had been tossed on by both Luca and Bruno, to keep the castle comfortably warm.

"So, you girls are going to need money while you're here," "shall we say ten thousand euros each?" Valentino still sitting back arrogantly in his chair, after being presented with a cigar by Luca, and he puffed away at it.

"Ten thousand each?" Alice looked bewildered and puzzled by the huge amount of money being offered to them.

"Well yes, that is, to begin with, there will be more, depending on how long you are here, then, we can look at finding you both somewhere safe to stay," what do you say?"

Alice looks over to Isobelle, still feeling slightly apprehensive at being in the castle, but the sound of so much money on offer, slowly starts to lighten up.

She grins over to Alice, still a little unsure, but Alice agrees, especially for now, they are out of the clutches of the police.

"Your friend has gone very quiet," the grinning Italian leaning forward in his huge chair, to flick cigar ash into the tall, stylish ashtray.

"She's never done anything like this before so, I think, after a good night's sleep, we'll both be looking forward to the adventure."

"That's settled then." "Right, go and get some rest, we will have breakfast, and then we depart on my friends' boat, and take you to parts of my country that you probably haven't seen before."

They leave their chairs, all finish their glasses of wine and put them on the dining table, as the girls start to climb the stairs, Isobelle not wanting to look at him, she felt slightly nervous about him still.

"Goodnight girls," he calls up to them smugly, with a slight smirk, "breakfast is at seven and we leave here at eight, make sure you are ready, I will speak with Giovanni and let him know to expect us."

He stands at the bottom of the stairs, looking up at them, like a commander-in-chief proudly looking at his troops, as the girls continue to walk up, Isobelle briefly glancing around and giving him a half-hearted smile, before carrying on going up with Alice.

They finally reach their room, and Isobelle sits on the bed.

"He scared the shit out of me Alice, I'm not sure we should be here."

"I think that is just his way, Izzy, he's an Italian remember, plus we are in his kingdom aren't we?" "Let's enjoy the time we have here, tomorrow will be amazing I bet, try and relax, and I'm sure you'll feel better about it all."

"I'm sure you're right, he just gave me the creeps a little bit but yeah, maybe because we are in his kingdom as you say, plus, it is beautiful here, I'm with you, and we are going to earn good money while we're here aren't we?" she smiled, trying to raise her spirits.

"Exactly, we'll get to see the sights tomorrow, never been to this part of Italy before, not even during my modelling days, so, I'm going to look forward to it, will make me feel better if I know you're having a good time too."

"I am, just the way he was at dinner, freaked me a bit."

The girls slipped out of their dresses and put on some silky nightwear that they had brought while they were out shopping, didn't want anything too warm, with the climate being warm anyway, the room itself also being cosy.

They lay on top of the bed, leaning in together, Alice putting her arm around Isobelle's waist, yet not wanting to curl up too close to her, with it being so warm.

"What are your dreams Izzy, you've never really said,

what is it you want out of life, not to be a maid forever surely?" Alice grinned.

"I want a life with children, with a man or woman, not fussed which, out in the country somewhere, maybe a bit of farmland thrown in, just a nice quiet, relaxed life."

"That sounds idyllic, maybe with the money you're going to earn here, it may set you up a bit hey, give you the step up you want."

Isobelle laid back away from her, to ponder what she had just said, and thought that she was probably right and that maybe she should try and just enjoy this new experience that had been presented to her.

Isobelle leaned back towards Alice, and gave her some loving kisses, before they both fell asleep, as they needed to be awake early for breakfast and the boat trip around the Azure.

Both girls woke the next morning, it was five-thirty, and the sun had already risen, it was going to be a nice clear, warm day.

"Sleep well darling?" smiled Isobelle, but Alice was still yawning, trying to wake herself up.

"Morning beautiful, I did thank you, did you, are you feeling a bit clearer this morning?"

"I am actually yes," she smiled, staring at the old marble ceiling, "let's shower."

"Thought you'd never ask," Alice smiled, and the girls quickly got out of their nightwear, threw them onto the bed, ran into the en-suite bathroom, and turned on the huge luxurious walk-in shower, their beautiful, bronzed bodies glowing in the sun that shone through the stained-glass window of the shower room.

They both got under the huge shower head that hung over them, again gold-looking in colour, they were unsure if it was real gold, but it certainly appeared to be.

Alice's long blonde hair was soaked by the water jetting down onto her, as Isobelle stood next to her, the dark shoulder-length being sprayed with the power of the water coming from the head.

They both put soap gel into their hands to wash each other, spending a few moments to lather each other's breasts, but not in a sexual way, but to just make sure that they were smelling their best while they were out, however, the girls kissed each other slowly, Isobelle almost wanting to have Alice have her in the shower, before she wrapped her arms around Alice's neck in a tender embrace, almost looking for more reassurance, and Alice embraced her lovingly, however much she wanted to make love to her in the shower, she didn't feel that the time nor the place was right, but she was sure there would be a time that she would have her, maybe after they had left this assignment.

They finished showering, grabbed the two large bright white bath towels, that looked as if they had come straight from a posh hotel, and wrapped them around themselves, water still dripping from their hair and bodies.

"Shorts and thin top weather today Izzy I think," Alice smiled, Izzy, nodding in agreement.

They had already put all of their clothes away, and both pulled out stylish shorts and tops; Izzy wore tight denim style cut shorts, and a thin grey top, that showed off her curves but, she didn't care, she knew that it was heading for a very warm day; Alice wore light-brown stylish shorts and a light cream thin top which again, also showed off her ample curves and, like Isobelle, she knew what a warm day it was looking.

They both put on a pair of light brown sandals, that had air pockets in them, so they knew that their feet were going to be nice and cool.

They both looked the picture of beauty, having already applied their makeup and perfume prior to getting dressed, and they were both ready to head down for breakfast, having also sorted out their hair.

"Let's have a fun day out, shall we?" Isobelle smiled; Alice was happier that she seemed much more like her old self again.

Alice grabbed her hand as they walked out of the bedroom together.

They started to walk back down the long windy stairs once again and were greeted by Valentino.

He wore a white short-sleeved shirt and beige trousers, some flat dark brown moccasins, with his greasy-looking, swept-back hair, looking every inch the smooth Italian he first appeared.

"Ah ladies, what a sight to behold you both are once again, come, let us sit for breakfast." "I hope your sleep was to your satisfaction, and the room is comfortable?"

"Yes, we slept very well thank you," Isobelle briefly grinned at him.

"My driver Bruno will drive you down to the boat yard, where Gio will take you and others around the Calabria, which is the region we are in now, you girls will have a great time, there is much to see."

"I took the liberty of arranging a full-English breakfast, as you call it, I hope you girls are hungry, there are also plenty of stops on your trip today, to go shopping, eating and drinking, oh, and you'll be needing those euros we discussed, I have arranged this with Gio also, he will give you this yes."

"*Luca, porta la colazione*" (bring the breakfast in) snapping his fingers, the men knew who was in charge.

The girls looked at each other at his arrogance, but this was his way.

They all tucked into the breakfast, as Luca came around the table, not saying a word, but pouring each of them fresh orange juice.

"We have a vineyard, where we grow all our grapes for the wine, and oranges and fruits, for this juice, you like?"

"Yes, it's very nice," smiled Alice, "wait, you said that your driver will take just the two of us to the boat yard?"

"Yes, I have business to attend to I'm afraid but, maybe next time I will join you yes," he sighed, sitting back in his chair forlornly.

Isobelle felt slightly better, knowing how her feelings towards Valentino had changed slightly due to the words he used the night before, but at the same time, not being too sure how Gio was going to be, but if there were other sightseers there, then she knew she was going to feel more relaxed, in the knowledge that he wouldn't be there.

They finished breakfast and Valentino showed them towards the big marble door of the castle, which boomed when opened and closed.

Bruno suddenly appeared behind him, walked out, passing the girls, got into the car, which was parked up beside the castle, started it up and pulled up outside, to wait for the girls to get in.

"Meant to ask you this when we arrived but, are they bullet marks on the side on the left there?" Isobelle quizzed, "I noticed them when I was walking up when we arrived.

"Where do you see this?" he sternly asked.

"There look, by that lion's statue on the left, there appear to be few bullet marks."

Isobelle went to take a closer look, just as Valentino met her halfway.

The stairs were flanked by two big commanding stone lions, looking hundreds of years old, but still appearing in near-perfect condition.

"Ah yes those," "they are from many centuries ago, when Italians used to fight each other, nothing for you to worry about, now go, Bruno is waiting for you, have a good trip."

The girls got in the back of the car, and it started to pull away from the castle, Isobelle looking back at him, and he gave them a wave goodbye and a grin.

They are soon arriving at the marina, where Gio is waiting for them, along with some other tourists which made Isobelle feel a bit safer.

Bruno opened the back door of the car, to let the girls out, and they look around their picturesque surroundings, with the boat *Buon Giorno* and Giovanni waiting for them to board.

Gio holds his hand out in the direction of boarding, looking in the girls' direction.

"Please, this way," he grins, the girls duly walk towards the boat, and get on, Gio holding their hand as they stepped on board.

"Waters are calm today," he tells everyone, "relax please, and enjoy your journey."

Gio seems pleasant; a bronzed, well-built man, with short dark hair, a goatee beard dark designer sunglasses.

The girls are greeted with smiles and a few greetings from the other passengers, around a dozen in total, all feeling very excited about the trip, with lots of laughter. Some had even brought some bottles of champagne with them.

"Please, safety rules," smiles Giovanni, "do not tip the boat over," he jokes, as the passengers laugh along with him.

"We carry drinks and snacks so no need to open that bottle you have there, unless you wish to share of course," he smiles, again the others laugh.

Isobelle and Alice manage to find seats at the back of the boat and sit next to a blonde lady.

"He seems nice," smiles Isobelle to Alice, today is going to be a great day, I feel like I can relax now," as she rests her head on Alice's shoulder.

"Ah, you're from England?" said the lady sitting next to Alice.

"You too?" smiles Isobelle, sitting up straight once again from Alice.

"Yes, I'm from a place called Jeromesly, have you heard of it?" she smiles.

"Can't say that I have," smiles Alice, but we're not from around that area anyway, we're from...well...somewhere else in England."

"Sorry, Jo's the name, Jo Franklin-Evans, nice to meet you both," she smiles, shaking their hands.

"It's my first time in Italy, never been here before so been looking forward to doing things like this," Jo continued.

"I'm Alice, this is my friend, Izzy, we're just here, erm,

sight-seeing ourselves really," Alice wasn't too keen on giving too much away, even to a stranger.

"It's good to see you looking more relaxed Izzy," as she put her head back on Alice's shoulder, Jo smiling at them being so close while watching as the boat pulls out from the marina.

The sun was beating down on the boat, and the passengers were wafting themselves with whatever they had, with it being so warm.

Alice and Isobelle put some sunglasses on to protect their eyes, and they were taking in the beauty of the clear blue sea, and the thousands of fish that were swimming beside the boat.

"I have snorkelling equipment on board if any of you wish to do this," Gio wanted his passengers to experience the seas as much as possible, "but I will inform you of this when we reach the point, and the sea this time of year is very warm yes so, you will have a nice bath time, hope you have all brought your rubber duck or submarine for you," he jokes.

"We will be going to caves and coves also on our journey, which is an experience, you will have a fantastic time, especially if you have never done this before," he said.

"We will be stopping later where you can get off and explore more of the Calabria; you can see Cathedrals, shops, things to see and do also," he smiled.

The passengers have taken to their skipper, and the girls also had taken a shine to him.

Gio was a very likeable Italian, slightly arrogant but nothing like Valentino appeared.

"Have you heard anything from Paul?" Isobelle was

curious, as Alice had not mentioned him at all since arriving in Italy.

"Yes, he's tried calling, but I'm here with you, and he's the least of our worries isn't he," she smiled back to her.

"Let's just enjoy this magical ride and day out together."

"Looking forward to the snorkelling," Isobelle shrieked.

"... don't forget the shopping and sightseeing too," Alice smiled.

Gio and the boat continued to take the trippers further in, before coming to a halt, turning the engine off.

"Ok everyone, this is where we stop for you to snorkel, for those of you who want to."

Isobelle and Alice were keen to, along with six others, while a few decided to stay on board.

Passengers took it in turn to get the equipment from Gio, before getting ready to dive in.

The girls were last in the queue to jump in, but they held each other's hands as they did so.

They swam around, coming across some starfish, sea urchins, a leatherback turtle, which neither had seen before, seahorses and as Alice pointed to Isobelle, in the distance, they could see a bottlenose dolphin, which they both stared in amazement at, this was certainly an experience that they would never forget.

The snorkellers continued to swim around, before being waved back in by Gio.

They all eventually climb back aboard, and revel with each other with what they had seen, the group had formed a good bond.

He then slowly started to steer the boat towards a large

cave, which was famous in those parts, and it seemed to go on for miles, yet was very beautiful at the same time.

He stopped the boat, so photos could be taken, before he turned his boat around, and headed out of the cave.

"I hope you enjoyed that experience everyone, now for our trip over there," as he pointed to what appeared to be a large island, "There you will find shops, restaurants, things to do and see and also an old cathedral, which carries a painting of Madonna, not that Madonna," he joked, but a painting of the other Madonna, which is known as our protector of these parts."

The boat chugged along, before reaching the island, where all the passengers started to depart, the girls getting off last.

"Ah ladies, I have something for you," he looked sternly at them, "I have been asked to give you this package from Valentino, I almost forgot," he smiled, "enjoy your look around, we depart back in three hours."

They give Gio a final look before they head off to shop and eat, Alice looking into the envelope as they carried on walking.

"This is the ten-thousand euros each that he promised," looking at Isobelle, "let's go and enjoy ourselves."

"Let's go and blow the lot," she laughed, jumping around with joy.

"Let's go, baby," Alice smiled at her.

They walked around the vast array of shops, and restaurants, passing the cathedral that Gio had mentioned to them, browsing in and out of shops, without buying anything at that point, they knew they had plenty of time to do that, especially with so much money, which Alice had stuffed in a bum-bag that she had brought with her, and would sit and split it with Isobelle when they got to sit down.

They came across a bar, *Bar Veneto*, and decided to call in for a coffee and a bite to eat.

"*Cosa posso fare per te?*" "*Excuse, hello, what can I get for you?*" said the waitress in slightly broken English.

Alice smiled up at her.

"Yes, can we please have two Aperol Spritz drinks, and a board of bread, cured Italian ham, olives, cheese and potato chips in a side bowl."

The waitress walks away, as the girls talk about the coming weeks.

"I'm quite looking forward to our modelling now, especially if we're going to be showered with money like we've been given," said a new excited Isobelle.

"Ah yes Izzy, here is your half, ten thousand euros."

"I've never had this kind of money before, and we're going to get more after it's all done aren't we," she smiled, "especially if we get brought back out this way to model, with all of this scenery."

"We can only hope," Alice chuckled.

"Right, come on, let's carry on exploring, there was a nice blouse that I saw on the way here, I think I'll go back for it," Isobelle was definitely in the mood to carry on with her Italian dream.

They got up from the table, leaving the bill on the table, along with a tip for the service, which was customary.

They carried on walking, and came across another quaint shop, where they both brought a stylish flowery blouse each, thanked the assistant, before walking out.

They headed back to the shop where Isobelle had spotted the blouse, which was still there, a beautiful white flowing top, with white streaks running across it, and an image of Tropea faded into the background of the blouse.

"That'll look lovely on you Izzy."

"... Out of it too I hope," she winked, laughing and smiling, "might even try it on for you later," she winked.

They came out of the shop, and it was time to head back to the boat, the three hours had flown by.

They saw one or two others from the trip, including Jo, who they had been sitting next to them, as they walked back to the boat.

"Oh, buy anything nice?" she smiled, noticing that they had some bags with them.

"Oh, you know, the customary blouses you wear when you're away, that sort of thing," Isobelle smiled at her, "have you brought anything nice yourself?"

"The same really, a few pairs of nice shorts that I saw", Jo smiled, "I also went to the cathedral, and saw the painting of Madonna, was an amazing sight, you'll have to check it out, depending how long you're here for."

They carried on chatting about the trip whilst heading back to the boat.

"Come, hurry everyone, there is something else I wish to show you, before we head back to the port," Giovanni was insistent on getting everyone back on board, so he could show them one last thing.

The sun was beginning to set over the horizon of the sea, which made for a spectacular sight.

Everyone was back aboard, as Gio pulled the boat back out from the island, and into the vast clear blue sea.

He carried on driving the boat for what seemed like an eternity, before stopping almost in the middle of the sea and switching the engine off.

"Now, if you all carefully go over to your left of the boat, you should be able to see what is known as a pod of dolphins, but you need to look carefully, you will see them over to the west if you look carefully," Gio confidently said, knowledgeable of the local seas, having skippered his boat for many years.

Lo and behold, he was right, many of the passengers pointing over to the west, the romantic setting of the sun setting in the background, the pod of dolphins, about six of them, bobbing up and down, as if they had come to show off to the boat and its passengers and they were only one hundred feet away.

Lots of flashing of the passenger's phones were going off, getting as much coverage of the dolphins as they could, even Gio was still taken in by the beauty of them, even though he had seen them a thousand times before.

"Come, we must go, before it gets too dark, and I won't be able to navigate my way back, only joking with you," he chuckled, the passengers breathing a sigh of relief.

Gio was soon taking his boat back to Tropea marina, and pulling up to the walkway, from where he had originally helped the girls on board.

Everyone started to get off the boat and make a payment for the trip, three hundred euros each, but everyone seemed to be paying extra, such was the excitement of the day.

"Was nice to meet you girls, maybe I'll see you back in England sometime," Jo smiled, as she was the last to get off, paying Giovanni before walking off.

"Thank you, Gio, what a very pleasant and amazing trip this was," both Alice and Isobelle starting to get money out to pay him.

"Oh no no," he smiled, "please, I do not wish to be paid, this was an arrangement I had with Valentino so please, keep your money," as he pushed his hand towards the girls' hands, to stop them paying him.

"But please, we would like to, even if it is a tip, we've had a wonderful time," smiled Isobelle to him.

"I'm sorry, I cannot accept this," giving them an almost stern look, before tying his boat up for the night, and walking away.

"Look, there is Bruno, waiting to take you back."

They started to walk up towards the car, as Bruno got out of the driver's seat, and opens the back door for them to get into, as they continually look back at Giovanni checking his boat over.

"Wonder why he wouldn't even take a tip from us?" she asked Alice, Isobelle was a bit puzzled but was thankful for the day she had had anyway.

Bruno, as expressionless as ever, was standing by the back passenger door, waiting for them to get in, like he was there to collect royalty or someone famous.

The girls got in, and the car pulled off, as they continue to glance back at Gio, still tending to his boat.

"I've got a real zest for this now Alice, I'm looking forward to whatever we have in store, what an exciting adventure we're on really."

"I'm glad you're a little more relaxed Izzy, still, we need to be on our guard because we don't know this guy, however a romantic country that we're in."

"Perhaps I can help relax us both later honey," winks Isobelle, as she caresses Alice's thigh, Alice giving Isobelle a huge smile, knowing what she had in mind, Bruno looking in his rear-view mirror at what the girls were doing.

"Don't you ever talk?" Isobelle snaps at him, leaning forward towards their burly driver, almost in a fit of annoyance, but he gives her a blank look again in his mirror, without saying a word, and carries on driving back to the castle.

"Ssssh Izzy, he's probably under orders, let's just get back and relax."

They pull up at the castle, and the girls get out and start walking up the steps, where the door is opened by Valentino.

"Ah, you are back, you had a good time, yes?" he smiles, his arms out-stretched in an almost welcoming manner.

"Yes, thank you, we did, this place is both amazing and beautiful, I'm hoping that you're going to take us back out there for our modelling shoots," Isobelle chuckles.

"All in good time but for now, let's eat, and rest and the hard work begins tomorrow," "we will have breakfast at seven-thirty, talk business and set up for your photo shoots."

"Is it just to be the two of us, or is that other girl joining us, you know, the one in England?" asks Alice.

"Ah, you mean Leona, alas no, she was not able to make it here, maybe another time."

The girls start to walk up the stairs, to dump their bags, and change for dinner.

We eat in thirty minutes so, please, do not be long."

The girls dump their bags and crash out on the bed as if they had been running a marathon, but it had been a long day, and they were both looking forward to modelling tomorrow.

They both slip into their evening wear; Alice this time, wearing a cream skirt and silky scarlet V-neck blouse, and matching scarlet shoes, whilst Isobelle wore a knee-length sky blue skirt, with matching V-neck blouse, and white flat shoes, again, both looking very elegant.

"After dinner and business chat, it's you and me honey," smiled Isobelle to her lover, Alice shaking her head and chuckling as they headed out of the door towards the stairs and dinner.

"Ah, as ever, two beautiful ladies, what a sight to behold," "come sit, dinner is about to be served," Valentino gleefully gestured.

Again, Valentino sits at the head of the table, swept back almost jet black glossy hair, black trousers and an open-necked perfectly ironed white shirt, looking and smelling as good as he did when they first met him.

Luca then appears, carrying three plates as usual, with silver covers over the top to keep them warm.

"Tonight ladies, we have for you chicken breast, how you English say, baby potatoes and some salad, with our famous red cherry tomatoes, I hope this is to your liking."

Again, Luca comes round to each of them in turn, to pour them all a glass of white wine, as Valentino is ready to toast, by raising his glass to them.

"*Lascia che domani sia l'inizio delle cose a venire,*" (let tomorrow be the start of things to come) "this means in my language ladies that, tomorrow will be an exciting time for the two of you, I will make sure of this," he smirks, as he begins to drink his wine, chillingly looking at the girls as he did.

"Eat your food, or it will go cold, and Luca has been patiently waiting for your return to cook for you," he smiles, arrogantly sitting back in his chair.

They all start to eat, as talk then turns to what is to happen the next day.

"Now, tomorrow, breakfast is seven-thirty as I've said, then, we head to a different part of my castle, where photos will be taken in my studio, and I will want various poses of you, in various positions," he added, rudely talking whilst chewing his food, "then we break, more food, then we carry on with photoshoot yes?"

"Don't worry, you will also get time to rest, but, hard work begins now, this is why you are here yes?"

"… and we get paid when?" asks Alice.

"Yes," he smiles, arrogantly wiping his mouth with his perfectly folded napkin, "yes, you will both be paid handsomely, at the end of the assignment, I will give you both ten thousand euros each, how is this?"

"Yes, that sounds good to me," smiles Alice, "Izzy?"

"Wow yes, ten thousand euros, that's almost ten thousand pounds now isn't it?"

"By the way, I want this all in writing, a contract, that we will be paid what you promise, I take it you have the legal documents drawn up, we're not going to be scammed," Alice was a shrewd business-woman when it came to these type of matters.

"Yes yes, it is all in place, of course, now, you have sexy clothing with you yes?"

"Don't you worry, we'll be looking our best for the shoots, just let us know what you need from us, and when we sign this contract, I want to give it a good read over first," Isobelle let Alice do all the talking regarding matters of business, with this being her expertise.

"I also have clothing for you in my studio so, I want you to look your best, as I know you will, there will be something good for you both."

They finished their meals and started to leave the table.

The girls start to walk the stairs when they hear a shout, something they had not heard before.

"What was that?" a startled Alice asked Valentino.

"Ah, Luca can sometimes get a bit heated in the kitchen, I have told him about his temper before, nothing for you to worry about, go and get some rest," the Italian smirked.

"That sounded like a female voice," Alice was still unnerved by the noise.

"Do you think Luca prepares all of your meals on his own? No, he has people in there helping, it was probably one of them smashing a plate or something, I'll go and sort it out, go and get some rest, down here for seven-thirty remember, glad you have enjoyed yourselves today," he again stands at the bottom of the stairs, hands in his smart Italian trousers, watching them walking up the stairs, as Alice looks back at him, as she grasps Isobelle's hand, to almost reassure her that everything was ok.

Valentino then arrogantly blows them a kiss from his two forefingers, in his bid goodnight to them, before he strolls off, almost in an angry walk, to deal with the noise.

The girls reach the bedroom, Alice still feeling a little uneasy as to what she had heard.

"You don't think he's hiding anyone do you, or kidnapped them or anything?" "I've not heard that noise before either," Isobelle again started to feel a little uneasy, especially with Alice's reactions.

"No, I take his word for it, I'm sure that Luca does get help in the kitchen," "look at me, I'm getting as jumpy as you, we could always cancel this modelling you know, get away."

"No, I'm here now and, like you say, it was probably a kitchen helper," "it has kind of put me off sex tonight though, would you mind?" Alice didn't want to upset Isobelle by refusing her advances, though she knew that she was feeling horny in the car heading back.

"No, of course not, we've plenty of time for each other haven't we," she smiled at Alice, "did you want to try and leave, if you're feeling a bit edgy?"

"No, it's ok, it has been a long day, and I'm sure he has things in hand, and I take his word that it was a kitchen maid, though it is strange that we've not seen her come out to us yet isn't it?" "Let's get some rest and look forward to an exciting time ahead, starting tomorrow."

They get out of their evening wear, tired from their long day, knowing that they had to be nice and fresh for the modelling in the morning.

They slip into their satin nightshirts and climb into bed, which felt and smelt like it had been freshly re-made for them.

Alice leaned over, giving Isobelle a kiss goodnight, Isobelle returning it with a long kiss, rolling her tongue around Alice's, almost wanting to make love to her.

"Let's sleep," chuckled Alice, plenty of time for me and you," "goodnight darling."

"Night Alice, sleep well."

The next morning had arrived, it was six o'clock, and the girls stretched to try and wake themselves up.

"Been thinking about that noise we heard last night Alice, do you think we should ask if we can see the kitchen maid, that'll help calm us won't it?"

"Yes, that's a good idea, we could ask if she's ok, maybe see if she can come out and say hello to us perhaps."

They get up to shower, both showing their beautiful curves, more so Alice, with her previous career, but Isobelle equally having a nice body.

"They get in the shower together, no sexual thoughts, but more thoughts on the day ahead.

"How do you think today is going to pan out Alice, you've been in this situation before."

"You just relax Izzy, follow my lead, listen to what he asks of you but, I'll direct you too, I'll show you what he's asking you to do ok."

"I'm both nervous and excited at the same time, this is going to be an amazing experience, just a shame that we're not going back out on the boat to model, that would have been amazing."

"We could always ask if he has any plans to do that couldn't we?"

"Yes, we could, now, turn round, I want to wash your back, and that peachy bum of yours, I can see why you used to model" Isobelle chuckled, as both laughed at her request, but she did as Isobelle had asked.

They had soon washed each other, come back in to dry themselves, had caught the sun from their excursions the day before, and were both looking and smelling like they had just come from paradise.

They elegantly strode out of the room after dressing, walking hand-in-hand, and were soon down the stairs, again, being watched at the bottom by a smiling Valentino.

"Ah girls, forever beautiful, perfect for today, come, this way, and I will show you to my studio."

They walked out of the back of the castle, a part that Valentino was yet to show them, about two hundred yards away from the castle, and in front of them stood a big white building, with three levels, that looked as beautiful as the castle, with huge gleaming windows, the sun shining through them, at least the girls knew that they'd be warm enough.

"This way ladies, we must start," demanded the Italian, pointing down in the direction that they must go.

They walk down a gleaming white pathway, around fifty steps, and into a huge room, where there were bright screens already set up and waiting, and the floor was comfortably heated. There were artistic photos of naked and partially naked girls adorning the walls, and it made the room feel and look very professional, and this relaxed both girls a lot more.

"Come, this way, I wish to discuss with you the order of the shoot," he smiled, again wearing dark trousers and a brilliant white shirt, that was undone at the top by a few buttons, he too looked like he could have modelled.

"So ladies, I will direct you, where and how I wish you to stand and pose yes, and I will snap away many times."

"I know Valentino, I have filled Isobelle in on this, as this is all new to her but, as you know, I have previously modelled."

"Ok so, let's get started."

The girls walk over and stand in front of the screen and start to pose in various positions for him.

Isobelle seems a natural and is starting to enjoy the attention of the camera, and is in full swing, much to the delight of both Alice and the Italian.

"Wow girls, you are both very good, Isobelle, you sure you have not done this before no?" he smiled.

"No, this is my first time, but Alice persuaded me, plus the money is going to be good," she smiled back.

Valentino's camera continued to snap away, as the girls carried on posing.

"Girls, I wish you to kiss, but maybe wear just these blouses I have here, I wish you to lose the dresses yes?" Valentino was wanting to push the boundaries.

Alice looked at Isobelle, wanting to know if she was happy to do it, but she was loving the attention of the camera so much, that she was more than happy.

"There is a screen over there where you can change if you wish, or just change where you are," but the girls felt more comfortable going behind the screens.

Valentino took the blouses over to them, and they went behind the screen, as the Italian waited.

"You sure you're happy for him to take pictures of us, we're going to be naked you know, apart from these blouses, which look pretty see-through anyway," Alice was happy to do it, having been in the same position for many years, but she wanted to make sure that Isobelle was again comfortable.

"Yes, I'm very ok with it, I'm loving it, and the camera seems to like me," she chuckled.

"Ok well, as long as you're happy," the girls disrobed,

their dresses falling to the floor, but wanted to leave their knickers on, Isobelle was a bit uneasy going out, where he would see her pussy.

The girls then slipped on two beaded tops, that had sparkly sequins all over them, and you could see their breasts peering through them.

They put their shoes back on and walked out from behind the screen, where Valentino was pacing up and down, in anticipation of seeing them.

"Ah yes, you both look magnifico, but, I ask that you lose your panties please," he smiled, "I will look away, and when you have done this, I wish you to be in a clinch close together, you to touch lips, with your right legs bent back please, and your hands on each other's hips, and eyes closed."

Valentino turns around, as the girls face each other, smiling at each other, as they remove their knickers.

They stand close together, in the clinch that he asked for, and tells them that they are ready.

"Wow ladies, what a sight it is for me to see two stunning girls like you, and the camera seems to like you also."

"Now, get in close together, your breasts touching through the blouses, and touch lips, close your eyes, and raise your right legs, your heels touching your buttocks."

They get into the pose that he requested, as Valentino gets down and continues to snap away, the pose looked amazing and would look very artistic in any fashion magazine on the planet.

The photoshoot had been going on for around three hours, and Valentino was starting to get hungry.

"Ladies, let us break for lunch, put your underwear and

dresses back on, and let's head back to the castle to eat yes, then we will continue."

Valentino turned around as the girls picked their knickers back up, and put them back on, as they disappeared behind the screen to get dressed.

They reappeared, and they all headed back to the castle.

"I have arranged to fix you up some pizza and fries, salad and something to drink if this is suitable for you yes."

They all sat down at the table, and Luca appeared, stone-faced as he always was, carrying their food on the silver tray.

As before, he walked around the table after pouring them each a glass of white wine, before disappearing back into the kitchen.

Again, there was a female's voice shout, coming from somewhere.

"Who is that shouting?" Alice asked, munching on her salad, intrigued by who it might be, "why don't you introduce us to the kitchen maid, it would be nice to thank her for such delicious food that she cooks us" she continues.

"She is very shy, and will not come out to meet you," Valentino suddenly looked very angry at being disturbed by the shouting.

"*LUCA! LUCA!*" he shouts, as his doorman comes from the kitchen, and leans down to listen, as Valentino whispers in his ear, so the girls don't over-hear his conversation, even though he'd be talking in his language anyway "*chiudi quella ragazza prima che sia necessario, stiamo cercando di mangiare*" (shut that girl up, before I have to, we're trying to eat) he says, in a menacing voice.

Luca heads back to the kitchen and is out of sight, and the noise suddenly stops.

"Sorry about that girls," he smiles, "please, carry on with your meals," gesturing with his hand for them to carry on enjoying their food.

Isobelle looks at Alice, with slight concern once again, but understands that he must have set rules in the castle, so she cast her fears aside, much to the relief of Alice.

They all finish eating and get up to head back for more photos.

Valentino leads them, but Alice hangs slightly back, with a little concern, so she can look through the small round window at the top of the black kitchen door, to see if she can see the woman in question, who had been shouting, but there was no-one in sight, not even Luca, Isobelle looks back at her, noticing that Alice wasn't walking next to her, before Alice catches up with her, also so Valentino wouldn't notice.

They all head back to the studio, and the camera once again begins to snap away, with the girls in the clothes that they first wore, when they entered the studio.

"This time girls, I wish of you to remove your dresses and your bras, keep your panties on, and your shoes, Alice, you to lay flat on the floor, looking up, your right hand covering your breasts, and you Isobelle, you to lay your head on Alice's tummy, looking at the ceiling please your breasts on show though yes," Valentino knew exactly what he wanted, as the girls got into position, and again, Isobelle felt very relaxed and had got into the moment of the camera snapping away.

This time, he removed his camera from the tripod and brings it in closer to where the girls were laying.

He stood a few inches away from them, as the camera snapped away.

"Yes ladies, this is very good, the camera loves you," both of the girls were enjoying the moment, and as more sexy snaps of them were taken, though tiredness was starting to set in, as this was visible to Valentino.

"So, when are we getting paid for all of these shoots again?" Alice took the lead in enquiring about their contract.

"Yes, all in good time, do not rush me over the contract ok, all in good time" he snapped.

Isobelle was about to angrily snap back at him before Alice intervened and shushed her quietly.

The atmosphere turned a little frosty, as the girls got up, gathered their clothes, and made their way back behind the screen.

"Do you think he's going to pay us, you know, as he promised?" Isobelle asked Alice.

"I hope so, I'm sure he's just a bit tired like us, it has been a long day hasn't it?" she smiled, trying to stay calm, and not un-nerve her lover.

The girls were soon dressed, and came from behind the screen, Valentino sat on one of the red sofas in the stylish studio, one leg crossed over another, patiently waiting for their appearance.

He looked on at them in silence momentarily.

"Come come please, I wish to show you something," he muttered, arrogantly and nonchalantly wagging his finger, but with his back turned, motioning them to follow him.

The girls slowly walked in his direction, as he walked slowly towards the door, sighing as he reached the exit.

They arrive back in the castle, the day starting to

darken, with the night drawing in, and he takes them in the direction of the kitchen.

"I wish to show you another part of the castle," he said, motioning them through the black kitchen door.

He opened a big thick fire door, and as they peered inside, being almost pitch black, next to no visibility, he stood back, and pushed them both inside, and they fell down a flight of stairs, crashing into some old boxes at the bottom, grazing their faces.

"Now be quiet, don't disturb me, and you'll be unharmed," he smirked, "the pictures will come in very useful, along with my other models who, unfortunately, couldn't be quiet so, I had to dispose of them," he said chillingly, "just make sure you don't go the same way," before he slammed the door shut and appearing to lock it behind him.

The girls were shaken and a little dazed by coming down the flight of stairs, as Alice gingerly raced back up, her legs and arms slightly cut but alas, he had indeed locked the door behind him.

"Let us out you fucking monster, LET US OUT!" but, no matter how much she shouted and screamed, she remained unheard.

Isobelle sat where she landed, sobbing, not knowing where fate was going to take them.

They looked around the dim cold room and heard a murmuring coming from one corner of the room.

Isobelle embraced Alice, as she was frightened as to who it could be, but they were both convinced that it was the female that they had been heard shouting a few times while they were upstairs.

They slowly walked over, to that part of what appeared to be the cellar where all of the wine was stored and seemed to shed a bit of smoky light, sat a woman, propping herself up against a post.

...it was Leona, the model who they had met in England.

She too was both dazed and bloodied, a few cuts to her face, her clothes looking damp, and seeming slightly dazed and confused.

"Oh my god Leona, are you ok?" asked a concerned Alice.

"Wha...wha... who are you?" she asked, shaking her head in a confused manner, still very dazed and bewildered.

"It's Alice and Isobelle, Leona, we met you at that FUCKING SCUMBAG's studio in England, do you remember us?"

"Oh yeah, you fell for his charm too did you, congratulations," she smirked, with her bloodied mouth, her eyes almost shut, sighing, trying to muster the strength to talk.

"WE'RE TRAPPED, WE'RE TRAPPED," Isobelle sobbed," how the fuck are we going to get out now?"

Alice went over, putting her arm around Isobelle, to both comfort and reassure her.

"Don't worry, we'll get out of here soon enough, the question is though, how but, don't worry, I'm sure with the three of us, we'll get out of here."

She glanced over to Leona as she said it, before spotting an old sack, that she managed to tear in two, and cover over Isobelle, to try and keep her warm, as they all snuggled up together, Alice pondering their next move.

GET US OUT OF HERE

Paul, Scott and Julie meanwhile, were busy pottering around the house.

"We must get you out soon Paul, don't want you going stir crazy in the house."

"I'm not a cooped up kinda guy either, I like to be out, so, this does feel a little claustrophobic at times but, I'm sure I'll be able to get out, without being spotted, and I'm sure I'll be able to help out in the garden or something," Julie looks at Paul, with fantasies of him stripping off running through her head, turning her on a little.

"Maybe I could get you out somewhere for a beer, maybe we might both need disguises, just in case they have anything on me, so they can trace you," Scott said.

"That's a good point, looking forward to seeing what you're going to wear, maybe the tutu you spoke about, was perhaps a fantasy for you," Paul replied as both men laughed.

"Have you tried getting hold of Alice again, and what was the name of the other girl she was with?"

"Huh, Isobelle, or pain in the arse as I like to think of her," Paul didn't want Isobelle around, and the sooner she was out of their lives, the better.

"Why is that?" Julie asked.

"... because she basically jumped in our car, when we were escaping Chammerley, I didn't even know she was in the car until we'd pulled away," "I had plans for it to just be Alice and me, now this girl has just ruined everything."

"You boys think about all that tomorrow, I'll go and sort dinner," Julie wandered into the kitchen and started to fix up a meal for them all, "chicken casserole ok for you Paul?"

He nodded in her direction, giving her a brief smile, while still thinking about the hassle that Isobelle had caused, and that things would be running smoother without her.

"We'll just chill tonight if you like, maybe go out for a pint and a game of snooker or something tomorrow," smiled Scott.

"Ah, that sounds like a great idea, I need to try and reset, it's all been really stressful."

"Thank you mate for being here for me, don't know how I'd have got through all this without you."

"My home is your home my friend, and everything in it," Scott continued, as Paul again looked over to Julie, who was still prepping the casserole, knowing what they did while Scott was out.

Dinner was soon served, and after finishing, the plates cleared and washed by Paul, they just chatted and also sat in silence in the lounge area, while the television was on, Paul was deep in thought, sitting in a chair on his own, while the couple sat cuddled up on the sofa, Scott often glancing over to Paul, but he seemed a million miles away in his thoughts.

"You ok over there mate?" Scott was letting Paul know that he was there if he needed to talk.

"Yeah, I'm just mulling over my plans, that's all."

"Don't you worry yourself about your plans for now mate, just concentrate on the here and now," "I have phone calls to make, I could set you up somewhere, I know a couple, who have a place that they own, a farm, but they're hardly there, and I'm sure that'll let you use it, they spend most of their time away, on cruises and things like that, living the life of Reilly, but for now, you just stay here with us and, when you find out where that wife of yours is, and that Isobelle, then I'll give them a call, I'm sure that they'd love it to just be lived in until they are ready to use it again, it just sits idle pretty much, well, apart from the helpers, girls who just feed the animals, make sure they're fed and all that."

They all then settle back down for the night, Scott and Paul knocking back a few beers and having a laugh before they all head off to bed, Julie looked back at Paul as she climbed the stairs, giving her a little grin, as if it was a tinge of jealousy, that it wasn't him in that position.

Paul sat on his own for a few more minutes, wondering how life events for him and Alice were going to unfold, he also knew that he needed to get rid of Isobelle as quickly as he could, but how?

Paul lay in bed, tossing and turning. He lay in a comfortable double bed, fresh clean sheets, but things were running through his head, and he was sweating, as if in a bad dream.

He suddenly shot up in bed, he'd had that bad dream, and it rocked him.

He was sweating more and panting faster, dreaming about what they did to Sarah back in Barnwood, but also where Alice was.

He had dreamt that a mysterious man had her in a headlock somewhere, her tied to a chair, and Isobelle was watching on and laughing, and he felt helpless, as he then watched the man have sex with them both, but that Alice was starting to enjoy it, going down on her, then Isobelle, before he got up and broke Alice's neck, that's what woke him.

He shouted a little, and this caused Scott to come into his room and switched the light on.

"You ok Paul?"

"Yeah, sorry, just had a bad dream, you go back to bed, we'll talk about it in the morning."

"Ok mate, as long as you're ok," Scott paused, looking at his friend, before he turned the light back off, and closed the door.

The next morning, Paul awoke to the smell of smokey bacon, drifting up to him from downstairs, he got dressed and ventured down, and saw Julie sitting at the breakfast table, while Scott is still rustling something up.

"Ah, just in time, a full English is it, heard you moving around," Scott watched as Paul's face lit up, he was feeling rather hungry, and sat down next to Julie.

"Sleep ok?" she asks.

"Yeah, sorry if I disturbed you last night, just a bad dream that's all."

Scott walked over and put the large plate of cooked breakfast in front of him.

"Get that down your neck, we'll go out today, you need

a breather out of here, but we need to disguise ourselves."

Paul ravished the breakfast like he hadn't eaten for days, drank his coffee that Julie had poured him, as she watched him, still fantasising about him in the garden, shirt off doing the gardening, earning his keep.

"That was delicious thank you, sorted for the day now," he smiled, sitting back in his chair, holding his stomach, like he had just eaten a horse, as Scott came over and put his plate in the sink to be washed.

"Right, let's go and have a rummage, see what I brought back for us to wear as disguises," smiled Scott, as both men went up the stairs to have a look in the bags that he brought back with him the day before.

Scott had stored the bags in the big walk-in wardrobe in their bedroom and pulled them out and emptied everything onto the bed.

"We don't want to look too outlandish, do we?" Paul joked.

"No, just normal clothes, but I've got things like fake beards and moustaches too, we need to be as inconspicuous as possible."

It was a fairly warm day, but they still didn't want to wear any shorts, otherwise, they might be spotted, just by possible markings on their legs, and Scott had a distinctive England badge tattoo just above his ankle, this being his only tattoo, but this might be something that the police may spot during surveillance, even though it wasn't him on trial, but it might lead the police to his friend.

Paul put on a smart pair of maroon-coloured chinos and a bright white t-shirt, and attached a goatee beard to his face, that stuck on with strong glue.

He also put on some large sunglasses and a baseball cap and white trainers, as Scott looked him up and down.

“Blimey mate, I wouldn’t recognise you, you look so different.”

Scott wore a pair of dark denim jeans, a yellow t-shirt and a baseball cap and moustache, they both looked like they had come out of a set of Miami Vice!

They walked down the stairs, and Julie almost fell off her chair, she was still sitting at the breakfast table, she was so taken aback by their appearance.

“BLOODY HELL! What have you done with my Scott and his mate?” she joked, “you just need a gun each now, have you both joined The Village People?” she laughed.

“Get used to it love, this is the new me, we’re off to sink a few beers, play some snooker, and then off to find a gay bar somewhere,” Scott nudged Paul in jest, as they all burst out laughing.

“We’ve got to be in as much disguise as we can, at least when we go out, otherwise, we’ll be spotted, and it’s goodnight Vienna for Paul.”

“I know, you do need to get out of here Paul, you can’t be stuck in all the time, but remember that the garden needs tending to at some point.”

Scott goes over, puts his arms around Julie and kisses her goodbye.

“Urgh, you’re all bristly,” wiping her chin, as it had made her itch.

They head out of the door and get into the car and pull off and into Jeromesley Centre.

They soon reach the centre and park outside the snooker hall, where non-members could just go in and play.

It was a huge smokey room, containing around twelve tables and a dartboard in the corner.

There were a few members and non-members, and it was also fully licensed.

Scott had used it a few times before, and they approached the bar and were greeted at the bar by the owner, Paul Cottingham.

"Yes sir, what can I… is that you Scott?" he chuckled, almost not being able to contain his laughter, "have you come as a Miami Vice extra?" he continued to laugh.

"Shush," Scott muttered firmly, "I'm here with my friend, who's in a little bother so, keep it down, he doesn't need any attention."

Paul glanced behind Scott at his friend and continued to serve him.

"Is it the usual, lager shandy, what about your mate?"

"Yeah, I'll have that, but get my mate a lager, and a few hours of snooker too, table four looks free, is it?"

"Yeah mate, it's free, how long?"

"Maybe two hours?" as he glanced back to his mate and got an approving nod.

"Paul served the pair their pints and turned on the lights for table four.

He also pulled out two spare cues and some chalk for them to use, and they wandered over, Scott setting the balls up as Paul sat down at a table nearby and started to drink his lager.

Scott broke off, as Paul continued to sit in the corner, almost not realising that it was his turn next.

He got up to play, his heart almost not in it.

"So, what exactly happened in Barnwood mate, you've not told me too much?"

"Huh, how long have you got?" "I got involved in a drugs run, as you know, lost my job, killed a few men, stole a bag full of drugs from a baron, so, a heap of stuff," he whispered across to Scott, who sat down at the same table while Paul played.

"WHAT THE FUCK PAUL!" killed people? Running… running from a drugs baron?" Scott whispered back, as he looked around him, making sure that no one heard them talk about what had happened.

"Do your Mum and Dad know?"

"They're dead Scott, it's been a bit of a roller-coaster," he sighed, as he aimlessly took at a ball before pushing his cue through.

"Oh my GOD Paul, you've been through the wringer haven't you?" "that's tough, I'm so sorry, I didn't know."

"You weren't to know mate but, I appreciate your support, and for bailing me out when I needed you."

"You mentioned that you knew someone who had a place where I could stay?" Paul asked, remembering that Scott had brought up the subject at the house.

"Yeah, got to make a few phone calls first but, yeah," "they have a farmhouse as I say, Mr and Mrs Greenwood, Anne and Steve, lovely couple but they're hardly there, and I'm sure they'd appreciate their property being lived in, maybe help out to look after the animals, while they go galivanting around the world," he smiled.

Paul stopped short of telling Scott about Sarah, something that he didn't need to know, or the sex he'd had with Julie in their house while he was out.

"Anyway, what about that wife of yours, are you going to try and get hold of her again, don't you think it's a bit odd, or maybe out of character of her to not contact you?"

"She's having too much of a good time with her girlfriend to even think about me, but yeah, I'll try and give her another call."

They continued to play on for the two hours that they had booked, and Paul sunk a few more pints in the meantime, almost to the point of being drunk, Scott switching to coke, just in case he was pulled over.

They take the cues back over to the bar and give them back to the owner Paul, Scott pays him for the table time and heads outside, and into the car and back home.

It was mid-afternoon, and Julie was sitting reading a book, with the television on in the background, a half-drunk cup of tea on the well-polished coffee table in front of her.

Scott unlocked the door, Paul leaning against it, and as Scott opens it, he falls through the entrance and onto the floor.

Julie looked up, to see why there was so much noise with the men coming back.

"Did you both have a…" she saw the state of Paul, "maybe a strong coffee for you," she said firmly.

"Maybe I'll have it in my room if you don't mind," he slurred, holding his head, the alcohol was starting to kick in and take hold, "I feel like my head is about to explode."

Julie made him a black coffee and told him that she would bring it up to him, worried that he wouldn't be able to hold it climbing the stairs, and being as drunk as he was.

"I'll come and knock on your door in a minute with your coffee, and when food is ready, go and get some rest," she smiled.

He thanked her and gingerly started going up the stairs to his room.

She put his coffee on his bedside table, Julie watching him crash out on his bed, and he was asleep in next to no time.

She came back downstairs and got talking to Scott after she'd come back from Paul's room.

"How many has he had?" "What has he told you about what's going on?"

"He's had a few, we had a chat, can't go into too much detail, only to say that he's had a rough time, and needs our support more than ever."

"It's great having your friend here, and he'll be useful in the garden, digging and pulling up the weeds for example but, he can't stay here forever."

"I know, don't worry, we've been discussing that, he knows that I'm going to be calling Anne and Steve about their place but, for now, let's just welcome him here, I'm sure you'll be nice to him, I know you have been so far."

Little did Scott know just how nice she had been to their guest.

Meanwhile, back in Italy, Alice was still trying to find out a way of escaping, and where they would hide out if they were able to get out.

"Leona, do we get fed, and what purpose do they have for us, there must be a reason that we're here?" Alice grabbed her softly around the arms, as Alice could still see that she was in a pretty bad way.

"What have they done to you?"

"Leona! Leona! You need to try and help us all get out of here," though she seemed either drugged up or very tired, as she kept mumbling words, and neither Alice nor Isobelle could get any sense out of her.

"I guess we're just going to have to wait to see what they do next aren't we," "I'm so sorry Izzy, it was all my idea, I persuaded you to do this, I feel totally responsible for you being here," Alice started to cry, something she wasn't used to doing, she was normally so strong, but it was a show of weakness that endeared her even more to Isobelle.

In a fit of pure anger and frustration, Isobelle got up from the floor, raced up the stairs, and started to bang the back of the cellar door.

"WHEN ARE WE GOING TO GET FED YOU USELESS PIECE OF FUCKING SHITS?"

"FUCKING LET US OUT," she screamed.

...but her shouting and banging were going unanswered, and she collapsed in a heap at the top of the stairs and hysterically begins to burst out crying herself.

"We're going to die here aren't we?" she says, her eyes stained with her tears, looking back at Alice and Leona.

"Now, get that out of your head Izzy, we WILL get out of here, we just need some sort of a distraction of some kind, we will find a way out of here, I promise," Alice needed to try and keep Isobelle's spirits up, but they needed to try and devise a plan, but rest assured, we will find a way out," even Alice was unsure how, but they had to think of something.

Suddenly, there was a noise, the cellar door was opening, and Luca appeared with a tray of food, as Isobelle raced back down, as he started to walk down, with food and drink.

He looked at them with his customary stone face, as he placed the food on the table, again, keeping his eyes on them, so they didn't try anything funny.

He casually walked over to the girls, who were now

cowered in one of the corners and stood mainly over Alice, who was in the middle of the three of them.

Suddenly…SMACK! as he struck her across the face with the back of his right hand, leaving Alice's right cheek red, as she began to rub it.

"WHAT THE FUCK WAS THAT FOR?" she snapped.

"*Voi ragazze avete fatto un grosso errore venendo qui, non scherzare con noi" (*you girls made a big mistake coming here, don't fuck with us) he smirked, arrogantly huffing in their direction, and giving them an evil stare, before he walked off and back up the stairs, slamming the cellar door shut and locking it behind him.

"Are you ok Alice, your cheek looks sore, let me see if I can find something to help soothe it," Isobelle started to rustle around them, to see if there was some kind of cloth to cover her cheek, "what the FUCK did he just say?"

"I don't know, but whatever he said, didn't sound too friendly to me," Alice grimaced, as she got up off the floor, still rubbing her cheek, which looked like it was starting to swell, grabbed the tray of food and drink, and took it back over to where they all sat, as it didn't look like Leona had any strength left in her body, she had hardly moved since they had been dumped down with her, and Alice even wondered if Leona knew that it was them who were there with her.

"We've got to try and distract Luca next time he comes down with some food for us, he must have a mobile phone on him or something," Isobelle said, starting to feel a bit more optimistic that they might get out, but they still had to try and get past both Bruno and the arrogant Valentino.

The cellar felt very cold, they all started to shiver, and after a bit more rummaging around, Alice managed to find a few more sacks, whatever they were used for, and she managed to rip them down the middle, to try and use them as blankets.

They had all finished the food that had been brought down to them and drank the water that had also been brought down.

They were starting to feel a little sleepy, as Isobelle rested her head on Alice's shoulder, Leona already having her head resting on the other.

"Tell me about your modelling career, where you're from, past loves, everything," Isobelle asked.

Alice proceeded in telling her about her life, marrying Paul, and, by the time she got to the point of meeting Stacey, then Sarah in Barnwood, Isobelle was fast asleep, her head feeling heavy on Alice's shoulder.

Alice herself was also soon asleep.

Morning broke, and the girls were awoken by the noise of the cellar door being pulled open, and at the top, stood Luca, with another tray of food for them all.

As he approached the table, Isobelle noticed that the cellar door was slightly ajar. Not having the energy to get up to make a dart for it, also knowing that Luca would chase her, and would be too strong for her, but instead, she shouted up, hoping that the slimy Valentino would be in earshot.

"YOU FUCKING SCUMBAG, JUST FUCKING LET US GO WILL YOU!" she screamed.

Suddenly, Luca's mobile phone rang in his pocket.

"*Capo*?" (Boss) Luca answered.

"*Quelle ragazze per tenere basso il fottuto rumore che sto cercando di mangiare*" (tell those girls to keep the fucking noise down, I'm trying to eat) Valentino replied.

Suddenly, there was a noise outside…

BANG! BANG! gunshots rang out, and it appeared a battle was about to commence, and there appeared to be a lot of shouting by men.

Luca raced towards the cellar door, his phone crashing to the floor after it was only halfway inside his pocket when the gunshots started to ring out.

The girls noticed it, Alice's eyes lit up, quickly scurried across the floor, before grabbing it and started to enter Paul's mobile phone number, her hand shaking with both cold and fear.

"Call the police Alice, they'll get us out," Isobelle wanted to get out as quickly as possible, by whatever means.

"I can't Izzy, if I do, my life is over, they will call the British police then, that's it, you won't see me again, I'm better off calling that shit husband of mine, get him to come and get us."

Ring…ring

Ring…ring

'Sorry, I can't come to the phone right now, but leave me a message, and I'll come back to you.'

"Paul, it's me, look, I'm not going to have long on this phone, and don't call it back but, we're in Italy, it's a long story but, we've been kidnapped, and we're in the main castle in a place called Tropea, and we're in the cellar, come quick, just PLEASE don't call this number back, it's one of the kidnappers phones… hurry."

She hung up, gunshots continuing to ring out outside, her hands continuing to shake, as she searched to delete the number from the call log.

The gunfire outside had stopped, Alice wiping the phone

casing as clean as she could get it with the sacks that they used to cover themselves to keep warm, so Luca wouldn't be suspicious that they had used it before she pushed the phone back close to where it fell.

Lo and behold, Luca had noticed his phone was missing from his pocket, and raced down the cellar stairs, to see it laying on the floor, close to where he had been standing after he'd been speaking to Valentino.

He once again gave the girls an evil stare, the girls looking scared and, without him saying a word, picked his phone up, keeping his eyes on the girls at all times.

"*Mangiare!*" (eat) he angrily gestured with his hand towards the food, before walking back towards the stairs once more, the girls watching as he climbed them.

"Let's get this food that they've left us, we don't know how long it'll be before we're fed again."

Leona started to come around, her mouth and face still bloodied from before.

Suddenly, they heard the cellar door opening once again, and when they looked up, they saw a rather dishevelled and a little bloodied Valentino standing at the top, as he walked down to speak to them.

"Sorry about the disturbance girls, just a visit from our Italian friends, but all is good now."

"What do you want from us, why are we here?" asks Alice.

"Questions… questions, oh, didn't I tell you, I'm looking to trade you," he smirked, "the Italian friends that I just had over, who you may have heard us with outside, they have a few of our *amici*, ah, this means friends to you English, and we need to trade to get them back so, what better way of doing this yes," the slimy Italian arrogantly gestured to them, "I'm sorry, it's just business, you understand don't you?" he grinned, wiping a splatter of blood he had trickling from his mouth, as Isobelle went to get up and attack him, before being pulled back by Alice.

"That wouldn't be a wise move now would it, I hope the food is to your satisfaction?" he smiled, "do not worry, it will not be long now, you'll be out of here, you'll be comfortable somewhere else, and we'll have our *amici* back, its er, how you English say, win-win," as he turned around, and started to arrogantly walk back up the stairs, hands in his trouser pockets.

"Ah yes, meant to add, there is a bucket over there in the corner if you need to, use the toilet as you say, and I will get Luca to bring you down some fresh blankets, it's cold down here but, we must keep it cold for the wine, you understand, don't you?" The cellar door is then slammed shut.

"I've got a great idea, let's go and smash all of his precious wine and champagne, that'll piss him off," Isobelle was in no mood to be messed around by such a slimy man, holding them against their will.

"We've got to think smart Izzy, that will only antagonise him, I'm sure he could and would easily get rid of us, kill us and dump us somewhere, we've got to think up another way, at least until that shit of a husband gets here, hope he hears my message soon."

"Before we get moved to god knows where, and possibly killed you mean?" Isobelle was starting to feel a bit anxious once more, and it was Alice who needed to try and reassure her that all would be ok.

"Your husband needs to get here quick, otherwise I

fear that we'll be transported, and no one will ever find us again," Isobelle began to shake and cry, Alice put her arm around her.

"Listen, get this negativity out of your head, we'll soon be out of here, one way or another, let's just sit tight, let's not do anything stupid to upset that bastard, and we'll figure a way out ok, ok?" Isobelle's sniffling started to soften, her crying and tears had stopped, as she nodded in agreement to Alice, seeing confidence glow from her that they would escape, but when, and how?

Meanwhile, Scott and Julie can hear movement coming from upstairs and Paul is soon downstairs, still holding his head.

"I'm so sorry, how much did I have to drink yesterday?" looking at Scott's direction.

"You drank enough," Scott chuckled, maybe it's what you needed, you had to let off some steam, with what you've been through so, you're excused," he chuckled.

"You ready for some food, beef stew, dumplings and veg, that ok?" Julie called, as she had already ventured into the kitchen, leaving the men to talk.

"That's great but, not too much for me, still feeling the effects," Paul continued to hold his forehead, sitting back on the sofa as if he had just run a marathon.

"I'll get you something for your head too, looks like you need it," Julie smiles, as she reaches for a glass in the cupboard, and some paracetamol, and brings it into him, he thanked her and takes his medicine, as much as he hated gulping down tablets.

"Weather is meant to be good tomorrow, if you fancy a spot of gardening with us, fresh air will probably do you good too," Scott nudged his friends' arm, to see what the response would be, after all, Julie was looking forward to seeing Paul maybe strip off in the sun.

"Yes, course I will, you've been good enough to sort me out."

They all sat to eat, Paul not quite finishing his food, however delicious it looked and was.

They sat and chatted for the rest of the evening before it was time to go to bed.

Paul made his way upstairs first, still feeling the effects a little of his and Scott's snooker, realising that he had drunk way too much, he wasn't used to it, since his drinking with John and the others in Barnwood.

He was soon in bed, as he heard Scott and Julie making their way upstairs before there was a tap on his door.

Scott opened the door, slightly ajar, to check to see how his friend was.

"You ok mate, anything you need?"

"No thanks, you've been great, might try and get hold of that wife of mine again in the morning, see what's going on."

"Ok, I'll let you settle down, talk in the morning, night."

Paul nods in Scott's direction, before he gets his head down, and drifts off into a deep sleep.

It's seven-thirty the next morning, and the sun has risen, making the bedroom feel really warm.

He again, can smell the aroma of bacon, and feeling hungry, is soon dressed, and starts to head down the stairs.

"How's that head of yours?" Scott smiles across to him, sitting at the breakfast table, smells coming from the kitchen.

"Morning," shouts Julie, "breakfast?"

"That'd be great, that sleep did me good," Paul was feeling more like himself and was gearing up for the day ahead.

Julie was soon putting the delicious cooked breakfast in front of them both, before bringing her own in, and they all sit to eat, Julie asked if Paul is still up for helping out in the garden, especially with the weather being so good.

"Yes of course, looking forward to helping out, just let me know where you need me, and what you need me to do, and I'll happily help," he smiled, Julie briefly looking at him and smirking.

"You going to try Alice again, see if she's ok?" Scott still thought it strange that he couldn't get through to her.

"Yeah, I'll give her a call a bit later," he smiled.

Julie opened the big beautiful French doors that lead out into the garden, the sun was shining as they all went outside, not before Scott had grabbed some wine for Julie and beer bottles for him and Paul, also grabbing a glass for her red wine, which she liked.

Julie and Scott started to weed, as Paul started to mow the rather large lawn, sweat was starting to drip down his face, his t-shirt starting to get wet, and he felt it was time to take it off, much to the delight of Julie, his muscular body glistening in the beaming sun.

Julie was still weeding with Scott, but down a different part of the garden, Julie kept glancing over at Paul's ripped chest, looking round, to make sure that Scott was not seeing her perving over Paul.

Paul had got up to the end of the lawn, close to where Julie was, and glanced over to her, Julie quickly looked back to see what she was doing, but he noticed her looking at him, and gave her a wry smile, Julie quickly looking back at him, giving him a wry smile back, before she carried on weeding.

Time had ticked on, and they were sitting down, having a well-earned drink, Paul guzzling his beer down, the bottle almost not even touching the sides.

"Wow, steady on fella, especially after how much you drank yesterday at the snooker," Scott chuckled.

"This sun has given me a bit of a thirst," he smiled back at his friend, "besides, you have a lot of lawn there, I need fuel," he chuckled back.

A few hours had gone by, they had sat down outside for lunch, and again, the drinks were flowing, but they were having a good time, with plenty of chat and laughs.

The lawn had been cut and the weeding had been finished, the garden was looking fit for a king, the lawn was looking in great condition, and the smell of freshly cut grass was drifting across the beautiful garden, and it felt like just the most beautiful day.

The sun was starting to set in the distance, and it was starting to get rather cool, the three decided to head inside.

Julie decided to head into the kitchen and make a start on dinner.

The boys sat down to talk about the fun of doing the garden, and Scott duly thanked him.

"Going to try that wife of mine again I think," Paul pulled the phone out that Scott had lent him, and it began to ring.

Ring…ring

Ring…ring

'Hi, can't come to the pho…' just as Paul decided to hang up.

"Don't you think it's a bit strange that you can't get hold of her, at least let her know that you're ok?" Scott was a bit concerned by the lack of contact.

"I'll check my other phone after dinner, you never know, she might have left me a voicemail message, that's if she's bothered about me, she's probably having a wail of a time with that girlfriend of hers" he grumbled.

"Just make sure that you don't put your sim card in, otherwise the police will track you," Scott said.

"Oh, don't worry, I won't."

Julie had cooked a fry up, they had all mustered up an appetite, and the food was soon gone.

Paul thanked her once again for a delicious meal, before wandering upstairs to go and find his phone.

'Ah, here it is,' after rifling through the sock drawer.

He turned it on, which took next to no time, and saw there was a voice message from a mobile number that he didn't recognise, so he decided to dial his voicemail messages and sat on his bed to listen to it.

He sat in silence, listening, almost stunned by what he was listening to… *"Paul, it's me, look, I'm not going to have long on this phone, and don't call it back but, we're in Italy, it's a long story but, we've been kidnapped, and we're in the main castle in a place called Tropea, and we're in the cellar here, come quick, just PLEASE don't call this number back, it's one of the kidnappers phones… hurry."*

'FUCK!' he shouted, as Scott raced to the bottom of the stairs.

"Are you ok mate, what's wrong?"

Paul raced out of his room.

"Alice has been kidnapped, and she's in Italy and..." "why didn't I think about checking this phone until now?"

Both men raced down the stairs, Julie standing at the bottom, listening to the commotion.

"What's going on?" she asked.

"Alice has been kidnapped, and she's in Italy, we need to get her out," Scott felt as anxious and panicky as his friend but realised that they both needed calm heads and to devise a plan.

"Is she there with that other girl, Isobelle did you say her name was?"

"Huh, no doubt yeah but, we need to try and get there quick, and we obviously can't fly, we'll be automatically stopped at the airport, can you get another car, because I bet yours will have been tracked by the coppers?"

"I can ask my friend, Helen Quigley, ask her if we can borrow hers, tell her that we're going on a road trip, which we kind of are," Julie wanted to help as much as possible.

"Oh no, sorry babe, you're not coming with us, it's going to be far too dangerous, we're going to need guns, we don't know what we're going to be facing out there, but if they've been kidnapped, in Italy, it isn't going to be pretty," Scott didn't want her to get involved, especially where violence was going to take place.

"Don't worry about guns, I have a gun in my room, don't ask, long story, and I'm going to ask a couple of guys who owe me a favour, Charlie Grunge and Karl Mahoney, do you know them, I know they'll be able to get you a gun, we're going to need to leave soon, will you contact your friend now Julie, we could do with moving soon, I'll give the guys a call, will you be ready to move mate when we have the car?" Paul was anxious about wanting to go sooner rather than later, not knowing if Alice was even still alive.

Both Julie and Paul got on the phone to make their calls.

"Hi Helen, it's Julie, are you ok?" "Is there any chance we can borrow your car for a few days, we're going away, and you know, ours is playing up, and we're wanting a few days away, somewhere in Europe, not sure where yet."

"I'm fine thank you Julie, yes, of course you can, we don't really need it at the minute, make sure you bring me something nice back, a souvenir would be lovely," Helen was a cheery lady, had been friends with Julie for years, and had many a good night out with her before she met Scott, but they remained close friends and often popped round for a chat when they were both free.

"I'll drop it round to you later."

"Any chance we could get it now, you see we're looking to leave in the next hour or two," Julie wanted to be as calm as possible, hoping that Helen wouldn't sense any anxiety in her voice.

"Erm yes sure, are you ok?"

"Yes, we're fine," Julie mumbled, "it's just a last-minute thing, and Scott wants to move as soon as possible."

"Ok well, I'll pop it round to you within the next half an hour, if that's ok, you sure you're ok?"

"Yep, we're absolutely fine, you know what Scott is like, when he gets an idea, thanks mate, you're a star."

Paul had been on the phone with both Karl and Charlie, and they were heading over to Scott's and would be with them within the hour.

"Right, that's them sorted, they'll be here in a bit, and they'll have you a gun too, just hope that the four of us will be enough, we don't know how many we're facing do we?"

"We could always try and recruit someone while we're out there, got to think about the room in the car," Scott though thought of one of his other mates, who would always help him when Scott needed him.

"I could ask my mate Conrad Brunswick to come with us, plus I know he owns a gun, that'll make five of us."

"Helen has that big SUV hasn't she Julie?" Scott asked.

"She did the last time I saw her."

"Great, that'll be big enough for us all to get into then, it'll be a long journey," Paul was pacing up and down, waiting for both Helen to come with the car, as well as Charlie and Karl to arrive.

Scott got on the phone to Anne Greenwood, to ask about the farmhouse that they had, and if Paul and his wife could stay there.

"Hi Anne, it's Scott, are you ok?" "How's Steve, is he ok?" "Listen, don't suppose we could make use of your farmhouse could we, well, not we but, my mate Paul and his wife, they need somewhere to stay for a little while."

"Hi Scott, yes, we're both well thank you, yes, of course they can, it just lays idle anyway, well, apart from the girls, I only really need someone there to make sure the animals are fed and watered, to help them out a bit, and the land is kept tidy, as long as Paul is a worker, that farmhouse needs a lot of looking after, we just keep it as somewhere to go back to now and again so, as long as they don't mind a bit of hard graft?"

"Hard graft is their middles names I think, don't worry,

it'll be well maintained, when can they go and stay, is it free from now, or in a few days maybe?"

"Yes, it's ok to go there from now, I'll let the girls know to expect you."

"That's great Anne, I'll let Paul know, he'll be delighted." "What's Steve doing now?"

"Oh, he's just resting up, works too hard, you know what he's like."

Suddenly, there is a knock at the door, and Scott needs to cut his conversation short.

"Got to go, someone at the door, give my regards to Steve, tell him we'll see him soon, and you of course," just as he was hanging up.

Karl and Charlie had arrived, and, right on cue, Helen was pulling up with her car.

Charlie walked over to Paul, and seeing Julie nearby, he stood as close to Paul as he could, passing him the gun that he asked for, still making sure that Julie could not see what he was giving Paul, though she had a pretty good idea.

"You sure you want to do this Scott, please come back safe."

"I'll be ok my beautiful one, there's plenty of us here, we'll be fine."

"Right, we all set?" Paul was in no mood to hang around, just as he was watching Helen get out of the car.

"Hang on, we should wait until Helen has gone really, so it doesn't look suspicious," Julie said.

Helen knocked on the door, as Julie answered it.

"Oh sorry, didn't realise you had company," Helen anxiously looked at all the men in the house.

"Ha-ha yes, just a few of Scott's friends, they were in

the area and said would pop in to say hi, but they're leaving soon too," Julie smiled, slightly nervously.

"My son is coming to pick me up, and he's having to come this way, we're heading into Jeromesley," she smiled, again, nervously looking around at all the men, who gave her a slight grin, before looking away.

Just then, Helen's son pulled up and beeped his horn.

"Ah, here he is, must go, let me know when you're back, and I'll come back for the car," she smiled, not being able to take her eyes off all the men in the house.

"Yes, we will," smiled Julie, trying desperately to usher her out of the front door.

"Bye then, bye Scott, Paul, and er... yes...bye," Helen waved, before gently walking to her son's car, again looking back at the house, with a sense that something wasn't quite right.

Charlie menacingly pulled part of the curtain back, to check to see if Helen had gone.

Scott had called his friend Conrad soon after coming off the phone with Anne, and he arrived soon after Charlie and Karl.

"Right, let's give it five minutes, give her a chance to leave completely, then we'll go," said Paul.

There was a slightly awkward silence, as the men just wanted to leave.

Scott took Julie into the kitchen, away from the others, and lovingly embraced her.

"Don't worry babe, I'll be alright, please don't worry will you, I'll text you and let you know when we've arrived ok?"

Julie held tightly around his neck and gave him a passionate kiss.

"Right, let's go, the coast will be clear now," Paul led first out of the door, followed by Karl, Charlie, Conrad and finally Scott.

Scott got in the driver's seat, Paul sat next to him, and the other three were in the back.

Scott beeped Julie, as she nervously stood by the front door, worryingly biting her nails at what was in store for her man, and watched them pull off, Scott giving her a wave and a beep of the car horn.

Next Stop… Italy!

Scott drives for around thirty minutes, and pulls into a service station, to get some food for their journey, it was going to be a while before they could stop, he also made sure that there was enough diesel in the car to get them there, so he filled the tank up too.

Ten minutes later, he came out, armed with two bags, full of food for them all; sandwiches, drinks, crisps and chocolate.

He then drove into the petrol station, and filled the car up, before pulling back out.

They were soon boarding the ferry, and crossing the channel, before pulling into mainland Europe.

They were soon at the border of Italy and were stopped at border control.

Two armed guards were patrolling the area, as Scott was pulling up slowly towards the checkpoint, before winding his window down.

The stone-faced guard walked up to the window and looked inside at the other men in the car, looking at each in turn, trying to suss them out.

"Papers," he muttered to Scott in broken English, Scott

looking around for the documentation that he needed, before pulling the sun visor down, and taking the papers out, before passing them to the guard.

The guard looked at them, again expressionless, before passing them back to him.

"Where is it you are all going?" "Business or pleasure?"

"Ah, just a bit of sightseeing, you know what us men can be like," Scott tried to joke with the guard, "one or two of us have never really seen Italy before, just want to check out its beauty," he smiled.

"How long you stay?" muttered the guard, whilst still looking in the back at the others with curiosity and suspicion.

"Probably just a few days," Scott said.

There was a momentary pause by the guard, still checking the men out in the back.

"On your way," said the guard, as he pulled away from the car, Scott giving him a slight nervous wave, the others looking at the guard as they drove by, and through the checkpoint.

They were now in Italy.

"Right, let's go and find this Tropea place, wherever that is," Paul wanted to get in and out of Italy as soon as they could, with as little disruption as possible.

Charlie got his phone out and started to search for the castle that Alice had mentioned in her voicemail.

They made it into Tropea and came across the marina.

"Someone here is bound to know where it is, let's ask this guy here," muttered Charlie, seeing a boat owner hovering around, it was Giovanni.

"Be careful Charlie, we don't know these people, don't give anything away."

Charlie looked at Paul, and got out of the car, as Scott had parked up.

Charlie approached Giovanni.

"Hello, speak English?"

"A little yes, muttered a cautious Giovanni, seeing that Charlie was very rugged looking, someone, you wouldn't mess with, and Giovanni answered him as best he could.

"Do you know the castle around here, I hear it's very beautiful, and wanted to go and show my friends, during our tour of Italy, do you understand?"

"Ah yes, of course, smiled Giovanni nervously, looking back at the car containing the other men, Charlie moving himself to try and block his view.

"I have not been in Tropea long so, I cannot help," he grinned at Charlie.

"Ok, thank you anyway, have a pleasant day," Charlie said, in a menacing voice, whilst walking back to the car, glancing back at the boat owner, like a gunslinger, getting ready for a shoot-out at dawn.

Giovanni immediately got on his phone as soon as the car pulled off.

"*Valentino, potresti avere compagnia un uomo e stato qui per chiederti dove sei* (Valentino, you may have company, a man has been here to ask about where you are)," Giovanni seemed a little ruffled by Charlie's appearance and visit, "*Hai bisogno di aiuto perche c'e una macchina piena di uomini* (do you need any help, as there is a car full of men?)"

"*il nostro andare non ti preoccupare ci occuperemo noi cose da questa parte* (Ah Gio, do not worry, we will handle things this side)."

"*Luca, Bruno, vieni con me* (Luca, Bruno, come with me)," Valentino was gathering his men together, to get them to guard outside, waiting for them to arrive, making sure they were both armed.

"*Luca, tu copri il dietro, io e Bruno coprirai il davanti* (Luca, you cover the back, me and Bruno will cover front)" he yelled, barking his orders at his men, preparing for what could be another shoot-out.

"Something's going on out there," Isobelle whispered to Alice, feeling a little startled, trying to listen as much as she could.

"You don't think your husband has come do you?"

"Hush, let's try and listen," Alice covering Isobelle's mouth up gently with her hand.

The five men suddenly spotted the castle, parked up behind some trees nearby, got out, and crept gradually towards the impressive white marble building.

They all got their guns at the ready, making sure they were all fully loaded.

They raced up to the surrounding wall and ducked down out of sight.

"They all gathered together, to work out a plan.

"Charlie, Karl, you head towards the back, me, Scott and Conrad will hit the front," Paul commanded.

Charlie and Karl ran round, to try and find a way to the back of the building.

The other three men suddenly spotted two men patrolling the front of the castle.

Shots were starting to ring out around the back of the building, while Valentino and Bruno still guarded the front.

Scott suddenly peered his head over the wall, and started

to fire shots, as the Italian men started to hide behind pillars near the castle entrance, shots were exchanged.

"Cover me, I'm going over," Paul wanted an end to this gun fighting as soon as possible.

There was a short pause of gunshots, as Paul managed to get over the wall, without being detected, and raced up to the side of the castle, to try and get more visual on the Italians.

Bruno suddenly spotted Paul nearby and began to fire in his direction, but Paul managing to dodge his bullets.

"Right, I'm going over the wall too," Conrad said to Scott, as he started to pull himself up and over the wall.

Valentino spotted him, and, just as Conrad was climbing over, managed to shoot him, Conrad flopping to the ground on the other side of the wall.

He was dead.

Scott looked over the wall, to see his friend lying motionless in front of him.

In a fit of anger, and fighting back tears, Scott too started to pull himself up and over the wall, just as Valentino was taking aim, Paul fired towards him, putting a bullet in his gun arm, causing him to drop it, before fleeing, holding his arm, which was now bleeding heavily, before leaving his other men to fight for him and his honour, there was no sign of him.

Meanwhile, both Karl and Charlie were having a shoot-out with Luca, the Italian himself hiding behind a pillar, and firing when he got the chance.

Karl ducked down, to try and get a clearer shot at Luca.

The Italian was in his sights.

He knelt up to take aim, Luca spotted him and managed to get a shot in first, a bullet hitting Karl straight in the head.

Karl was also now dead!

"YOU FUCKING BASTARD... FUCKING BASTARD... AHHHHH," Charlie raced up, firing at will at Luca, putting a fatal bullet into his chest, as the stone-faced Italian collapsed behind the pillar that was now splattered with blood.

Charlie raced up, in a fit of anger, and began to pump bullets into the now dead Italian, one bullet after another into the lifeless body, bullets pumping into his chest, before he fired one more bullet into his head.

Luca was well and truly dead!

Bruno came out from behind the pillar, not knowing that Scott had climbed up and over the wall, started to walk arrogantly towards Paul, spotted him and, just as Bruno was about to pull the trigger, Paul felt that his fate was about to be sealed, a blast rang out, Scott had shot him dead.

Charlie ran over to Karl, whose eyes stared into the bright sky, sadly, life had left them.

He paused momentarily with his friend, knelt down and closed his friends' eyes shut with his hand.

The girls in the cellar had heard the gunshots but also noticed that the fighting had ceased.

They were waiting for Valentino to reappear, just as he did before, but there was no sign of him this time.

"ALICE! ALICE! WHERE ARE YOU? ALICE?" shouted Paul, as he pushed the heavy doors of the castle open, and raced around.

"GOD... IT'S PAUL!" Alice excitedly smiled at Isobelle, and as much as she didn't like the man, she was glad that they were going to get out of the hell that they were currently in.

"ALICE?" he continued to shout, frantically looking around for her.

"We're down here," Alice shouted, feeling an enormous relief that they were about to be rescued.

Paul managed to unlock the cellar door, to find the three girls almost cuddled up in a corner of the cold, dirty room.

"What the FUCK are you doing here?" snapped Paul.

"Yes, nice to see you too," she chuckled, trying to raise the mood a little.

"... and I bet this was all your fucking idea wasn't it?" he snapped at Isobelle, just as he was embracing Alice, glad that she was still alive.

"Don't have a go at Izzy, it was all down to me, can we not just get out of here?"

"... and who's this?" as he looked at Leona.

"It's a long story like I say, I'll fill you in, are you here alone?"

"No, I came with four others but, one is dead."

Where's that FUCKING SLEAZEBALL Valentino?" Alice snapped.

"I hit one guy, but he fled, don't know if that's your Valentino that you mentioned, don't know if he's dead or not but, we shot one of them dead, there was another guy round the back, just wanted to get in to find you.

"Now, can we go please?" Paul commanded, as all the girls got up off the floor, Alice and Isobelle helping Leona, putting her arms around their necks, as she was still pretty weak, and dragged themselves towards the stairs and out of the building.

They pulled themselves out, to be met by both Scott and Charlie.

"Where's Karl, and Conrad?" he muttered to Charlie and Scott.

Charlie shook his head.

"... Karl didn't make it, but I sorted that greased ball out who got him, good and proper."

Tears started to well up in Scott's eyes at losing his friend Conrad, and Paul felt a real loss for his friend.

"I'm not leaving our friends here, Charlie, me and you go round the back, and we'll take the boy's bodies back with us, not leaving them here," Paul was the man in charge, and he was clearly in no mood to leave friends bodies on foreign soil.

"Scott, take the girls to the car, and we'll go and get Karl, we'll load him in the boot as best we can, and then we'll come back for your friend Conrad." "I'm so sorry Scott, I know you were friends."

Scott shed another tear, before quickly wiping it away.

He took the girls to the car, as Paul had instructed him to, as he watched Paul and Charlie go around the back of the castle to get Karl's body.

Only a few minutes had gone by, and Scott saw Charlie and Paul carrying Karl's body to the car, before struggling to open the boot, and dumping his body inside, slamming it shut, in case any cars passed, and seeing a body inside, before going back to collect Conrad's body.

Moments later, he and Charlie had got Conrad's body, Paul once again opening the boot and piling it on top of Karl.

"Right, let's get the FUCK out of here," as both men climbed into the car, Scott skidding away as fast as he could.

"YOU FUCKING OWE ME FOR THIS ARNOLD!" snapped Charlie, who had sat in the front with Scott, not even glancing back to Paul as he'd said it "we'll talk about this when we get back to England shall we? Charlie said menacingly."

"Hey, leave my mate alone, or you can fucking walk back to England," "I've just lost someone too, not just you," Scott snapped.

"Who the FUCK do you think you're talking to?" Charlie snapped back.

There was a little tension in the car, but Scott just carried on driving.

Paul was checking that Alice was ok, she was his main concern, he didn't care how Isobelle or Leona were, or what Charlie had just said, he was just glad to be getting out of there.

They were finally heading away from Tropea, and back to their homeland, passing safely through border control.

Things back in England were soon to take a turn for the worse, and the sinister character was still lurking, hunting Paul down.

NO ONE WILL FIND US HERE

They arrived back in England and decided to drive to Gordon Howell's Hospital, which was just outside Jeromesley, and find a quiet spot, where they could lay Karl and Conrad's bodies out on some grass, but somewhere where Paul knew that they would easily be found, but not too close to the hospital, so as questions were not asked of their deaths.

"We need to drop Leona off first, looks like she could do with being looked at, will you take her in Scott, because there's likely to be cameras around?" Alice was quick to say that Leona needed help, as she still looked both battered and bruised by her ordeal.

"Yes, of course, then we must get those bodies out of the back and put them on that grass we spotted on the way into these grounds," Scott didn't want to leave Karl and Conrad's bodies in the back too long, as they desperately needed to get away as quick as they could.

Scott drove over near the A&E entrance and quickly called a nurse over for assistance.

"Nurse, nurse, I need your help," found this woman wandering down the road, sorry, I don't know who she is but, looks like she could do with being looked at," he stated.

The nurse quickly grabbed a wheelchair close by that had just been dumped outside and sat her in it.

"Sorry nurse, I have to go, can I leave you to it?"

The nurse nodded to Scott that it would be ok to leave Leona in her hands, so he quickly got back in the car, getting ready to drive around to the grassland that they had spotted on the way in, both Isobelle and Alice peering their eyes over the back seat, sadly waving to Leona on their way past.

'Take care of yourself Leona,' Alice whispered to herself.

Scott then saw the patch of grass that they had spotted coming onto the grounds, pulled over, checked that no cameras were looking out from the hospital, and quickly got out with Paul, to get their friends' bodies out as quickly as they could, before they pulled away.

Conrad was pulled out first, before being laid on the fresh grass.

"Goodbye my friend," Scott pauses momentarily, a few tears filling his eyes once again.

"SCOTT! WE DON'T HAVE TIME FOR GOODBYES, COME ON" Paul whispered sharply, as Scott then helped lay Karl next to where his friend lay.

Both men got back in the car, Scott glancing across to Conrad for one last time, before driving as casually off as they could, and out from the hospital grounds.

"You going to tell me how the FUCK you ended up in

Italy, if it wasn't for your SHIT of a friend?" he snapped to his wife, "… and who were those slimeballs?"

"I suggest we dump her as soon as we get back, she's nothing but trouble, I didn't fucking want her with us in the first place," he snapped."

"Look, as I said, Italy was MY IDEA, not Izzy's," Alice angrily snapped back.

"She's still trouble and anyway, Izzy now is it?" Paul was angry that he had to come all the way to Italy to get his wife out of trouble.

"Paul, this farmhouse of Anne and Paul's is big, you might need Alice's friend about to help out, especially with there being livestock, you're going to need all the help you can get, there's a lot to be done," Scott trying to be the man of reason.

There was a deathly silence in the car for some time before they arrived back at Scott and Julie's house.

She saw the car approaching and flew out of the front door, face beaming with the broadest smile, like Scott had been away for weeks, just as they pulled up to a halt.

They all got out, and she immediately flung her arms around him, and almost squeezed the life out of him, holding him tight for what seemed likes hours.

"You didn't text me to tell me that you'd arrived," she said crossly.

"I'm sorry darling, it was all a bit manic, I didn't get the chance.

"Hi again Alice, are you ok?" Julie also raced up and embraced her, kissing her on the cheek, "Who's this?" as she looked at Isobelle.

"Oh, this is my friend Izzy."

Julie briefly embraced her; she was a very touchy-feely woman.

"Nice to meet you, Izzy," how are you both and what the hell happened?"

"Another time darling, I've got to get these to a place of safety, to the farmhouse, I'll fill you in when I've dropped them off," Scott said.

"Right now, have you got any clothes that might fit these girls, at least for the time being, get them started, until they're all on their feet?"

"Yes, I've got a bag of clothes that I was looking to throw away, nothing wrong with them, nice clothes, just stuck in the wardrobe, and I don't wear them," "come in the house, I'm sure we can sort through a few things between us," she smiled.

"Yes darling, then we really must leave," Scott didn't want to hang around the house too long, just in case they had been tracked coming back from Italy.

"Hang on, where's your friend Conrad, and the other guy who came to the house before you left?" she noticed, looking in the car for him, that he hadn't got out of the car with them.

"They're dead!" Scott's eyes began to well up, and he let out a few tears and a bit of a cry.

Julie momentarily stood stunned at the news, before giving her man a comforting hug and ushering the rest of them inside.

They all sat waiting, as Julie took Alice and Isobelle upstairs to look through the clothes that she had bagged up, along with some unused underwear.

Julie could sometimes be a bit of a hoarder, so she was glad to be getting rid of some of the clothes.

Alice and Isobelle sifted through what they wanted, as Julie looked for a suitcase for them to put all the things into, so it was going to be easier for them to be taken, as opposed to bags.

There was an awkward stance between Charlie and Paul, Charlie glancing menacingly over to Paul every so often.

"Remember what I said in the car Arnold, you owe me BIG TIME for this," he growled, yet doing so in a quiet way, so that Scott wouldn't really notice, and the girls upstairs wouldn't hear him getting angry with Paul, "maybe we can do some business with some people I know, you know, they need their fixes, and you can help me do this, you can take Karl's place, it's the least you can do," he snarled.

Paul glanced over at him briefly, Charlie wasn't the type of character to be messed with, and he was on hand to help him get his wife out of Italy, so Paul felt that he did owe him in some way, so he nodded to him in agreement.

The girls were soon downstairs, with a suitcase carrying the clothes that they had sorted through.

Scott had needed to take a moment in the kitchen, to think about his friend Conrad, shedding a few more tears.

Alice put the suitcase down, and the three of them noticed a slight tension in the room, between Paul and Charlie.

"Is everything ok here?" Julie says, looking at both Paul and Charlie in turn.

"Yes, we're just upset with Conrad and Karl getting shot, that's all," Paul was quick to put any possible rift out of their minds.

Julie noticed Scott taking a moment in the kitchen,

glancing out of the window, overlooking the garden, and went to see if he was ok.

"Right, are we all ready?" smiled Scott, wiping his drying tears from his eyes.

"Yeah, I guess we are," Paul grinned, looking towards Alice and Isobelle.

Charlie's car that Karl had driven, was still parked outside.

"Don't you want to take anything to eat on the way?" said Julie, "hang on a minute, let me grab you some bits together.

She grabbed a bag and put crisps, chocolate, and some sandwiches that she had got in for them all, which were neatly tucked away in the fridge.

"Where is this place anyway Scott, is it safe?" Paul didn't know the Greenwoods; they were friends of both his and Julie's.

"It's about an hour away, in a place called Forston Dean, it's so in the middle of nowhere, you're surrounded by nothing but trees, hills and great views, it's out on its own, no neighbours so, you'll have peace and quiet." "There is a village nearby called Lunshill, about a fifteen-minute walk, a really quiet place, not many people there but you'll find all the things you need there; shops, places to eat, a few bars, nice little place, believe me, you won't be disturbed."

"Great, sounds idyllic, let's go," Scott, Paul, Alice and Isobelle headed towards the door, and Paul put one arm around Julie to thank her for her hospitality.

"Please don't tell Scott what we did while he was out will you?" he whispered into her ear.

"I'm not that stupid Paul," she whispered back.

"What are you two whispering about?" smiled Scott, turning round to see them embracing, as he was wheeling the suitcase towards the car, "come on, we need to go," "I won't be long darling," he shouts to Julie, as he climbs into the driver's seat of Helen's car, thinking it would be safer again, just in case his has been tracked.

Charlie walked out of the house, Paul looking back at him.

"We'll be catching up soon then Arnold," he shouts menacingly once again, giving an almost sarcastic wave to him.

Paul pauses before he joins Scott in the front, the girls getting in the back of the car before it pulls off.

Julie gave Charlie a cold stare, almost in a scared way, before she closed the front door, leaving him to get in his car before he pulled away.

"What did that guy mean Paul, we'll be catching up soon?" Alice quizzed him, "I mean, he didn't sound very sincere, almost sinister wouldn't you say?"

"Alice, he's just lost his best friend, you know what grief can do to you, he's just saying he's looking forward to catching up, maybe talking about what happened back in Italy," he smiled back to her, but he didn't want to let on about the kind of man that he was, and what dealings he had with him and Karl, before his death.

Isobelle began to sob, so Alice put her arms around her.

"Can you not fucking shut her up?" Paul snapped, angrily looking back in their direction.

"Do you not realise the ordeal we have been through Paul, will you stop having a go at her, she's still in a bit of a shock with it all."

Paul huffed, before sitting back in his seat.

"Don't think we're too far away now," smiled Scott, trying to break the frosty atmosphere in the car.

Scott was a cheery man, always wanting to see the good in people, and would do anything for anyone, as he had Paul, putting his life on the line for him, although they had gone back years as friends.

He never really got on too well with Paul's friend John, and it wasn't long after that he met Julie.

Isobelle had managed to pull herself together, both she and Alice wiping her tears, and they started to see signs for Lunshill.

'Lunshill two miles' said the sign.

They arrived in the village and, as Scott had described, it was small, with just a handful of people wandering about.

They had spotted a small convenience store, so Scott decided to pull up outside it, so they could grab some supplies.

"You all stay in the car, I'll go and grab you some things, at least to keep you going and yes, I'll even get your lady things," Scott chuckled, "I won't be long, maybe keep your heads down, just in case anyone recognises you, or have seen your picture anywhere."

It had turned a little chilly, with spots of rain in the air, and was going a little dark angry-looking rain clouds above them.

Scott walked in, and was greeted by the shop owner, Jack Turnbury, 'Lunshill Stores.'

Jack was a friendly elderly man, as were most of the residents of Lunshill, everyone knew everyone, so he was a little surprised to see Scott coming in the door.

"Good afternoon sir, weather not looking too good outside, is it?" said the owner, "just passing through, your face isn't familiar?"

But Scott was too engrossed by getting the shopping basket full, albeit the basket wasn't very deep, so he couldn't get much in, and realised that he was probably going to need another basket.

Scott had filled the basket up, and took it over to the till, before going and grabbing another basket.

"Sorry, I wasn't being rude, did you say something, I was down the other end of your store?"

"I was just saying sir how it looks like we're getting ready for a downpour, weather-wise," Jack raised a smile to Scott.

"Oh yes, doesn't it just," Scott smiled back, as he grabbed another basket and walked back up the aisle that he had left, to carry on grabbing some bits and pieces for them.

Scott had filled the other basket up, bits almost falling out of the basket and onto the counter.

"Wow, maybe I should close early for the day," Jack chuckled, "don't think I'm going to get much business today, with the storm clouds approaching."

"Storm clouds approaching, huh, you can say that again," muttered Scott to himself.

"Sorry?" said Jack.

"No sorry, just saying about how it's about to chuck it down," smiled Scott, wanting to be courteous.

"You're not from round here?" Jack smiled at him, as he started to scan the goods from the baskets that Scott had put on his counter.

"No, we're from out of town but, some friends of mine might be popping in now and again so, you probably won't be seeing me, unless I go to visit them," Scott smiled.

"That's good, always up for seeing new people, seeing the same faces all the time can get a bit tedious sometimes," Jack chuckled.

"I get that," Scott smiled, as he reached into his pocket to grab his wallet.

Jack bagged the goods up, Scott paid him what was owed and then thanked Jack for his hospitality, before leaving the store, Jack waving him off.

Scott opened the back door where the girls sat and proceeded in passing them the bulging bags.

He got back in the driver's seat, and pulled off, heading to Forston Dean.

They soon arrive at the farmhouse, with both Alice and Isobelle gawping at the size of it.

The house looked modern, with various outbuildings also attached, an older-looking barn at the back, and what looked to be about five acres of land, it was both stunning but bigger than the girls had expected.

Alice and Isobelle looked excitedly at each other, embracing like excited schoolgirls, but also realising that there was going to be some hard work ahead.

"Fucking hell Scott, you weren't joking were you that it was big, and would be hard work?" chuckled Paul.

"I did say didn't I, luckily, the Greenwoods have said that the two girls living here will be helping you with its upkeep, I think you're going to need them," as he slowly pulled up onto the gravel driveway, protected by a stylish wooden gate before entry.

Steve Greenwood had asked the girls here to keep the gate open, as people were coming to stay for a while.

As the car ground to a halt, they were met by the two helpers, coming out of what appeared to be the area where the barn was situated, Gabriela and Maria, two girls who looked like they were in their late teens.

"Hola Scott," smiled Gabriela, so good to see you again."

"Hola Gabriela, Hola Maria, good to see you both too, hope you're well."

Alice, Isobelle and Paul got out of the car, and walked up to Scott, Paul pulling the suitcase and the girls with the bags, getting ready to be introduced to the two Spaniards.

"Gabriela, Maria, this is Paul, Alice and Isobelle, they will be here for a while," Scott smiled at them.

Both Maria and Gabriela took turns approaching the three of them individually, embracing and planting a kiss on each side of their cheeks, giving them a warm and welcoming greeting.

"Please, let us take those bags for you, show you the farmhouse and your rooms," smiled Gabriela to them.

Alice and Isobelle followed the two girls into the farmhouse, still not being able to get over the size of it.

Scott pulled Paul back a little.

"This is where I leave you my friend, head back home to Julie."

"I can't thank you enough mate, you've been a godsend but, if anyone catches up with you, you've not seen us ok?" Paul said, not that Scott was going to do anything like that to his friend.

Paul shook hands with him and pulled him in for a hug, before Scott got back in the car, before pulling off, giving Paul a wave, and beeping his horn, as he pulled out and through the gate.

He watched as Scott drove away, giving him a final wave, before walking towards the huge house and going inside.

It felt very welcoming, and as he walked through the wide reception area, he turned left and into the very large lounge area, which had a very high, huge, beamed ceiling, the beams looking fairly new and the whole house felt both warm and cosy.

He heard the chattering of the girls who had gone upstairs with the young helpers, no doubt showing them around the rooms.

Paul decided to look around downstairs, turning full circle, looking up and down at the walls and the blazing fireplace and the thick red curtains, keeping the sudden change of weather firmly outside.

He then strolled towards the equally large kitchen area, with an exquisitely large island in the middle, it felt like a proper farmhouse.

There were extra doorways, which he opened, and they led to the extra buildings and the barn at the end.

He walked through, again looking at the cosy feel of the room.

This was used to store food, as he noticed that there was an endless supply of additional foods, like a gigantic larder, with a ladder attached to the wall, on wheels, so it could easily be pulled around by someone underneath.

The food seemed to be stacked up high and would keep them well-fed for months.

He came out, closing the door, before walking to another part of the lounge, walking into a well-lit and again warm conservatory, that overlooked five acres of land, seeing sheep, horses, cows, pigs and a chicken coop outside.

He stood looking over the land, and was awestruck at the size, but also thinking what hard work it was going to be, but they were all there so, between them, should be manageable, plus the two young helpers were there to show them the ropes.

He wandered upstairs himself, seeing all the hanging pictures on the wall of various scenes; portraits, beautiful landscape paintings of what appeared to be land that he had just been admiring, family photos, which made him think of his own mum and dad, who he still thought about constantly.

He got to the top and saw Maria and Gabriela showing Alice and Isobelle around the bedrooms.

"This is a six-bedroom farmhouse, and each room has its own en-suite so no queuing for bathrooms, which I know you English people do not like?" chuckled Gabriela.

"I have shown these ladies the rooms sir, do you wish me to show you also?"

"Oh please, call me Paul and no, it's ok, we're going to be here a while so I will find my way around, but thank you, Gabriela."

"Please sir, sorry, Paul, call me Gabi," she smiled, "and if there is anything you need or wish for, please do not hesitate to ask," she walked off and left the other three to get used to their new surroundings.

The girls were in awe of their new home, for however long that was going to be for, but also knew that they were going to need to work hard along with the helpers to maintain it.

"I'm finally in my happy place," smiled Isobelle, still turning full circle, with the biggest smile on her face, "this is just what I've always wanted, it's amazing, and I cannot wait to start going out and feeding the chickens, seeing to the horses," she smiled.

"That's good then," Paul said sharply to her, "maybe you can sort out mucking out the pigs and horse shit while you're about it too."

"Paul, was there any real need for that?" snapped Alice, going and putting a comforting arm around her.

"No Alice, I'm more than happy to do that, I'm used to his shit so I'll be used to it," she replied sarcastically.

In a rage at what she had said, Paul stormed over to her to take a swipe, before Alice stood in front of her to protect her.

"Just stay out of my way, do what you have to, and we'll be just fine," he snapped, before he walked off and onto the very long stairwell, to take a look around the other bedrooms, maybe deciding which one he and Alice were going to have.

"We will eat in a few hours, yes?" shouted Maria up the stairs to them all, "chicken ok, yes?"

"Thank you, that'll be lovely" Alice called down to her.

The girls realised that they were going to need to go into Lunshill at some point, but would have to make sure they were well disguised, just in case there were any cameras around, plus, they were looking forward to checking out what was around them, as they didn't want to be stuck inside all the time, despite the views from the land being stunning, all they could see was beautiful woodland and the animals, nothing else around them, apart from the tiny village, which wasn't visible from the farmhouse.

"At least any fucking that goes on here won't be heard by the neighbours," Isobelle joked, making Alice laugh.

The day had ticked on, and it was time to go and eat.

They had all sat down to the fresh chicken that Maria had cooked for them.

Gabriela had come out with potato salad, coleslaw and salad, crusty white rolls, and put it all on the table.

She had also poured all of them a glass of white wine.

There was a feast to be had, they were sure not to go hungry that day.

"We weren't even fed like this back in that horrible place Izzy," smiled Alice.

Suddenly, Paul's phone started to ring.

He got it out of his pocket, and looked at everyone, before getting up from his chair, with a mouth full of food, walking through into the conservatory that he had found earlier during his look around.

"That's probably that Charlie guy, he looked a nasty piece of work back at Scott and Julie's didn't he?" Alice said to Isobelle, turning her head back to see him walking off, his phone firmly fixed to his ear.

"He certainly doesn't seem the type you'd mess around with does he?" Isobelle replied.

"What does he want with Paul anyway?"

"Paul was saying that he wanted to talk to him about his friend Karl, and to catch up with him so it's probably that."

The girls carried on eating with the two Spanish helpers and left Paul to it.

"Look, I can't right now," Paul snappily answered the caller, in an agitated whispering voice, "I said we'll sort something but give me a bit of time to get settled first ok, I will call so we can make some arrangements."

"Don't bail on me Arnold, I know where you are, a few

phone calls with the right people if you fuck with me and… BOOM, you all go up in flames ok."

Paul gulped but knew that he had to follow the instructions, he knew that he was a sitting duck, and he had to return a favour.

"I won't bail on you, I said that I wouldn't didn't I, so, let me settle in, I've just got here, and I'll be in touch ok?"

"Just make sure you don't Arnold, or things could get very nasty for you," the caller then rang off.

Things for him had gone downhill since his time in Barnwood, and his life felt very different to the one he had then.

He put his phone back in his pocket and strolled back to the table to carry on eating.

"Was that that Charlie guy?" Alice quizzed.

All eyes drew to Paul, waiting for his reply.

He put on a brave face while he started to eat once more.

"Yes, he just asked how we were settling in, and if there was anything he could do to help, then for me to give him a call." "He is hoping to catch up with me so we can talk about Karl, think he's suffering a bit, and needs someone to talk to about him, not sure Karl had much family to talk about," he muttered, his eyes now firmly fixed to his food, stabbing his fork into a chunky piece of chicken breast and stuffing it into his mouth, not even giving any eye contact to any of them, so he had hoped that he wasn't going to be asked any more questions about his call.

Alice and Isobelle gave each other an awkward glance, as did Maria and Gabriela, before looking back at Paul, who just continued to eat.

They all sat in silence, drinking their wine, waiting for

Paul to finish, which he did after a few more minutes.

"That was delicious, thank you," he smiled at the helpers.

"So, did he say when he wanted to… "Alice was soon interrupted by Paul thumping his fist on the table in anger.

"LOOK, IT'S MY BUSINESS OK, JUST LEAVE IT NOW!" he snapped.

This startled Maria and Gabriela, and Isobelle to some extent, the helpers had certainly not seen this before, as both Steve and Anne had a warm, caring, down-to-earth nature, there was never a cross word said, certainly not in their presence.

"I will clear the plates," a shocked Gabriela said, nervously looking at him, and then the other girls in turn.

"I'm sorry Gabi, it's been a stressful time, I didn't mean to get angry, please let me apologise," Paul was feeling a little bad that he had upset Gabriela and Maria, as they would not have been used to seeing him get that way.

"It is ok," Gabriela said, again feeling slightly nervous at his actions, "if you'd like to retire to the conservatory, I will bring in some more wine if you wish, give you all a chance to wind down, how you English say," raising half a smile, as the mood had slightly changed with his behaviour at the table.

They wandered into the large bright white conservatory, which was again aligned with paintings and a few white drawings of naked men and women embracing, someone in the family was very artistic. They all sat down on the comfy red leather sofas and conversation suddenly turned towards who was going to do what on the farm.

"We'll maybe talk to the girls in the morning, ask them what needs to be done, and who's best suited to doing what," Alice said in a slight whispering voice to Isobelle.

Just then, Maria came in with fresh glasses for them, followed by three bottles of wine, two white and a red.

Paul sat separately on his own, slightly away from the girls, looking out of the French windows and into the sudden darkness of the land, being in a world of his own.

"Are you girls not joining us Maria?" asked Alice.

"Thank you no, but Gabi and I need to settle the animals down for the night, this is our routine yes?" she smiled, whilst again giving Paul a slightly awkward glance.

"There is some nightwear upstairs if you do not have your own," she smiled.

"Thank you, Maria, but we are all ok, we have something to wear," Alice smiled.

"I will leave you all to this," Maria smiled, before leaving the room.

"*Buenas Noches,*" this means good night, if you do not know this," she smiled, as she was leaving the room.

"Goodnight," the girls shouted in unison, Paul sitting quietly.

Not long after, they all finished their drinks, leaving the half-drank wine on the table, one of the bottles not even opened, and made their way to their rooms.

Paul walked into the bedroom that he and Alice were due to share, without even as much as a goodnight to Isobelle, while she had a bedroom a little further down the landing from the couple.

Both Gabriela and Maria had a huge bedroom that they shared in another part of the grounds, the other side of the barn to the main house.

Alice and Isobelle shared a tender embrace, giving each other a kiss, Alice glancing round into their bedroom, making sure that Paul was out of sight, so he couldn't see them doing it.

"See you in the morning sexy," winked Alice, "a hard day ahead tending to the animals but, at least we've escaped the hell of Tropea."

"Phew, we had to get out of there didn't we?" Isobelle breathed a big sigh of relief, "I honestly thought we were goners, didn't you?"

"Well, we're not so, let's count our blessings," "I hope that slimeball Valentino crawled under a rock somewhere and died after he was shot."

Isobelle smiled at her, brushing her hands with her fingertips on the way to her bedroom and sleep, a nice comfy bed as opposed to the cold cellar in Italy.

Alice watched Isobelle walk further away and round the corner to her room, which was a fair distance from Alice and Paul's room.

Alice walked in, to find Paul pacing the floor.

"What's wrong Paul?"

"Nothing, I'm just…"

"Just what… tired?"

"Yes and, how fucking long is she going to be here?"

"Oh, she as in Izzy you mean?" Alice angrily remarked.

"Yes, your precious fucking Izzy, she's becoming like a bad fucking smell," he snapped.

"Why can't she just FUCK OFF NOW?" he angrily banged his fist on a bedside table, partially making the room shake, he hit it that hard.

It was a wonder that the table didn't break, but it was made of solid oak wood and would have taken a sledgehammer to shatter.

"Maybe you should see a counsellor about that temper of yours, you need to try and get a handle on it."

"Don't tell me how to fucking be, you married me, if you don't like it… FUCK OFF."

Alice was startled by his behaviour, but they had all had a traumatic time, the drinks had been flowing since they arrived at the farmhouse, and maybe they were all a bit stressed by the whole thing, things would be better tomorrow and the time they were going to be at the farm, she was sure of it.

They climbed into bed, Paul's hands were starting to caress Alice's body under the sheets.

"After the way you've just acted?" she snapped, pulling herself away from his amorous advances, "think about your actions first, then maybe I might be keener to have sex with you."

Paul huffed, before turning his back to her, and soon fell asleep, Alice likewise.

It was seven the next morning, the squawking of chickens could be heard outside, along with the chirping of other birds, a cockerel crowing and even some geese squealing, flying over-head, they could also hear the noise of the horses, this was to be their lives, at least for the time being.

Alice got up first, stretching her arms out wide, letting out a big yawn and wearing a white see-through negligee, displaying her almost perfect curvy body in all its splendour, bright sunlight shone into the bedroom as the curtains were pulled open, with the warmth on her almost perfect breasts, her body was in full view of the large bedroom window.

Paul got an almost instant erection seeing his wife this way, realising just how perfect a body she had, he wanted her.

He got out of bed, pulled his designer boxer shorts down and began to caress her heaving breasts from behind, his erect cock pressing on her peachy bum.

He wanted her.

He pulled her away from the window, lifting her negligee up and over her head, and started to suck on her now erect nipples, pressing her up against the bedroom wall, kissing her around her neck and licking her earlobes, Alice wasn't feeling as mad with him now, she wanted him too, she had a sense of passion starting to run through her near naked body, longing and yearning for him, she had not felt this for a while, but she wanted him deep inside her.

The couple's passion rose, Alice grabbing his erect cock in her hand, giving it a gentle squeeze, before she moved it down to his full balls.

He pulled her knickers down, and she managed to kick them away, their passion and love-making now starting to get more intense, sweat starting to roll down them, as he penetrated her, lifting her onto his erect shaft, whilst still pressing her up against the wall, Alice wrapping her legs around his waist, so he could get deeper inside her, wrapping her arms around his neck.

Paul's thrusting became harder, kissing each other as they both moaned and groaned with exasperated pleasure, she was loving the feeling of love and desire finally coming from him.

"OH GOD BABY... DON'T STOP FUCKING ME," she let out a big sigh, as she could feel him getting faster, his panting getting deeper and deeper, the longing for his penetration had never felt more needed.

His balls were slapping on her arse, his pace quickening,

before he let out an almighty groan, he had spurted his load deep inside her, just as she had cum on him.

They panted, Alice still pressed up against the wall, both trying to catch their breath from the intensity, they both felt that it was very much needed and released some tension that had built up since arriving back in England.

Alice dropped her legs back on the laminated bedroom floor, a now limp Paul stretching his naked body across the bed, in exhaustion.

"I hope you're ready to have the same energy for farming now Paul," Alice started to put on a stylish pair of lacy underwear, followed by some beige shorts and thin blue cotton sleeveless blouse, and some black shoes, she felt very dressed down.

Paul slipped on his designer pants, clinging to his muscular frame, navy blue designer shorts of his own and a bright white t-shirt, carrying his equally designer baseball cap.

They head down for breakfast, smelling the delicious aroma of bacon, sausages, eggs and mushrooms.

Isobelle was already down, sitting at the breakfast table, one coffee already drunk, not long after having got up and dressed herself.

She was wearing some bright white shorts with sparkly grey stars and a sky-blue cotton t-shirt, also with a blue baseball cap, ready to cover her face from the bright sun.

Gabriela was in the kitchen doing all of their breakfasts' and had heard Paul and Alice getting up.

Maria had been outside, doing some work in the barn, just as she was walking back in through the big front door, as Paul and Alice were sitting down at the table, taking her bright green Wellington boots off just inside the door, before joining the others.

"Did you all sleep well?" she asks, just as Gabriela is coming in with their first cooked meal of the day.

"We did yeah," Paul smiled, this taking Isobelle slightly by surprise that he was being courteous for once.

She glanced at Alice with amusement at his change of mood, waiting for an answer, but Alice was gently shaking her head as if to tell her not to ask the question.

Isobelle was slightly bemused, but at the same time pleased that finally he may be in a better mood than he has been, yet still not forgetting that she had seen him with a dead body back at the house in Lansburton.

They all finish their breakfasts and drinks, as Maria started to clear the plates and cups up.

"Let me help you with that," smiles Isobelle to her, as Maria gleefully accepts.

Gabriela goes to another part of the farmhouse and fetches out some dark green overalls for them all.

"Put these on, you will need these, and there are some wellington boots that you must also wear, which are just outside, as it can get very messy yes?" she smiles.

"Today will be very much hard work but will get done a lot quicker if we all help each other," she continued, in slightly broken English.

Paul and Alice get up from the table, which has now been cleared, Isobelle joining them after helping Maria.

They all slip into their work outfits and walk towards the front of the farmhouse, where there was a large selection of Wellington boots, all in different sizes.

"You must have known we were coming," smiled Alice,

never seen so many boots but, have you got them in light pink with blue stars?" she laughed.

"Erm, I am sorry, but we only have them in this colour yes?" Gabriela not quite getting Alice's sense of humour.

"I was only joking," Alice smiled, the girls starting to laugh, as Paul raised a smile.

"Erm Paul, could you please go and do the feeding, of all of the animals; the chickens, horses, sheep, pigs and cattle, you will find all the foods you need for them, call please if you need any help," Gabriela smiled, as Paul walked away to carry on with his duties.

"Girls, could you help us please with the mucking out, it is not the best smelling and I hope that this will not affect your breakfast but it is not as bad as you think and, like I say, it will get done in half the time if we all help each other yes?" Gabriela said.

Alice and Isobelle were directed towards the horse barn to muck out, as Gabriela and Maria went off to sort out sorting out the other animals, close to where Paul was.

They found the pitchforks that they were shown, as well as the fresh hay to spread out for them.

"What has got into Paul this morning Alice?" Isobelle beamed, he's suddenly become very chirpy and happy.

"He fucked me this morning Izzy that's why," she laughed, "hopefully from now on, he stays like this.

"Yes, a happier Paul is a happier us, well, all of us, including the two lovelies here," she smiled, "god knows what they make of him."

"Missed you last night I did, masturbated thinking of you," Isobelle winked, as Alice smiled and gave her a gentle kiss on the lips.

"You do look very fetching in your overalls, I could just rip them off now, but we would never get this mucking out done, would we?" Isobelle chuckled, clearly still feeling very amorous towards Alice, and still wanting her.

"I think Gabi and Maria will notice the fact that we've had a roll in the hey won't they!" Alice joked, "come on, let's crack on with this, we'll soon have it done, it'll be lunchtime before we know it."

The girls were taking their time doing the mucking out and putting it all in a wheelbarrow that they had found nearby.

"So, Izzy, you've not told me too much about home life for you growing up, Tandesford in Canada wasn't it, what was it like, parents? friends? that sort of thing?"

"It was a usual growing up process I guess; friends, lots of them, I was an only child though so, no brothers or sisters to bounce off, I was popular at school, it was an all-girls school though but, I still messed around with some friends there, a few boyfriends along the way, though my parents were quite strict, wasn't allowed to bring any boys home until I was about seventeen, and only then we couldn't get up to anything, lost my virginity at eighteen."

"What about friends?"

"I had quite a large circle of friends, both girls and boys but, I had some close girlfriends, but I was particularly close to one boy, nothing like that, and he was straight, a lot of my friends thought that we should get together, we were that close, inseparable really."

"So, why didn't you get together, I'm intrigued now?"

"He died, in a motorbike accident, he was only eighteen," Isobelle's eyes began to well up with tears, as she bowed her head, her hand covering her red eyes, trying to not show too much emotion, but breaking down thinking about him.

"Aww Izzy, I'm so sorry, I didn't realise, that must be so hard for you, especially with the fact that you were so close." "Try not to cry, we'll raise a glass in his memory later shall we, what was his name?"

Alice walked over to her, putting her arms around her, and giving her a consoling hug, as Isobelle continued to fight back the tears, burying her head in Alice's chest.

"His name was Ben, Ben Everley, huh, we even used to talk about getting married, but that was more when we were younger, it was the sort of thing you did as kids isn't it?"

"Then a toast to Ben Everley tonight it is!"

"How long have you been in England, long?"

We moved here when I was about twenty, it was mums' choice, she could see that staying in Tandesford was affecting my mental health, what with Ben, and seeing that dad wasn't around anymore, he left us for some floozie when I was young, we decided to move here."

"Do you not see much of your mum now?"

"No, she passed away a few years ago herself, don't like to talk about it much so, it's just me now, well, I guess I have you too!" she smiled, sniffling, tears still rolling down her puffy red cheeks.

"What about you, where did you and Paul meet, you haven't told me much about that either really."

"… and also, why do you stay with him, knowing about his temper, and also the fact that he's killed?"

"We met in a place called Barnwood, a few hundred miles away, still in England." "I used to work as a model, as you know, and I was at this modelling assignment event, there were loads of girls there, some far prettier than me, and he came into the bar with a few of his friends, he came over to me after the shoot, brought me a drink, we had a few laughs and that was it really, the rest as they say…"

"In answer to your other question?" "I'm not too sure why we stay together sometimes, yes he frightens me, I worry about what he is capable of, and we both know what he is capable of, but then I also feel secure with him, he does love me, I know that it's just his temper that scares me, but he's a great lover, as you know."

"Has he ever hurt you, as in, physically?"

"He's lost his temper with me a few times, you've seen how angry he can get, but he's never hurt me, and we've been married a few years now, probably five."

"I couldn't be with someone like him, forever on a knife edge."

"I guess I've just got used to it now," she smiled.

Just as the girls had cleared the rest of the used hay, Maria popped her head around the corner.

"It's time for lunch ladies."

"Is it that time already?" Isobelle smiled.

They put their pitchforks down, and walked out of the barn, and saw Paul coming walking over in their direction, heading towards the farmhouse, looking tired and weary.

"This is why I don't do this for a living!" he huffed to himself, but he was grateful for the rest.

They all took their boots off outside, along with their overalls, and Paul, Alice and Isobelle went to the bathroom upstairs to wash their hands, Maria and Gabriela washing theirs in the kitchen.

Paul, Alice, and Isobelle were soon back downstairs and

sat at the table ready to eat, sighing at the relief of having a rest for lunch, before they finished off outside after, but most of the hard work had been done.

Gabriela had also sat down to join them, sitting next to Isobelle, Alice facing Paul, with Isobelle between the two girls.

Gabriela looked at the three of them in turn and chuckled at the exhaustion on their faces.

"This has been hard for you all yes?" she smiled.

"I take my hat off to you both Gabi, how do you two manage on your own with all that's got to be done?" sighed Alice, still trying to catch her breath at the hard work.

"Ah yes, you tend to get used to this, my parents had a farm in my home city, Valencia, so I am used to this."

"How did you team up with Maria?" asked Isobelle.

"Ah, she has come also from Valencia, we hmmm knew of each other yes, but we were not friends until we arrive here, now we are best friends," she smiled.

Maria then came out carrying plates, and another plate, that was covered with foil, but the aromas coming from the kitchen were to die for.

She put the plates out in front of them before she uncovered them… they contained large pieces of chicken breast.

She walked back to the kitchen and came out carrying a large bowl, which contained boiled potatoes, then a large bowl of salad, followed by a basket full of brown and white crusty rolls, along with some side dishes, it was a feast fit for a king.

"Please help yourselves, then we go back out to finish off, then tonight we rest," smiled Maria.

They finished their feast and washed it down with freshly squeezed orange juice, which was so refreshing.

They rested for what appeared to be a lifetime, but in reality, was only around thirty minutes, before they got up to go back out to finish off what they were doing.

Maria and Gabriela had gone around to help Paul with the sheep, pigs, horses, chickens and cows, sorting out feeds as well as doing a bit of milking of the cows but, with that being a technical job, always by hand, it was something that they were experienced at, and it was something that they had to do themselves.

The day had ticked on, and they had all finished doing what they needed to do, and it was getting quite late into the afternoon.

"Let's call it for the day," Gabriela smiled at Paul, as she, Maria and Paul started walking back to the farmhouse, Maria popping her head around to see if the girls had also finished.

"Yes, we're done here, fresh hay laid for the horses, food for them to eat so, I'm ready to rest up now, we're both enjoying it though," Alice smiled, as did Isobelle.

"Come on in then, let's go and eat," smiled Maria, before disappearing out of sight.

They all remove their boots and overalls one last time for the day, all feeling very tired from all of their work, but realised that they needed to work for their keep.

They all again went to wash their hands for dinner, the girls and Paul upstairs and Gabriela and Maria in the kitchen, where they had started to prepare food, a thick beef stew and dumplings, with lots of vegetables thrown in to make it more filling, after all the hard work that they had all put in.

Paul and the girls came down and went to sit at the table.

"Let me come and help you put food together," Isobelle smiled.

"Yes, how rude of me, me too," Alice called to them.

"This is ok, maybe tomorrow if you wish yes?" smiled Maria, popping her head around the corner to them all, who sat patiently waiting for the food to come through.

It had already been prepped earlier so it was just a case of heating it back up, and, like the meals that they had previously, there was enough to feed an army.

Maria walked in with the huge brown metal pot, steam rising from it, and put it in the centre of the table.

Gabriela came through with some large bowls, cutlery and some side plates for them all.

She then went back to the kitchen and once again, came in with various sizes of both crusty and soft rolls and put them next to the steaming pot.

"I'll play hostess shall I?" Alice smiled, getting up from her chair and going over to where the pot sat, asking everyone individually to pass her their bowls, starting with the two Spanish girls.

She had served everyone, with just herself to go.

She dished hers up and took it over to where she sat.

"Thank you, girls, this looks delicious," Isobelle smiled, looking forward to tucking in.

Suddenly, Paul's phone went off, it was on silent, but even the silent mode was loud with its vibration, it made everyone jump.

He took his phone out, and the expression on his face suddenly changed.

"Erm sorry, I've got to take this," as he walked off once more in the direction of the conservatory, all the girls looking at each other in turn.

There was a deathly silence suddenly at the table, Gabriela and Maria sensing that there was something wrong with the girls, due to their change in mood.

"Is everything ok?" Maria asks.

"Oh yes, he has these business calls he needs to take sometimes so, no, it's fine," Alice was unsure who it was on the phone but found it odd that he needed to take it elsewhere.

They continued to devour their food, Paul's sitting going slightly cold while he was away from the table, while Alice continued to glance back in the direction of the conservatory, to check to see when he was coming back.

After five or ten minutes, he reappeared from the room, quickly putting his phone away in his pocket, expressionless and walked back to his seat.

"Sorry about that, I erm… had to take a call, it was Scott, just checking that we had settled in ok," glancing over to Alice, while he settled back in to eat.

"Shall I warm this food back up for you Paul?" Maria asked.

"No, it's ok, it's still pretty hot so it will be fine."

Paul picked his knife and fork back up, and continued to briefly glance over to Alice whilst he carried on eating, Isobelle giving her a concerning look also.

Alice knew that Paul was lying and that it wouldn't have been Scott, but probably Charlie, who he had a secret chat with before they came to the farmhouse.

Food was all finished and both Gabriela and Isobelle

cleared the plates, which were swiftly put in the dishwasher.

Both girls then returned to the table, before Gabriela returned with bottles of wine.

"Let us go to the conservatory yes, as we know so very little of you," Maria smiled.

"That sounds like a plan," Isobelle smiled, she had taken a liking to the two Spanish girls, who had been so warm and welcoming from the start, and it was going to be just as nice to get to know their hosts, seeing that they were going to be spending so much time together.

Once again, Paul's mobile phone vibrated in his pocket, before taking it out to answer it, just as he too was heading to be with the others in the room.

"I'm just going to go and take this, pour me a wine and I'll be with you in a minute," he said, sheepishly, before again heading to the conservatory.

"Paul, honestly!" Alice snapped, but he continued to head off to answer the call.

The girls all sat down, the atmosphere going slightly cold with Paul's erratic behaviour.

"So, where do you all come from?" Gabriela asked.

The girls waited for the other to answer, chuckling as they were butting into each other trying to answer at once.

"I'm from Canada, in a place called Tandesford on the Chadley Islands, not sure if you have heard of it, very beautiful if a little cold," Isobelle smiled, "but I've lived in England for a few years now and I've settled here now," she smiled.

"That sounds very nice Isobelle," Maria smiled.

"What of you Alice, what is your story?" she continued.

She didn't want to go into her beginnings with Stacey,

or being with Sarah, just in case she had heard anything, so decided to tell them about her time in Barnwood.

"Well, I met Paul in a place called Barnwood and we became instantly attracted to each other, more so him than me, you see, I'm a model as a profession," she exclaimed, "I was only telling Izzy the other day how I met him," she smiled, wondering herself if she had made a mistake, knowing how his temperament had changed, but she knew that he loved her, and he was a good lover too.

Just then, Paul reappeared and sat down with the others, picking up his white wine, and taking big gulps.

"Wow, Paul are you thirsty?" Isobelle asked.

Paul though just looked at her with disdain, he was back to his moody self.

"I'm taking my wine up to the bedroom, are you coming Alice?" he snapped.

"I'll be up in a minute, just chatting, I won't be long."

All the girls topped their glasses back up, having already drunk most of it during their chatting.

"Goodnight," he said, with his back to everyone, not even giving them a look as he walked off, the Spanish girls just taking him for how he was.

"He seems a very angry man," remarked Gabriela, "why do you stay with him Alice?"

"He wasn't like this when we met, she was very charming, but he has had a few things happen recently and I think it's shaken him and he's not able to snap out of it, he's a good man really once you get to know him," she smiled a slightly false smile, to once again try to reassure them, and looking at Isobelle whilst also sipping her wine, knowing that she knew the truth about him.

"Right girls, today has been exhausting but enjoyable so, we're going to go up if that's ok with you," Alice yawned, starting to feel tired.

"Of course ladies yes, you have worked hard on the farm today so thank you, we managed to get everything done, though Gabi and I will go out soon to put the animals away for tonight," Maria smiled, "we will see you in the morning yes?"

"Looking forward to it, goodnight" grinned a tired Alice, as she and Isobelle started walking up the stairs.

"Goodnight," Gabi shouted, both girls looking back and giving them a wave.

Alice started to head towards Isobelle's room, as they still wanted to raise a toast to Ben, as they said they would.

"You don't have to toast him with me Alice," Isobelle smiled.

"No, he obviously meant a lot to you Izzy so, it's important to me too," Alice was a pillar of strength to Isobelle, and she appreciated it.

They walked into Isobelle's spacious room and sat on her bed and started to talk about Ben.

"So, a toast to Ben, no longer with us yet never forgotten," Alice smiled, whilst having an arm around her, pulling her in for a cuddle, whilst both were holding their wines.

"Bet you miss him, don't you?"

"I do yes, he was taken from me way too soon," Isobelle's eyes started to well up once again, as she took a big gulp from her glass.

"He'll be very proud of the woman you've become and knowing that I am here to protect you, though I still feel bad about Italy."

"You weren't to know what was going to happen with that sleazeball though were you, neither of us did, plus it was me who was all excited about going."

"Oh god, he's taken all of those photos too, where are they likely to go?"

"I'm sure the police will be swarming all over the place by now so, don't worry, they'll probably be seizing as much from that place as they can, including his camera equipment."

"Anyway, forget him, let's focus on the here and now," Alice tried to get a sodden-faced Isobelle to re-focus.

"TO BEN!" Isobelle raises her glass, kisses Alice on the lips, putting her glass on the table, Alice responds by doing likewise.

Their hands were starting to caress each other, Isobelle lying flat on her bed, as Alice started to kiss her around the neck, her hands exploring her body, when suddenly, she heard a commotion from down the hallway, so jumped off the bed to find out what was going on.

She opened Isobelle's bedroom door and hurried towards the room she had with Paul, to find him coming out of the door, almost in a hurry, clutching a jacket.

"Where are you going Paul?"

"I've got to be somewhere, I won't be long."

"But it's late, can't it wait until the morning?"

"No, it can't wait, you just go to bed, and I'll be back."

"It's that guy back at Scott and Julie's, Charlie, isn't it?"

"As I say, go to bed and I'll be back," he gave her a menacing glance, before he walked away, down the stairs, and out the door, startling Maria and Gabriela in the process.

Isobelle came out of her room to see what was going on, Alice glancing down the hallway to her.

“I think he’s been speaking to that Charlie guy on the phone, and I don’t think he’s going to meet up with him for a few drinks either, something isn’t right.”

Isobelle came down the hallway to put her arm around Alice’s waist in a show of support, as the two Spanish girls also joined them upstairs, having been chatting with each other after the others had gone up to bed.

“Is everything ok?” Maria looked concerned at Alice’s angry face.

“Not really, and I’m tempted to follow him, to find out exactly what he’s up to, I’m not going to be treated like a mug.”

“Maybe that’s not the best idea honey, wait till he gets back, and ask him to be honest with you,” Isobelle still clinging on around Alice’s waist.

“Yeah, maybe you’re right but, I’m going to get to the bottom of it when he gets back, I don’t trust that Charlie one bit, and I aim to find out exactly what the hell is going on, one way or another.”

WHAT'S GOING ON?

All four of the girls waited for Paul to return, he had been gone for some hours, Isobelle sat with Alice in the bedroom that she and Paul shared, as Isobelle didn't want Alice to wait alone.

"You go to bed Izzy, I'll be ok."

"No, you've been there for me, I'm going to wait with you until he gets back, even if that fucking twat is drunk, I don't care, better in numbers, isn't that what they say?"

"Aww Izzy you really are very sweet but honestly, I will be fine, but, if you do want to wait with me, I won't say no," Alice smiled, giving Isobelle a peck on the cheek, in a non-sexual way, it was neither the time nor the place, but she was sure that there would be plenty of time for that with her.

They had sat waiting for well over an hour before they heard the front door go.

They both paced out of the bedroom, to check that it was him returning and, sure enough, he was walking back in.

"So, you going to explain where the hell you've been?" Alice snapped, clearly in no mood to be lied to anymore.

"Oh, I've just been to see Scott, have a drink with him," he said, quite stone-faced, but she didn't believe a word that was coming out of his mouth.

"Ok so, shall we try that again, where have you been?"

"Not here, I'll talk to you in the bedroom."

The two Spanish girls had come up the stairs to make sure that both Alice and Isobelle were ok, Paul had practically barged past them on his way to the bedroom, Alice ushering them away with her hand, as she also did with Isobelle, that she was going to be ok.

Paul stormed into the bedroom, the door thumping against the wall, he paced the floor up and down almost in a fit of rage, before he sat down.

"What the fuck is wrong Paul, don't lie to me about seeing Scott."

"Yes yes, I've met up with Charlie, he wanted something from me, ok, so we've been to discuss it, so it's my business."

"I think you'll find it's my business too, depending on what he's wanting you to do, I am your wife remember."

"We're talking drugs here aren't we!" she snapped.

"We're running out of money, the pay is good, and it's just a few runs so, yeah."

"Don't you ever learn?" "I thought we'd got passed all that?"

"Like I say, we have to live so, what do you expect me to do?"

"Well, for now, we're ok aren't we but, maybe go out and get a job, we're starting a new life so, isn't that what normal people do?"

"This… normal?" "What fucking part of any of this is normal?"

"Well, that's all down to you isn't it, being on the run, being chased by unscrupulous people and just being in this situation, which, let's be honest, isn't great is it?"

"I'm not taking this fucking shit, I'm off out, don't wait up!"

"But Paul…" but he was out of the bedroom in a flash, and was soon down the stairs and back outside, into the deep of the night, and it had also turned slightly cooler, with the night having drawn in.

Isobelle, Maria and Gabriela were all heading over in the direction of Alice and Paul's bedroom, giving her a show of support.

"I am so sorry girls, you should not have to put up with this attitude, and you have been so kind and welcoming to us as well, I'm so sorry, you don't have to put up with all this shit of his."

"He will get cold in the night here," said a concerned Maria.

"FUCK HIM!" snapped Alice, "sorry, I didn't mean to swear but he has made me so angry."

"God knows when he'll be back if at all, I've got to the stage where I'm past caring."

Paul carried on trudging away from the farmhouse, getting his phone out of his pocket and making a call.

"Hi, it's me, can we meet?"

Meanwhile, Detective Neil Buchanan got a phone call from headquarters, but not where Neil was stationed.

"Is that Detective Buchanan?"

"Yes, it is."

"It's Inspector Garrison here from Lansburton station, fifth division," Inspector Garrison was a well-respected officer, who had been in the force for over thirty years and was coming up to retirement, "I hear you are chasing the Paul Arnold case?"

"Ah Inspector Garrison, not heard from you for a while, how are you and yes I am, do you have any news for me?"

"We have had a call from the Italian police, there has been an incident in a place called Tropea, and you may want to fly over there, take your forensics with you, and see what you find."

"Hang on, what has this got to do with Arnold?"

"There have been reports of sightings of five English men, and a man that has been seen, fitting his description, being in that party, "they've also got some footage to show you but they want to discuss it with you directly, as opposed to sending it over to us, you know what our Italian counterparts are like." so, get yourself over there pronto, there's a good fella."

"You'll be met at Tropea airport by Detective Luigi Contalini, he'll take you to where the incident has taken place."

"Ok, I'm on it, thanks for the heads up, I'll get a team together," Neil hung up on the Inspector, and gathered the other officers up from where they were.

"Come on guys, let's move out, a possible sighting of Arnold in Italy, we've got to get ourselves over there, and fast, I want to catch that fucking son of a bitch more than life itself, if it's the last thing I ever do."

They drive away from Lansburton after a fruitless

search for any clues as to their whereabouts and pick up visas to get over to Italy.

Neil thought that this was the closest he had ever felt in getting to them, and this was just the news that he had been waiting for, wherever they were hiding, they weren't going to escape his clutches for much longer, and any clues in Italy would help.

Neil got on the radio to his station, to organise the entry visas that he needed for him and a few other officers, as well as the forensics team.

The team were soon back at the office where Neil was stationed, and visas had been arranged for a dozen of them to fly to Italy.

The force had arranged for taxis and flights to be commissioned for them all, and they were soon at Lansburton airport, to take the first plane out, it was going to take two hours, and the force back at Neil's station, had e-mailed their Italian counterparts that Neil and his team were en-route.

The detective and his men had soon arrived at Tropea airport, had gone through security and customs, and were met by a man holding a board up showing 'Neil Buchanan,' missing out the word Detective, so as not to draw any suspicion or intrigue.

"This way please," said the gentleman with the board, as he started to lead them out of the airport, and towards a waiting car.

As they approached the line of cars, they were met by another man, tall, about six foot, slim, greased back black hair, chewing on some gum and looking suave in a navy-blue designer Italian suit and wearing dark sunglasses, Neil could almost see his own reflection through them.

"Neil Buchanan?" "Detective Neil Buchanan?" the Italian asked.

Neil had nodded in his direction, waiting for him to introduce himself.

"I'm Detective Luigi Contalini, nice to meet you," the Italian detective held his hand out to shake Neil's hand, while also showing Neil his police badge as confirmation as to his identity, "this way with me please, I will take you and your team to the site."

Neil and Luigi got into the waiting car, the other entourage getting into the cars behind, following the front car, to go to the murder scene.

"We were tipped off by someone that there were some gunshots here, at the castle, and we have some footage of a vehicle and what appears to be some men from England, so we wanted you to see this for yourself."

Luigi was putting Neil in the picture as to why he felt the need to get them to fly to Tropea, to see the scene first-hand.

"Is it not something that you could have just sent to us, we are both fighting the same cause aren't we, or so I thought?"

"Yes of course but, I thought it important for you to come here, get a sense of what has happened, and any clues you may wish to take back to England with you."

Neil was a little bit uncomfortable with Luigi, having a different mentality, but also their forces working in different ways, and Neil wanted to do things his way, and he felt a little forced to fly in, yet was also thankful that there may be some clues for him to take away, just as the Italian had said.

They arrived at Tropea castle, and the forensics team

from England immediately got to work with blood stains that had been scattered around from the shootings.

"How can you be sure that the men involved here were English Luigi?"

"They had an English look, plus I have spoken to the man at the marina, Giovanni, and he said that there was an English man asking questions as to the location of the castle, and other men in a car, you may go and speak to him if you so wish".

"Yes, I will, that might be an idea, get an idea of what was asked," "Where is this Giovanni now?"

"He is still at his marina, but he is being guarded by our police, so he doesn't take his boat out."

Luigi took Neil down to the marina and saw a man being guarded by an Italian police guard.

"Hi, you must be Giovanni, I'm Detective Neil Buchanan from Barnwood British Police," Neil showed Giovanni his police identity, "I understand that you have been visited by some English guys at your boatyard can you tell me a little about them?"

"Now, I'm going to record this conversation, just to let you know, but it's just as evidence, do you understand?"

Giovanni looked at him, pausing, before nodding in agreement.

"Yes, I see around five of them in a car, couldn't make out their faces, and the man who came to me was asking where the castle was so I directed him there," Gio was wary about telling the detective too much, as he didn't want to implicate himself with Valentino, as he could see himself being dragged into what had happened, and he had his business to think about.

"Ok, that's helpful, what did this man look like who came to see you, did he give his name?"

Giovanni was feeling very uncomfortable with the questioning, he didn't want to be a part of whatever this was but knew that he had to still answer the detectives' line of questioning.

"He was a very stocky man, around five foot nine maybe, rough looking, dark hair, not the sort of man you'd mess with and no, sorry, he didn't give his name."

"Is there anything else you can tell me about the other men, you must have got a sighting of the others in the car, the driver, the front seat passenger maybe, the men in the back?" Neil didn't feel that he had much to go on with the info that Gio had provided him with, "you must know something else, you sure you aren't hiding something?"

"That's all I know I swear, now, do you have any more questions because I have a business to run?" Giovanni was getting slightly irritated by questions that he didn't have answers for and had told the detective everything he knew.

"Ok, but don't go far, just in case I have more questions for you," Neil gave Gio a cold stare before walking away and back to where his team of forensics were.

He wanders around the crime scene, where there was a scattering of blood, and checked with his team, to see what they have found.

"There are different scatterings of blood," said one of the forensics team, "some by the front wall and more around the back," he continued.

"Make sure you get the blood samples over to the lab as soon as you can, good work," Neil said.

He then went over to speak to Luigi.

"Do you have any photos of the car, it would be a massive help to track that."

"No Detective we don't," "we have gone over CCTV and nothing appears, we do have tyre tracks and we do have images of one of your Englishmen," Luigi then calls one of his officers over, to bring him the electronic tablet, and he shows Neil the photo of one of the men who had turned up at the scene at the time of the shootings, as well as images of the tyre tracks that they had found.

Neil takes a closer look at the man in the photo on the tablet and thinks he may recognise him.

"I know him," he said to Luigi, "that's Scott Connelly, he's been known to us some years back for some petty thefts, he's kept clean since well, until now that is, thank you Luigi, that's a massive help.

"Can you take me to take a look at the tyre tracks, are they still there?"

"Yes, they are, the scene has been cordoned off, so everything has been kept for you to examine."

Neil walks off towards where the tyre tracks were, and bent down to take a closer inspection, looking around to see if he could see any more clues, any cigarette ends for the forensics team, or anything else that may help.

He stood up, got his phone out and took a picture of the tyre tracks, to see what vehicle they would match.

"There is no need to take pictures of the tracks, I will e-mail them over to you,"

Neil thought back to how this could have been done before he jetted across to Italy, but there was no communication from the Italians.

"It's ok, I need it for my evidence but if you still want to forward it over too, as a backup, that would be good."

"How many were killed here?" Neil asked his Italian counterpart.

"There were at least two, Italian men, and I do not know how many of your English."

"Where are they now, your morgue?" Neil asked.

"Yes, the deceased have been taken there, I can get one of my men to take you to the morgue if you wish, but your English are not at the morgue, if any of your men were killed, but indications show other blood so, make your own conclusions."

"Yes, can I go now, while my forensics team carry out their work?" Neil was keen to get as much information as he could, any clues that may help him find Paul.

Luigi called one of his men over to take Neil to the Tropea morgue.

Neil and the Italian officer were soon at Tropea mortuary, and both Neil and the Italian officer walked in, the Italian officer sitting down to wait for Neil.

Neil produced his police card to the mortuary technician and asked to be taken to see the Italians killed at the castle.

The technician checked his list to see which cold storage unit the deceased men was stored in.

He took Neil over, pulled the freezer door open, and pulled the bright white sheet down, so Neil could see who it was.

"This is Bruno Lucetti Detective," said the technician, "do you wish to take a look at the other man, Luca?" he continued.

"No, it's ok, this one will be enough, thank you," Neil responded.

The technician walked off to sit down at his desk, to allow Neil to examine the body a bit more.

There was lots of powder residue on his nostrils, from various drug-taking occasions, but also noticed the bullet wound that killed him.

Neil continued to look over his body, but there was nothing there that would help him get any clues.

He covered the body back over and nodded over in the technician's direction that he had finished his examinations, before thanking him and walking back out into the corridor where the Italian officer was waiting.

They went outside and got back in the car, the officer not saying anything to Neil, although it was only a short journey from the mortuary to where the castle was.

The car pulled up, and Neil got out to see that the forensics team were packing their things up and switched on his phone.

"I'm just going to go back and speak to Giovanni again, he must know something else."

He walked back down to the marina, and Giovanni was tying his boat up, and checking it over, to see if it needed mending or fixing in any way.

"Giovanni, is there anything else you can remember, anything that might help my investigations?" "There have been men killed here, you must know more than you're saying."

"Detective, I really can't help you any more than I have already, I know nothing else."

"Why were the English men here, were they looking for someone or something?" Neil wanted to probe Giovanni more, having a business in Tropea, he must have had a lot of people coming and going and must have known why they might have been there, but Giovanni didn't want to share his links to Valentino or what he got up to.

"Are there any Mafia links here that I should know about?" "Were they here to fight with any of them?"

"Detective, I have told you everything I know now, if you don't mind."

"Here's my card if you think of anything else." Neil walked away from the Marina for the last time, whilst looking over his shoulder briefly at Giovanni and heading back to the castle.

"One more thing Detective, I'm puzzled where these other dead men, or women, may be, if not at the morgue, if you say there were other blood trails," Neil was curious as to where the other dead were.

"I have no idea Detective Buchanan, this is something for your team to work out," Detective Contalini felt that he had helped as much as he could.

I think my team have got everything that we need thank you Detective Contalini, I think we'll wrap it up here, if you get any more information, be kind enough to send it over to us as soon as you get it, don't need any more delays on this case," he smirked at his counterpart.

"Yes of course Detective, I'll get my men to drive you back to the airport so you can catch your connection, don't want to keep you waiting."

There was a slight frosty atmosphere between the two Detectives, and Neil departed without even so much as a handshake for Luigi, to thank him for his co-operation and accessibility to the scene.

Neil and the forensics team headed back to the cars that

they arrived in, and the Italian officers drove them back to the airport for their flight home.

A few hours passed, it was quite late in the afternoon, and they had landed back at Lansburton airport, and they all headed back to the office.

"You guys get yourselves off home, there are a few things I need to do here, a few phone calls to make, the forensics report can wait until tomorrow."

The team that had flown out to Tropea with Neil all got their things together and wished Neil a pleasant evening before they headed out the door for home.

'Right Scott Connelly, let's find out where you are and bring you in for questioning' he thought to himself, he was determined to get some answers from him, and he didn't want to let a second slip.

'... and where are the other deceased, I'll have to get someone to ring around hospitals tomorrow, maybe they were brought back here,' he thought to himself.

Neil wanted to be the one who went to wherever Scott lived, to see the look on his face when he opened the door.

An hour or so had passed, and Scott and Julie were settling down to have some food before the evening ended, when suddenly, there was a knock on the front door.

"Who can that be this late in the day?" Julie looked at Scott, he equally looked puzzled.

Julie opened the door, to be confronted by a group of around five men.

"Can I speak with Scott Connelly please Miss?"

Scott then immediately came to the door, hearing that it was men's voices.

"Ah, Scott Connelly, long time no see," smiled Neil to him, "can you come down the station with us please?"

"What do you want, I've kept myself out of trouble for years now, so I don't know how I can help you with anything Detective."

"Ah Connelly, that's not exactly true is it, you staying out of trouble I mean, let's discuss it more down the station shall we, I really don't want to have to cuff you," Neil was in no mood to be messed about, and wanted Scott to just do as he's been asked.

"So Detective, am I under arrest?"

"No, you're not, we just have a few questions to ask you but, down at the station if you don't mind" Neil gave him a fake smile, one hand on his hip, whilst leaning against the frame of the front door with the other hand.

"I won't be long love," smiling to Julie as he walked out of the house and to the waiting police car, Julie had a look of concern on her face, wondering if he was going to be kept in.

Scott was quiet in the car heading towards Lansburton police station and was soon led to an interview room, where he was asked to sit down by Neil.

The pair were joined in the interview room by an officer guarding the door, who remained quiet throughout.

Before going to get Scott from his home, Neil had printed off the information that had been gathered in Italy, and, true to his word, Luigi had e-mailed the information from their tablet across to Neil's e-mail address, including the tyre track and Scott's picture.

Neil had brought with him a file containing the information, as well as evidence from Giovanni, that Neil hoped would get Scott talking.

Neil shuffled his paperwork inside the thin beige coloured, slightly creased folder, before plonking it on the table in front of him and clasping his hands together, forming a fist.

"Right, I am just going to start recording this interview, I'm sure you've seen all this before," Neil pressed down the button on the recording machine, as the tape started rolling.

"Ok so, the time is now eighteen-thirty-four, in the room is Detective Neil Buchanan of Barnwood police, Officer James Gladstone, and please state your name for the tape," the Detective looked sternly at Scott.

"Scott Connelly," came the reply, almost taking an age to answer, so as to delay matters, knowing it would infuriate Neil.

"Now then Connelly, let's cut to the chase shall we… where is Paul Arnold?"

"What are you asking me for, I've not seen him for years, where has this come from and what are you implying?"

"Right, let me tell you what I believe shall I?" "I am feeling pretty tired, and I should be at home having a nice glass of whisky, as I'm sure you wish you were right now, all curled up with your lover, you see, I have flown to Italy today, a holiday you might be thinking," he smirks, "no, I've been to a place called Tropea, lovely looking place, very scenic, a marina, you should go, oh wait, you have already haven't you, along with some of your friends, Paul too maybe?" Neil was trying to put pressure on him to divulge as much as he could, which would lead him to Paul.

"I don't know what you're talking about, I haven't seen Paul for years, like I've just told you."

"Ok, and what about Tropea, visited recently?" Neil was starting to get very agitated that Scott was holding things back from him.

"COME ON CONNELLY, let's not waste any more time… what were you doing in Tropea recently?"

"I don't know what you…"

Neil suddenly thumped his fist on the table in anger at Scott's reluctance to share vital information.

"STOP FUCKING AROUND WITH ME!" "I will ask you again, what were you doing in Tropea?"

Scott paused, hoping he could think on his feet.

"Ok, I was there, sight-seeing, it was a part of Italy that I hadn't been to before, and I wanted to see what it was like," Scott quietly said, looking down at the table, not wanting to look Neil in the eye.

Neil looked at him and chuckled.

"Ah you see, this is where we are at Connelly, let's take a look at these photos shall we?"

Neil pulled out a photo of Scott and laid it out in front of him.

"Exhibit P-one point one," he smirked at him.

"Now, can you confirm who that is in the photo Connelly?" Neil smirked.

Scott leaned forward, pausing to look at the photo.

"It's me," he said, almost in a resigned way.

"Yes, yes it is, isn't it?" Neil smiled, feeling that Scott was showing signs of cracking.

"… and what of these tyre tracks as well Connelly, your car is it?"

"I will say again, I went sightseeing, I had not been there before, and I was just visiting with friends."

"Ah, friends, now we're getting somewhere, one of these being Paul Arnold?"

"No, I don't know how many more times I've got to tell you, I've not seen him in years."

"So, during my trip to Tropea, like I say, lovely place, don't you agree?" "I had a chat with a guy called Giovanni, down at the marina, I'm sure he described you to a tee, where were you going?" Neil was getting insistent that Scott answered his questions truthfully.

"Who's Giovanni?" "I've never heard of him," Scott was getting tired with some of the questioning.

"CUT THE FUCKING BULLSHIT CONNELLY," there was a shoot-out there, as I think you well know, two Italians were killed, and maybe even one or two of your friends, and I think you and whoever these friends were, were there at the scene, and I think you were there with Paul, why don't you just admit it, so I can just go home, and we can look to release you on bail."

"As I say, I was there sight…"

"Yes, yes, as you keep saying, you were there sightseeing, right, we're going to keep you in overnight, so maybe you can have a think about the questions I have asked you, so I can question you some more in the morning, take him away officer."

"Interview terminated at twenty-eleven hours."

Neil pressed the recorder button to stop the interview.

Neil looked at the officer at the door, who took Scott by the arm to lead him away to be kept overnight.

"I need to make a phone call to Julie, let her know that I won't be back, I'm at least entitled to my call."

"You might want to get yourself a solicitor as well, or I can issue you one from the station if you'd prefer."

Scott looked at Neil before being led away to a cell.

Neil gathered his folder up, as Scott was taken away, he didn't want to be handcuffed and would go to the cell willingly.

Not being where Neil was stationed, he decided that he was going to take the evidence back home with him, so it was easily accessible in the morning.

The Detective left the building, got in his car and drove home, after an exhausting day, flying to and from Italy, as well as questioning Scott.

It was time for a whisky, put his feet up, look at the evidence in the folder and listen to the voice recording from Giovanni.

It was going to be an equally long day tomorrow!

The next morning arrived, Neil was feeling tired from his excursions the day before, as well as the intense questioning of Scott.

He made himself a coffee and some toast, grabbed the evidence folder that he had taken home with him, and took the toast out to the car with him, he wanted to go and interview Scott again as quickly as he could, as he knew that he was on a strict time schedule, knowing he could only hold him for twenty-four hours, and either release him or arrest him.

He arrived at Lansburton station within half-an-hour, and quickly walked up the steps leading to the front desk, with the beige folder clenched tightly under his arm.

He went to the officer at the front desk and showed him his badge.

"Can you get Scott Connelly from the holding cell for me please, and bring him into Interview room one, and his solicitor, if he hasn't had one appointed from here already?"

Neil goes into the interview room and waits for Scott to be taken from the holding cell, along with the station-arranged solicitor and brought into the interview room, where Neil was already sitting down and waiting for him.

Scott walks in, followed by the solicitor, and sits down opposite Neil.

Neil re-started the tape machine, before starting the conversation.

The date is Wednesday the fourth of August twenty-twenty-three and the time is o-nine hundred hours," going through the same people in the room as there was yesterday, even with the same officer on the door.

"So, Connelly, did you sleep well?" "I know I did, nice coffee and a bit of toast this morning, stretched out in my nice comfy bed, you could be in your comfy bed too, all curled up with your partner once you've told me where Paul Arnold is!"

Scott looked stone-faced at Neil, not budging an inch from his statement the day before.

"I'll tell you again, I haven't seen him for years so, you can badger me and interrogate me all you like, but you'll keep hearing the same thing."

"Ok, let's go back to Italy then shall we, what were you doing there, because I have witnesses say that you were involved in the shooting at the castle, tell me what your involvement in that was?"

"I do not have a clue what the hell you are going on

about, you're not dragging me into that, you're not putting that on me."

"Oh so, you do recognise that there was a shooting there do you, why can't you just own up that you were part of this group?"

"All you're doing is trying to fix someone up for whatever happened there, and you're trying to frame me for whatever you want."

"So, can you prove your whereabouts during your trip to Tropea, shops visited, bars museums?" "You must have some receipts on you to prove you were where you say you were?"

"No, I don't, because I didn't think I'd need to keep my receipts oh, just in case I get questioned by the police, so I MUST keep hold of them!"

"The man I questioned, Giovanni, described you to a tee, how do you explain that?"

"Well, how should I know, because I wasn't there, like I keep saying, I don't know this guy that you keep referring to, so you're barking up the wrong fucking tree I'm afraid."

"Maybe we should go and speak to your girlfriend, Julie, isn't it?" "I'm sure she could shed some light as to your whereabouts and hey, she might even be able to tell us where Paul is, why didn't I think of that before?"

"Now you're clutching at straws!" Scott huffed, sitting back in his chair, his station solicitor making notes yet keeping very quiet during the whole interview, Scott not giving Neil an inch of what he was hoping to hear.

"If I haven't seen Paul, then how do you expect Julie to have seen him, she hasn't even met him yet!"

"Do you have any more questions for my client,

because, unless you're going to arrest him, I think it's time you released him, you sure haven't got enough to detain him any longer" the solicitor piped up to Neil, telling him that he needed to decide as to what he was going to do.

"Interview terminated at ten-twenty-two hours," "you're free to go Connelly but, don't go far, I'm sure we'll have more questions for you once the progress of the investigation, give our regards to your girlfriend," Neil smirked at Scott, as the solicitor got up with him from his chair, before leading his client out of the room, that the officer at the door had opened for them, before Scott walked out of the building, to find a taxi to take him back home to Jeromesley.

Neil got up from his chair, shuffled his paperwork back in his crumpled folder and made his way towards the open door, before turning to speak to the standing officer.

"There's more to come from this, just you wait and see, and I'm going to get that fucking son-of-a-bitch Paul Arnold, and I think Connelly knows where he is, I'm going to put some surveillance on him," the officer smiled slightly at Neil, as the detective was about to walk out the room door, as the officer had no involvement in the case that was being investigated.

Meanwhile, back at the farmhouse, there was still no sign of Paul, and some hours had passed.

All the girls decided to go to bed, and it was the early hours of the morning and even if he didn't return, they had decided that they were going to carry on regardless, feed the animals and muck out, as they had been doing, besides, Maria and Gabriela had been doing it on their own before their arrival.

Alice decided to get into bed with Isobelle so they could both have a cuddle up together, the feeling of being safe.

The two Spanish girls bid the girls goodnight, as they watched Alice and Isobelle both go into Isobelle's room, before closing the bedroom door.

"si te gusta ese tipo de cosas" (if you like that sort of thing) they smiled at each other, and giggled like little girls, at the thought of what might be happening in the bedroom between the two of them, but Alice was not in any mood to make love to Isobelle, she was too upset with the way Paul had been with them, so she was just looking forward to cuddling up with her and just talking.

"What the hell is Paul playing at, I'm sure he's probably with that nasty Charlie guy that he knows, and I don't trust him at all," both girls were starting to disrobe, putting a nightshirt on each, before pulling the fresh sheets back and climbing into bed, Alice kissing Isobelle on her lips, then resting her head at the top of her chest, Isobelle running her fingers through Alice's hair, like a protective mother to her child.

"I guess we've just got to wait until he gets back haven't we," "we've just got to concentrate on us, he's a big boy, he can look after himself," Isobelle was trying not to let Paul get to Alice, and at least she had Alice to herself for the time being.

The girls were soon asleep, wrapped in each other's arms.

The next morning came and there was still no sign of him.

It was seven-thirty, and Alice and Isobelle got up, Alice went to her room to put something different on, knowing that there was work to be done, looking after the farm.

When both girls came from their rooms, they once again had the aroma of cooked breakfast downstairs, and they felt that they could almost float down the stairs to it, it smelt that good.

They casually walked down the stairs and, with it once again being a warm day, both had shorts and a thin t-shirt on, knowing that they would be putting their overalls on over the top of what they wore.

"Good morning girls, did you sleep well?" Maria asked, setting up the table for their delicious first meal of the day.

"Yes we did thank you, stressing about that man of mine, glad I have Isobelle here to keep me in check," she smiled.

"I'm sure it's something and nothing Alice though I must admit, he's not my cup of tea, I don't know how you do it," she continued, putting the cutlery aside the table mats.

"It has been challenging Maria, I must admit, not sure how things are going to go forward from here, but we have had worse moments than this so I'm sure we'll get through it," Alice was trying to put a positive slant on the events of hers and Paul's marriage.

"Well, you've got a delicious breakfast being cooked by Gabi as we speak so you've got that to look forward to, and we'll have lots of fun today, with Paul not being here, while we tend to the animals, but we're here too if you need us Alice, that goes for you too Isobelle ok, please do not think that you cannot approach us if you need us to listen."

Gabriela comes out with the breakfast, a tasty feast, before coming out with a jug of freshly squeezed orange juice and a huge silver pot of percolated coffee.

All the girls were finished in no time, Alice couldn't

help but occasionally look at the empty chair where Paul sat, but it was particularly quiet, and the atmosphere had a feeling of being a lot more relaxed.

Both Gabriela and Maria noticed Alice looking at the chair, the Spanish girls both looking at each other, while continuing to eat, but wanting to change the mood a little, with whatever Alice was feeling.

"Would you like to do something different today girls, feed the chickens and pigs today, but you can do whatever you wish, maybe brush the horses too if you would like this yes?" "Gabi and I can do everything else; you can do this at your hmm, own pace yes?"

"Brushing horses!" smiled Isobelle, I've never done that before, I'd love to give that a go, what do you think Alice?"

"Yes, yes, we could do that, that would be great, let's do that."

Suddenly, all the girls are jolted, Alice's phone starts to ring, it's him.

Alice looks at all the girls, breakfast is as good as finished, the plates are clear, and they are just resting for a few minutes to let everything go down.

"I've... I've... got to take this," she smiled, getting up from the table and walking as far from the table as she could.

Suddenly, there is another mobile phone going off, this time it is Isobelle's, Gabriela and Maria once again looking at each other, Isobelle also leaving just the two helpers at the table alone.

Alice returns from her phone call from Paul, and sits back down, noticing that Isobelle wasn't there.

"Where's my friend gone?" she asks the girls.

"Ah, she also had a phone call so she has gone to the

conservatory to answer it," Gabriela nervously smiled, unsure who it might be, because they had not seen Isobelle on the phone with anyone before.

"I'm just going to go and check to make sure that she's ok, I won't be a second," Alice said to them, before walking off towards the conservatory.

Alice reaches the conservatory and sees Isobelle still on the phone.

"... yes, I can meet you, but not yet, I'll call you," Isobelle whispers."

She can sense that someone is at the entrance of the room, and quickly goes to hang up.

"... ok, I've got to go," she again whispers, before she hangs up, and turns around, to notice that it was Alice standing looking at her.

"Everything ok?" Alice, with a slight concern in her voice.

"Oh, yes erm, just an old friend, wanting to catch up, knew her when I was in Chammerley, said we'll have to catch up at some point, just unsure when," she smiles, before she brushed past Alice, not before giving her a kiss on her cheek.

"Let's go and see to those animals shall we, I'm looking forward to brushing the horses," looking back at Alice as she carried on walking towards the front of the farmhouse to get into her overalls.

Alice felt a little puzzled, as Isobelle had never really spoken about her friends before, especially any from Chammerley.

All the girls get kitted out in their workwear and head outside to see to the waiting animals.

Gabriela directs the girls to where the chickens and the horses were and shows them where the chicken feed was.

Alice was keen to talk to Isobelle a little bit more about her friend in Chammerley, and why she hadn't mentioned them before.

Isobelle went over to the chicken coop, grabbed the feeding bucket full of seeds and started to throw them in through the door that she was able to open, the chickens ran over to feed on them, Alice grabbed a bucket, filled it with water, and filled their drinking containers with it.

Isobelle had gone a little quiet, so Alice decided to ask her about her friend back in Chammerley.

"It was so nice that your friend called you Izzy, you've not spoken about them before, is it a male or a female?"

"Oh erm, he's a male, Henry, yes, Henry is his name," she nervously said, not wanting to look Alice in the eye while talking about him.

"Oh ok," Alice smiled, "might I get to meet him at some point do you think, I bet he's nice?"

"Oh erm no, I don't think so, he's a little shy when it comes to meeting new people so, I doubt it," glancing briefly at Alice, giving her a very brief smile.

"So, tell me a little about him, is he originally from Chammerley?"

Alice was a little curious, wondering if Isobelle was holding something back from her.

Suddenly, Isobelle's phone went off again.

She glanced briefly at Alice, before walking away to take the call, her back turned to Alice.

"... I've told you, I will call you when I can, and I'll

arrange to meet you ok, how did you get this number anyway?" Alice could just about hear her say.

Once again, a concerned Alice started to slowly walk over to her, worried that she might be in some kind of trouble.

Isobelle looked over her shoulder, hearing that Alice was approaching, and quickly hung up.

"He's persistent isn't he, he must like you, I've got competition," Alice smiled at her, but Isobelle just walked passed her, giving her a slight grin, without saying a word, to carry on seeing to their jobs.

"What did Paul have to say anyway?" Isobelle wanting to change the subject.

"He just said that he would be back at some point, but he had some things he needed to do first, he was being very vague, but I can imagine he's getting up to all sorts with that horrible excuse of a man," she sighed.

"Maybe he's needing to do it Alice, whatever IT is," she grinned.

"You've changed your tune about him haven't you?" Alice, feeling slightly puzzled.

"No, not really, I'm just saying that maybe he's been put in such a difficult situation, maybe this Charlie is putting pressure on him to do what he's telling him to do, we don't know what's going on do we?"

Alice noticed that Isobelle had changed a little towards her, and Henry may have changed her attitude, and Alice didn't like it, she wasn't used to Isobelle being a little cold in her sudden change of attitude.

"When are you planning on seeing Henry anyway, that'll be nice for you, is he planning on coming here, love to meet him," Alice smiled, trying to lighten the mood between them that had shifted for whatever reason, maybe Isobelle was feeling slightly isolated being at the farmhouse, and the feeling of being too cooped up.

"Erm, I don't know, I said I'd arrange to meet him somewhere, so there's nothing concrete."

"It'll probably do you good to get out of here for a while, maybe go into Lunshill, there's a few bars there aren't there, you could maybe have a few drinks with him there."

"Yeah maybe," Isobelle seemed distracted by something, but Alice knew that she was there as a support and that he could talk to her about anything, after all, they had both been through a lot since they had met.

"Are you sure you're ok Izzy?" Alice was a little concerned that her attitude had changed slightly.

"Yes, I'm fine, just tired I guess, this farm work is exhausting, maybe meeting up with…"

"Henry?" grinned Alice.

"…yes, Henry, would probably do me good."

The girls carried on with their farm work, and it was soon lunchtime.

"Coming in girls for a bite to eat, we have already done some chicken and cheese rolls, some cake and of course juice and coffee," smiled Gabriela.

Isobelle and Alice put down the things they had been using to sort out the chickens and headed back to the farmhouse, taking off their overalls and boots, before going off to wash their hands, to get ready for a delicious-sounding lunch.

They went upstairs to wash their hands, the bathroom being big enough for the two of them to wash their hands together, but this time there was no chat between the pair, instead it was deathly silence, Alice kept glancing over to Isobelle, but she not giving Alice any eye contact at all.

'There is something very clearly wrong with her, but she's shut me down suddenly' Alice thought, whilst still rinsing the soap from her hands, 'but maybe it is just tiredness so I should give her the benefit of the doubt.'

They dried their hands on the fresh lime green towel that was hanging up on a towel hanger in the bathroom, a bathroom that smelt so fresh and clean like it had just come out of a showroom.

They head downstairs, the frosty atmosphere between them continuing, before sitting down next to each other at the table, ready for lunch.

Maria came in from the kitchen, carrying a plate full of chicken and cheese soft rolls, and a selection of cakes, before heading back to bring through the big pot of coffee and the fresh orange juice.

All the girls sat down for their feast, again, except for Paul, who had still not returned.

There was very little chat at the table, Isobelle eating her food in almost stone-cold silence, something that Maria and Gabriela picked up on, glancing at each other, whilst continuing to eat.

"How are you getting on out there, are you far off finishing do you think, don't worry if not, as long as the animals are fed, that'll be ok," smiled Gabriela, trying to break the frosty atmosphere that had suddenly come about.

"We haven't fed the horses yet, or brushed them, that's our next job when we go back out, I know Izzy and I have been looking forward to doing the brushing, haven't we Izzy?" Alice grinned at Isobelle, waiting for her to respond, but she just carried on eating her chicken roll, grabbed a cheese one, and nodded her head again, without even giving any of them a look, just looked down at the table.

Alice moved her hand under the table, to go and grab Isobelle's hand, to see what response she got, but she slowly slid her hand away from Alice's, immediately realising that this was more than just tiredness.

"Have I done something wrong Izzy?" she whispered.

"No, I erm, I just need a break from here, go and meet James in the town, that's all."

"James?" "I thought you said his name was Henry?"

"Yes…no well, yes, his name is Henry, but erm, his middle name is James, so, he prefers that sometimes now, can we just change the subject?"

The table fell silent, all the girls eating and drinking in silence, the atmosphere felt slightly frosty as if Paul was there, the Spanish girls thought that that atmosphere was a bit tense, but something was troubling Isobelle, and she wasn't letting on.

"I'll help you clear the table," Isobelle got up and collected the various plates off the table, with most of the food being eaten, "thank you too, it was all delicious," she smiled to Maria, who was also clearing the plates with her, along with all the empty glasses and cups, dregs of coffee in one or two of the cups.

"Is your friend ok?" whispered Gabriela to Alice.

"Your guess is as good as mine but she said that she's tired, and needs a break," "she's going to meet some guy, I think, soon, in Lunshill, I think that the break away from here will probably do her good, though I've never seen her like this, though I've not known her overly long so, here's hoping that the mood she's in now, will change once she's met up with this guy, let her hair down a bit."

Isobelle and Maria were soon coming back from the kitchen, Alice giving Isobelle a smile and a wink, Isobelle just raising a grin in Alice's direction.

"Right ladies, shall we go, yes?" Gabriela realised that the day was starting to race away from them, and there was still so much to be done.

They all went outside to put their overalls and boots back on, Isobelle and Alice heading round towards the back of the barn, to where the horses, pigs and chickens were, and the atmosphere was just as fraught as it had been during that morning, the call that Isobelle had taken, had shaken her, but Alice didn't want to interrogate her about it more than she already had, whatever was bothering her, she had to just be there for her, but something clearly wasn't right, and was Isobelle lying about who this man was?.

Alice and Isobelle went to sort out the pigs and feed the horses, before they were brushed, again, this was done in almost complete silence, Isobelle was upset by something.

"Are you sure nothing is bothering you, Izzy, you know you can always talk to me, it's just that you've gone strangely quiet all of a sudden?"

"Sorry no, I'll be ok, just need to get away from here, the night out will do me good."

"Well ok, so long as there's nothing on your mind."

Isobelle looked at Alice, giving her a half-hearted grin while starting to groom the horses.

'Maybe she just needs a break, I'll give her a bit of space,' Alice thought to herself, 'we have been spending quite a lot of time together after all.'

They had finished feeding the pigs and grooming the horses whilst also giving them some food, and the day had dragged on.

"You girls finished, yes?" came the shout from behind them, seeing Maria's face as they turned round.

"Yes, I think we're done here now," "would you like us to bring the horses in?" called Alice.

"No, this is ok, we do this a lot later in the day, when you go upstairs to bed we do this, it doesn't take us long," Maria smiled, "it is time for us to hmmm, go inside to eat yes?"

Both girls sighed, as it had once again been hard work, Alice was starting to feel that she too needed a night out, and maybe ask the two Spaniards to perhaps join her.

They all got ready to go inside, taking off their boots and overalls before they did, and as per the usual routine, both Alice and Isobelle went upstairs to wash their hands.

"I know what you mean about a night out Izzy, starting to feel like I could do with one too, I'm exhausted" she chuckled, hoping it would raise a smile from her.

Again, Isobelle raised another half-hearted grin at Alice, to acknowledge that she had heard her, but as usual, Isobelle was deep in thought.

They headed towards the stairs, before casually walking down, the aroma of the food that was being cooked was simply divine.

"Maria is cooking a beef stew with, how you say, hmmm suet balls?" Gabriela was unsure if this was the correct terminology.

"Ah, do you mean dumplings?" Alice chuckled, raising a smile from both Isobelle and Gabriela.

"Ah yes, I hear this before, hmmm, how you say, yes, hmmm, dumplings?" she chuckled.

Gabriela had a slight look of horror, "I mean to ask, you are not vegetarians?"

"No, it's ok, we're not, plus we've been eating the chicken haven't we so no, it's ok, we're not," Alice replied, Isobelle also shaking her head, with a brief smile to Gabriela, who in turn briefly smiled at Alice, Gabriela also picking up that something wasn't quite right with Isobelle, even she had sensed that something was troubling her.

Maria was soon coming in from the kitchen, carrying another big pot of food, and the smells coming from the pot were just delicious.

"I have made a big pot of beef stew with some su…"

"Hmmm, dumplings!" Gabriela laughed.

"How do you say this word?" Maria chuckled.

"They're called dumplings," Alice smiled, chuckling as she did.

"Ah, ok, I am not hmmm familiar with this English word but yes, hmmm dumplings it is," she chuckled once more, Isobelle raising a smile but still not saying anything in response.

They were partway through their meal, Maria had made so much, but it could be carried over for another day, maybe have it for lunch the following day.

Once again, Isobelle's phone rang in her shorts pocket, and she pointed towards the conservatory that she needed to go and take it.

"He must be some guy this man if she is so hmmm, secretive, this how you say this?"

"Yes, that's right, I don't know this guy, she's only told me about him herself today," she frowned.

The rest of them continued to eat until all the food on their plate was finished.

Isobelle was soon coming back to the table and had been away for around ten minutes.

She ate the rest of her food like she hadn't eaten for a week, and was soon starting to clear the table.

"Thank you Isobelle, I will help you with this," smiled Gabriela.

The plates and cutlery were soon in the kitchen, and it was time to relax.

"I'm just going upstairs to get changed, I'm going out," Isobelle grinned to them all, and off she went to almost run up the stairs.

Maria, Gabriela and Alice all looked at each other, not quite knowing what to say, but Alice was determined to give Isobelle the space that she needed.

"Within the hour, Isobelle was downstairs, wearing a beautiful navy-blue one-piece dress, off the shoulder, make-up and hair done, and looking like she too was ready to walk a catwalk.

"WOW Isobelle, you look… you look…AMAZING!" smiled both Gabriela and Maria, almost unable to take their eyes off her.

"You sure do Izzy," smiled Alice, as she had rarely seen Isobelle look so stunning though she had when she dressed up for their fateful trip to Tropea.

"I'm not sure what time I'll be back but, is there a spare key I can have, just in case it's late?"

"… and Alice, whatever you do, PLEASE do not even think about following me!" Isobelle said, in an almost snappy way to her.

Isobelle practically brushed past Alice, without even looking at her.

She was carrying some red heels and smelt incredible, but her comment had almost infuriated Alice, so she followed her to the conservatory, noticing that Isobelle was about to get her phone out of her bag to call the man she was meeting.

"What the HELL is going on with you lately?" "What is it you're hiding from me?" Alice had angrily grabbed Isobelle around the arm, as she had had enough of this sudden change of attitude from her.

"Sorry, I didn't realise that you had suddenly become my mother, now, get your hand off of me, and give me some space, you're suffocating me!"

"… and don't even think about following me either, as I said!"

Isobelle had arranged for a taxi to come and pick her up, and she was meeting her mystery man in Lanshill.

Within twenty minutes, there was a beep outside, and the taxi had arrived.

Maria had given her a key to get back in, but she wasn't sure what time that was likely to be.

"I'll be as quiet as I can when I get back… don't wait up!"

… and with that, she was off and out the door, almost slamming it shut but, that was not hard to do, with it being a big farmhouse door.

"How do you fancy a night out girls, on me, don't worry, we won't be following Izzy but, we too need a night out, if you'd like to that is?"

"Yes ok but, if we catch sight of Isobelle, we either go

to another bar, or we come back here to home yes?" smiled Gabriela, "I do not wish to think that Isobelle thinks that we follow her."

"That's absolutely fine, of course, but no, we need a night out, not sure how long it's been since you were last out."

"It has been for some time yes, we have been so busy here, we are normally so tired to think about going out but yes, a night out with you feels like it will be nice, yes?"

All the girls went to their respective bedrooms to get changed and do their hair and make-up.

Alice went for a quick shower, the large green towel slightly damp from it being used by Isobelle, but it was still ok for her to use.

After another hour, they were all ready to go out, it was around eight in the evening, and the night was still light, the sun was still shining, and it was still relatively warm from that day.

Gabriela was wearing an almost traditional Spanish red dress, and with her long dark curly hair tied up, looked like a Spanish temptress, herself looking incredibly stunning.

Maria wore a silky off-the-shoulder dark blue silky dress, again, with her hair also tied up, and looking equally radiant.

Alice came down, wearing a bright yellow off-the-shoulder one-piece dress, and the three of them could have passed as models, even though Alice previously was.

"WOW girls, you both look a million dollars, look at you, you should have modelled, and you both look breath-taking."

"Hmmm, *gracias* Alice, this is very kind, you too look very nice," "I have already called a taxi, and they say will be here in twenty minutes, and we go into Lunshill yes?" "Hopefully we do not see Isobelle."

"If we do then we will just keep walking or cross over the road, I am not there to spy on her, but we need a night out too," Alice smiled, though secretly wanting to see who this mystery man was that Isobelle had been chatting to.

The taxi seemed to arrive before time, and the girls were ready to go, filtering out of the door in single file, Alice heading out first, with Maria locking the door behind her.

The taxi pulled into Lunshill, as the girls pile out, and into the first bar they come across 'Lunshill Lounge' a swanky wine bar, music pumping and lots of middle-aged people having a quiet drink, but the wine bar was quite popular, people would come for miles to drink there.

Thankfully, there was no sign of Isobelle and her mystery man, Lunshill being a popular place for drinkers, and it would have just been a coincidence had they bumped into her.

The three girls were having a good time, a few men buying them drinks, due to how stunning the three of them looked, but they were also enjoying the attention they were getting, not so much Alice, she was more concerned with how Isobelle was, and if this mystery man was looking after her.

They came out of the bar to look for another one, and, in the distance, she spotted Isobelle, with her mystery man, who, at first sight, looked vaguely familiar.

"Look isn't that Isobelle?" Gabriela pointed a lot further away, some three hundred yards up the hill, they could only just make her out.

"It can't be!" a shocked Alice said, not quite believing who she thinks she may have seen.

"That is Isobelle yes?" smiled Gabriela once more.

"Yes, it looks like her but, the man she is with, has been talking to on the phone… it can't be… surely!"

"Who is this man you speak of Alice?" quizzed Maria.

"It looks like… no… it really can't be… we're here, and… he is there!"

"Who?" said Maria.

"It looks like… it looks like… Valentino, the man who kidnapped us in Italy but, how has he found us, he cannot be, it really cannot be!" Alice was almost quivering with fear, for both Isobelle and the three of them.

"OH MY GOD, what if it is really him, what are we going to do?" Alice was shaking and was in no mood to carry on drinking, and this also struck fear into both Gabriela and Maria they jumped in a waiting taxi, and headed back to the farmhouse, to wait for Isobelle.

Alice needed answers.

NO WAY BACK

They arrived back at the farmhouse and sat down to ponder what they had just seen in Lunshill, but maybe she was wrong, maybe it wasn't him, how would he have found them to start with, and he was in Italy so, maybe she was just imagining it, but she needed to know for sure.

Maria had made all of them a percolated coffee, sitting down to discuss the day's events, whilst also trying to calm Alice, who was still convinced she had seen Isobelle with Valentino, but until she had spoken to her, she couldn't be one hundred percent sure, after all, it was this guy that she knew that she was arranging to see, but, was she, seeing that she had been so secretive on the phone to him?

'What do I say to her, that I saw her with someone resembling Valentino?' 'How do I even approach the subject without upsetting her, after all, we've become close, and it would seem to her that we followed her, even though I agreed that I wouldn't?'

They suddenly heard footsteps near the thick wooden farmhouse door, and in walked Paul.

"Where the FUCK have you been, with that low life no doubt?" Alice sat shaking with anger, still agitated by seeing Isobelle with who she thought was him.

"Yes, I've been with Charlie, just discussing a few things, business, and a catch-up, besides, you've got Isobelle to keep you company!"

"Where is that girlfriend of yours anyway, tucked up in bed waiting for you?"

"Don't be a FUCKING DICKHEAD, she's not here, we are waiting for her to come back from going out, for your information, not that it's any of your business anyway."

"Just remind yourself who got you out of Italy, you've got me to thank for that, without us, you'd probably still be there, or even dead, just remember that!"

He walked off to head upstairs for a shower, Alice being more concerned about Isobelle, and wondering if she was ok.

"Why don't you try calling her?" "I'm sure she's ok, and I bet she would be ok hearing from you," Maria smiled, trying to reassure Alice.

"Do you think I should, don't want her thinking that I'm checking up on her?"

"I'm sure she'd appreciate hearing from you," Gabriela agreed with Maria.

Alice got her phone out of her bag, as they all appeared to huddle around it.

Alice made the call…

Ring…ring

Ring…ring

Ring…ring

Ring…ring

It seemed an eternity for Isobelle to answer, but she finally did.

"Oh, hi Alice, I hope you're not checking up on me!" Isobelle answered.

"I'm ok if that's why you've called me," she continued.

"No, I'm not checking up on you, just making sure that you're having a good time, and seeing that we're somewhere we don't know, that you haven't got lost," Alice smiled, trying to raise her spirits and to almost bring a calmness back to herself.

"Yes, I'm having a good time, stop worrying, I'm fine."

"Ok, I wasn't worrying, looking forward to hearing all about it when you get back," "see you soon," Alice smiled, just as Isobelle was disconnecting her end.

"How does she seem to you Alice?" Maria asked, clearly concerned with how Alice had been feeling about the whole situation.

"She seems, normal, maybe I was seeing things, let my imagination run wild, I need to get a grip," Alice was starting to feel less anxious about how Isobelle was, and she was sure that she would be straight on the phone to her if she had got herself in any kind of trouble.

There was movement from upstairs, Alice putting her mobile phone down beside her, waiting for him to come down the stairs, so they could talk.

"Maybe this is the right time for us to put the animals away, you should have some space to talk," Gabriela looked in Maria's direction, and they got up to go and put their overalls on, and bed the animals down for the night.

"Thank you for tonight Alice, Maria and I had a good time, we will do this girls' night out again yes," Gabriela smiled, as she trotted to catch up with Maria to see to the animals.

Paul thunders down the stairs, almost in a hurry to come down.

He sits down, letting out a puff of his red cheeks from his blistering hot shower.

"So, what is this business that you said when you walked in?"

"He just wants me to help him, sort out some stuff, now that Karl isn't with him now, he needs someone to replace him."

"REPLACE HIM?" What the hell is meant by that?" Alice was angry and wanted an explanation.

"What the FUCK is meant by that?" "Drugs you mean?" she continued.

"Well, it's not selling candyfloss is it!"

"I thought that all that stuff was done when we left Barnwood, to start a new life, I don't want us going through all that again."

Alice got up, pacing the floor, trying to digest the words that had just come out of his mouth.

"I'm not going to be dragged back into that world, not by him, or by you as a matter of fact, I'd sooner get out."

"Get out?" "You don't mean us surely?"

"Yes, I fucking well do mean us!" "I know you had that bagful of drugs from that other scumbag, and you want to carry it on?" "Not with me you won't be!"

Paul looked at her, almost speechless by her statement.

"So, you're willing to give up on us, just because I'm doing a little bit of running with someone?"

"Paul, WAKE UP!" "Can't you see how this will all end,

you will get caught up with him and his seedy little world, with whatever else he gets up to, and you will only end up dead like his partner, is that what you want, does our marriage really not mean that little to you?"

"Look darling, it's easy money, besides, Karl was shot dead in Italy wasn't he, not drugs related at all was it so, you cannot say it was, they've been doing it for years, and Charlie said that they have never been caught, they are always really careful."

"Don't DARLING ME," "it's dangerous, and you know it." "I don't like him, I don't trust him as far as I could throw him, and I think you are only asking for trouble."

"There's more than just him doing it, but he needs more help, and it's easy money for us, we need the money, and we can't stay here forever, and I wouldn't want to stay here much longer anyway, the cops will soon catch up with us here, so it'll only be for a short time."

"Where is that girlfriend of yours did you say anyway?"

"She went for a well-deserved night out, she met up with this guy she knows, and they went into Lunshill."

Alice was still pacing the floor up and down, trying to decide what to do.

He was right about one thing, they couldn't stay there forever, and she realised that the police would soon catch up with them if they stayed at the farmhouse for too long.

"Where is he getting these drugs from?"

"There's this drugs baron that he's got in contact with, someone gave him his contact, and he's set up with him, it's easy money for us, we are running out of money, and it won't be for long, and it'll allow us to get out of here."

Alice stopped pacing the floor and came and sat down next to him.

"I'm going to pretend that I've not heard you tell me about, you know, what you want to do with that fucking imbecile," "don't you even think about bringing anything back here, especially that the girls have been so good to us, you do that, then we are over, do you understand?"

Paul nodded stone-faced in agreement.

"I wouldn't dream of bringing anything back here, I'm not that stupid," he smirked.

Suddenly, the sound of the big chunky wooden door being opened, rippled through the house, as Isobelle walked in, expressionless.

Paul got up and walked back upstairs, with her not being his favourite person.

Alice was conscious of letting on that she had seen her in Lunshill.

"Hi Izzy, have you had a good time?" "Did your date turn up?"

"She glided across the floor and walked in Alice's direction.

"He wasn't a date!" she remarked, "but yes he did."

"Did you go anywhere nice?"

"We just went around Lunshill, just a few drinks, nothing spectacular."

"Are you arranging to see him again, love to meet him?"

Isobelle was wanting to change the subject, without answering Alice's question, giving her a blank look, wanting to keep her night out a closely guarded secret.

"What did you all get up to while I was out?"

"Well, we also went into Lunshill and NO, we weren't

following you, didn't even see you in truth," though Alice knew that that was a lie, wondering what kind of reaction she would get from Isobelle.

"You WERE following me, weren't you?" she yelled, "I specifically asked you not to, you went against your word."

"HANG ON!" "I NEVER gave you my word, besides, we weren't following you and, like I say, we didn't see you anyway, and I wanted to treat the girls for how kind they have been to us, so I thought I'd treat them to a night out, and there's not really anywhere else to go around here is there?"

Isobelle got up from sitting next to Alice, and immediately headed up the stairs, slamming the door of her bedroom shut, like an angry teenager.

Maria and Gabriela then also appeared at the front door, closing it shut behind them.

"Isobelle is back so, at least we can rest easy now." Alice felt mentally drained with having to deal with Paul arriving back at the house, but also Isobelle being coy with her mystery man and storming off in the process.

"Yes, we saw her walking up towards the pathway, she saw us, but she didn't say a word, we assumed that he either didn't show up or it was a bad night, she didn't look happy," Maria said.

"How is she now, is she not with you, I thought she may be telling you about her night?" Gabriela and Maria were intrigued to know what had happened.

"I asked her about her date, and if she'd had a good time, and she got all defensive and has now just stormed upstairs, something isn't right."

"Hmmm, how do you mean by defensive, this word I do not understand?" Gabriela replied.

"Not wanting to give too much information away, not wanting to tell me too much, so she got angry and is now in her room I assume, I heard a door slam anyway," Alice had an uncomfortable feeling, wondering why Isobelle had reacted the way she had, surely it was a happy meet-up, seeing that she hadn't seen him for a while now, maybe he had given her some bad news, maybe she was pressing Isobelle too hard, especially if she had heard something from him that she didn't want to hear.

"Perhaps tomorrow she will talk to you Alice yes," Maria smiled, Alice was starting to think that maybe she was right, that she was maybe jumping to all kinds of conclusions, and a good night's sleep was maybe what they all needed, it was starting to get into the early hours anyway.

"Think it's just been a long day for all of us, I think I'm going to head upstairs to bed, a good night's sleep and things will seem a lot clearer tomorrow, I'll say goodnight girls, I did enjoy our night out though, sorry it was so brief, maybe a longer night out soon?" she smiled and waved to them both, on her way up the stairs to bed.

She went to go into the bedroom she shared with Paul, to see the door slightly ajar, he was seemingly fast asleep, so she crept along the landing where Isobelle's bedroom was, her door closed, Alice quietly opening it, with no squeaking came from it, Isobelle was also seemingly asleep, her back turned away from the door.

Alice crept over, and peered her head around, to see her asleep, she looked lovely and peaceful.

Alice kissed her on her head, before quietly walking out of the room, closing the door gently behind her.

She quietly walked towards her room, Paul was still fast

asleep, closed the door and got undressed, ready to climb into bed herself, it had been a hell of a day, but tomorrow would be a new day.

Alice got into bed, Paul only just moving from his deep sleep, huffing that the covers were being tugged slightly off him.

Alice was a little restless, not being able to switch off from Isobelle coming back, and a little bit with Paul too, especially with what he had told her.

The night had soon become the early hours of the morning and Alice realised that she needed to get some rest, as she had her farm work to do, and she also wondered what the next day was going to throw at her.

She awoke to the sun glistening through the thinly veiled curtains of the bedroom window, Paul was already up.

She gave herself a few minutes to wake up, peering up at the smooth plastered light blue ceiling and the glass chandelier hanging from the light fitting, the sun shining on and off above her.

It gave her time to ponder a little, what was going on in her life, what the hell was going on with Paul, who was this mysterious man that Isobelle was seeing and speaking to on the phone and, also what their next move was going to need to be?

'What time is it?' she thought to herself, 'it feels late into the morning, and I feel that I'm the last one to get up.'

She looked at her watch, that she had taken off before she got into bed, it was seven-forty-five, and she could smell breakfast.

She slumped down further into the bed and covered her

face over with her pillow, she hadn't realised it was so late, she was always an early riser.

She was quickly up and dressed, in white shorts and a thin blue t-shirt, ready for another day's work on the farm.

There was no sign of Paul.

Gabriela was sitting at the table, breakfast was being cooked by Maria and Isobelle in the kitchen this time, and she was glad to be waited on for a change.

"Where is he?" Alice asked, in a slightly agitated tone.

"He asked for a bit of toast and a coffee, and he was gone, left about half an hour ago," Gabriela shrugged, "he did not say where he was going, sorry."

"Don't be sorry Gabi, it's not your fault that he's so secretive but I can imagine where he's gone, don't worry, shirking his farm responsibilities too, I'm sorry for his behaviour."

"Please, do not say sorry also, many men act this way and, it's ok, there is the four of us, we will manage the farm, as we did before yes," she smiled to Alice.

Suddenly, breakfast was coming in, cooked, and piping hot as usual, carried by Maria and Isobelle.

The usual scattering of eggs, bacon, sausages, beans and toast, with fresh juices and coffee.

They all sat down, Isobelle, sitting next to Alice, giving her a brief glance and grin before she started to tuck into her feast.

"Do you girls wish to swap roles, you only have to say, if you wish to do something different," smiled Maria, who, despite being young, was the slightly older of the two Spanish girls, and she was more of the spokesperson than Gabriela, who could sometimes come across as a little shy.

"What would you like to do Izzy, do you want us to carry on doing what we have been doing, or do you want to do something different, I don't mind either way?"

Isobelle once again glanced at Alice, without saying a word, just a shrug of her shoulders, not seeming bothered.

Alice paused, giving her a brief look of annoyance.

"We'll just carry on doing what we have been doing if that's ok, it has been nice brushing the horses and feeding them, as well as the pigs or sheep, didn't think I'd enjoy that, but they seem to enjoy us being there, hey Izzy?"

Again, Isobelle just gave her a brief grin as she carried on eating her breakfast, her mind elsewhere.

Breakfast was all finished as Gabriela and Alice cleared everything from the table, and took it into the kitchen, both loading up the dishwasher while they chatted.

"Your friend has gone very quiet lately Alice," Gabriela frowned.

"Yes, I know, and I'm going to find out once and for all who this mystery man is," she sighed, leaning back on a counter, arms folded in an angry gesture.

"How are you going to do this without her seeing you, or are you going to confront her with him?"

"No, I'm going to catch this guy unawares, because I don't think that Isobelle is telling me the truth somehow, she is hiding something from me, and I intend on finding out exactly who this guy is," Alice was determined to get to the bottom of this saga, she had had enough of this change of mood from Izzy, and, if it was that slimy Italian, she needed to go armed.

"I need to ask you a serious question Gabi… do you possess a gun in the farmhouse at all?"

"A GUN?" "Why would you need this?" "We have a gun yes, in case of hmmm, how you say, people who come in when they shouldn't be here," Gabriela was struggling to explain exactly what she meant, but Alice realised.

"A burglar you mean?"

"Ah yes, this is the word I search," "but why you are needing this?"

"If this man who Izzy is meeting, is who I think it might be, he's dangerous Gabi." "There was this man in Italy who kidnapped us, Valentino, and he's not a nice man, and if Izzy has been coerced into being with him, then I need to take action, if it is him, it certainly looked like him when we spotted them together but, they were a distance away so, I could be totally wrong."

"Maybe a gun is not wise Alice, if you are needing to protect yourself and Isobelle then, maybe take this instead," Gabriela pulled a sharp army knife out from a box that was hidden underneath the sink.

"Where did you get this?" "Actually, don't answer that, I don't want to know but, ok, thank you, I'll grab it the next time Izzy goes out, and I'm going to follow her, find out who this man really is."

"We must go back to work on the farm, Maria and Isobelle will wonder why we are in the kitchen so long," she smiled, brushing past Alice and back into the dining area, "please, I hope you do not need to use the knife, please be careful."

Maria and Isobelle had already headed outside to put their farm workwear on, and Gabriela and Alice were soon outside with them.

Alice stopped Gabriela in the doorway of the farmhouse before they joined up with their prospective partners.

"Please don't breathe a word of this to anyone what we discussed, not even Maria, please," Alice whispered to her.

"Hmmm, breathe a word, I do not understand this?" Gabriela looked puzzled.

"Sorry yes, it just means do not tell anyone, about the knife idea," Alice continued to whisper.

"I just wish for you and Isobelle to be safe, and if this is what it takes then hmmm, it is best," "now go, they may see us whispering and may wonder," Gabriela ushered Alice away in the direction of where Isobelle was, who had already started to feed the chickens.

She trudges over, hands in her overall bottom pockets, kicking up some leaves along the way that had blown into the yard overnight.

"Where abouts are you Izzy, I saw you feeding the chickens, I'll sort the pigs and sheep, unless you have already done it, then we could feed the horses together shall we?"

"No, not done them yet, so yeah, if you wanted to, then we can sort the horses out can't we?"

The girls carried on with their work, Isobelle hadn't finished feeding the chickens, and Alice wandered over in the direction of the pigs and sheep to feed and water them.

"I'm heading back out tonight so I won't be around for long, sorry," Isobelle mumbled, not even looking Alice in the eye to tell her.

"Ok, seeing your fancy man again, Mark was it?" she tried to catch her out, seeing what name she gave this time.

"Henry yes," she grinned, glancing back at her briefly, before carrying on feeding the rest of the chickens.

"That's ok, I'll probably just be chilling with the girls anyway, have a good time," she smiled back at her.

The chickens, pigs and sheep had been fed and it was time to go and feed the horses before they were brushed, something that both the girls enjoyed, Alice was less so lately with how Isobelle was being, her head definitely wasn't in it, or indeed Alice.

"What time do you think you'll be going out Izzy, just curious?"

"Not sure yet, but I'll be meeting him before dinner tonight, so I won't be eating, probably grab something while I'm out with him."

They went to feed the horses, and, before long they were called for lunch.

They all headed inside to eat and were soon back out to finish off what they were doing.

"Right, I'm going back inside to go and get ready, is it ok you carrying on?" Isobelle was clearly wanting to get out.

"Yes, you carry on Izzy, I'll finish off brushing the last horse, then I'm done too," "you shoot off."

Isobelle went inside to go and get ready, passing Maria and Gabriela on the way, who gave her a blank look, wondering what had happened.

"Voy a comprobar que Alice esta bien," (I'm going to check that Alice is ok) Gabriela said to Maria, before heading over in her direction, Maria watching her trudge down the yard.

"Is everything ok Alice, is what we discussed in the kitchen hmmm, needed?"

"Yes, it will be, I'm going to give her time to go and get ready, then I'm going to disguise myself and follow them, I'm determined to find out who it is she's seeing."

"Please be careful though, if he is dangerous, as you say, you do not know what he is capable of."

"Don't you worry, neither does he with me," she huffed in defiance.

The work had all been finished for the day, and the three of them wandered back inside, after removing their overalls and boots.

Isobelle was coming down the stairs, wearing a flowing flowery dress and red heels, her hair looking silky soft and smelling as fresh as a summer breeze, like a bunch of red roses.

"You look lovely Izzy, I hope he is worth it," Alice grinned, clearly missing the attention that Isobelle had previously given her, wishing it was the two of them going out instead.

Beep… beep.

"That's my taxi, don't wait up, I've got the spare key from the side, see you all later," Isobelle was soon leaving the farmhouse and closing the big heavy door behind her.

Maria got up to go to the bathroom, and this gave both Alice and Gabriela the chance to head back to the kitchen, so Alice could grab the army knife that Gabriela had shown her earlier.

"Please be careful Alice, I hope you know what you are doing if this is this man you speak of," Gabriela almost reluctantly handed the knife over to her.

"Is this something you cannot tell the police of?" she continued.

"I cannot get the police involved, we are then done for, the police must stay out of this, I need to deal with it my way Gabi, please trust me."

Alice concealed the knife as best she could, before heading upstairs to get changed, making sure she also had a baseball cap to disguise herself from both of them, as well as any surveillance cameras, when she reached Lunshill.

She was soon downstairs, wearing faded jeans with holes in the knees, a black t-shirt and a baseball cap, her hair put up inside it.

She too had also called for a taxi while she was getting ready, and this had soon arrived.

Gabriela had sat down with Maria on the sofa when Alice came down the stairs.

"Ah, you are going out Alice?" Maria asked.

"Yes, I'm just popping into Lunshill, something I need to get," she smiled.

"We can give you a lift there if you…" Maria smiled, as she started to get up.

"No no, it's ok, just need to go there on my own, get a bit of fresh air, but thank you," Alice noticing that Gabriela had put her hand on Maria's arm, as if to pull her back, Maria giving Gabriela a puzzled glance as to why she had done that.

"I won't be too long," "if Paul gets back before me, tell him I won't be long if you would."

Alice was out of the door and heading towards the taxi, to go and find Isobelle and her mystery man.

"Anywhere particular in Lunshill Miss you want dropping off?" said the taxi driver, looking in his rear-view mirror at his passenger.

Alice was miles away, deep in thought, and wasn't sure if she had heard the driver properly.

"Hmmm?" "Oh, just drop me anywhere around the centre, a few places I need to go so yeah, anywhere is fine," she instructed, looking up from her pulled-down black designer baseball cap.

The driver pulled up on the High Street in Lunshill and let her out after she had paid him.

She wandered around, looking in shops, looking to see if she could see the two of them, but there was no sign of her.

She felt like she had been wandering around aimlessly, window shopping, with little to no direction, yet keeping an eye out as she walked.

She decided to go to the Lunshill Lounge for a drink, as she had not found them as yet, and ordered herself a glass of wine before she sat down.

She sat alone, looking like the glamorous former model that she was, despite her wearing dressed-down clothes.

"Well, hello, not seen you in here before," came a strapping man's voice, "mind if I join you unless you're waiting for someone, date not turned up?" he smiled.

"Not being rude but PISS OFF, I didn't ask for your company, did I?" "Plus, I've eaten men like you for breakfast, gorging on a small sausage, small like yours probably," she smirked, sipping her wine, the smartly dressed man soon walked away with his tail between his legs.

Just as he sheepishly walked away, going past the window outside, was Isobelle and her mystery man, Alice felt more convinced than ever that it was Valentino but, how?

She quickly put her half-empty wine glass down and rushed outside.

She had left herself enough time for there to be distance between her and them, and she slowly walked behind them, a crowd of other people in between, for cover.

Alice pulled her cap down a bit more, to disguise herself, just in case Isobelle was to turn round and spot her.

Sure enough, she did turn around to look back, Alice's quick reaction was to turn into the doorway of a shop, she hoped Isobelle hadn't spotted her.

The couple carried on walking down the High Street, Alice came away from the shop doorway and continued to track them, checking that she still had the army knife in her pocket, feeling a sense of power, in the knowledge that she was in control of the situation that she had put herself in, even though her breath was quickening with fear.

The couple stopped, turning sideways to Alice, yet facing each other, and Alice's worst fears were confirmed, it WAS him!

'WHAT THE FUCK IZZY… WHAT THE HELL HAVE YOU DONE?' were the thoughts running through Alice's head.

'How has that fucking slimeball found us?' she had so many questions running through her head, and she was determined to get answers.

Alice watched him from a distance as he kissed her on her cheek, grabbing the top of her arms, as if he didn't want her to escape, giving her a wry grin, Isobelle staring coldly at him, no reaction, no expression that Alice could see, standing only a hundred yards away, her baseball cap pulled down as far as she could get it, but still enough to see what was happening, with the feeling of protectiveness towards her lover.

She casually walked away from him, not turning back to watch him, as he arrogantly strode towards what appeared to be a side street, Alice quickly rushed to catch up with him, yet making sure that Isobelle was far enough away to not see her.

On the side of the street, there was an alleyway, dirty and dingy and he was soon getting further into the dark of it, before she walked quicker to see where he was.

There was no sign of him.

She looked around, going further into the dark, smelly alleyway, but she still couldn't see him.

She felt empty, that she had lost him, and turned around to go and walk away, feeling her chance was missed.

As she did, he sprung out from a side hole in the wall and grabbed her from behind, his right arm wrapped around her neck, and his left hand covering her mouth, to prevent screams.

"I should have killed you bitches when I had the chance, but I got distracted looking through your phones while I had you locked away," Alice was trying hard to break from his vice-like grip, she felt like she was being strangled, she tried to find the knife that she had on her, reaching into her pocket to grab it, as Valentino started to drag her further into the dark mess of the alley, choking her as he did, but she managed to finally get the knife out, unclicked it before stabbing him in the leg. He let go of her, clutching his now blood-soaked trousers and writhing in agony, collapsing onto the floor.

"FOTTUTA PUTTANA!" (YOU FUCKING BITCH!) he yelled at her, before she plunged the dripping blade into his chest, again and again… he tried to reach for a gun that he had in his inside jacket pocket, but his injuries had got the better of him, and he breathed his last breath, he was finally dead!

She stood over his lifeless body momentarily, shaking, as she never thought she'd need to kill anyone again but, it was either kill or be killed, and she was relieved, as, kicking open his jacket, saw the gun on the inside, she was sure it was going to be loaded, so she knew she'd done the right thing.

'Alice, you need to go and hide this body' she thought to herself.

She saw some old sheets at the bottom of the alleyway, so she grabbed his legs and dragged him down to where they were.

He was heavy, and it was taking all her strength to pull him, but she finally managed to get him down to the end of the alley.

It smelt of old urine and dirt 'just where you belong this isn't it!' she thought to herself, as she pulled the sheets over the top of him, making sure that he was completely covered up.

There were dust sheets and tarpaulin to cover him over with, as well as old rubbish bags.

She made sure that he was well covered over, throwing the dirty bags over the top of him.

It appeared that no one came down there anyway, apart from the smackheads, drunks, and rough sleepers so she felt that he wouldn't be found for some time, plus, who would miss him anyway?

She found a piece of cloth on the floor, and wiped the blade clean, along with the splattering of blood on her hands, as clean as she could get them, putting the knife back in her pocket after she had closed the now cleaner blade, before she casually started to walk away, stopping, as she had come into a shed of light from the entrance, so she could compose herself, pulling her clothing together from the initial struggle with him, before she looked around, seeing no-one around, so she casually strode out and back onto the High Street.

She wandered around, not quite sure what to do with herself, she was almost in a state of shock.

'I need to go for a drink, calm my nerves a bit' she thought.

She saw another bar across the road, 'The Setton Arms,' so she casually crossed over and walked in, heading straight to the ladies' bathroom, to first check that no one was in there, to wash the excess blood from her hands.

She ordered herself a white wine and a packet of crisps and sat alone in the centre of the pub, very few people were in, mainly elderly people, so she knew at least that she wasn't likely to be bothered.

She sat in the pub for what appeared to be hours.

Suddenly, her mobile phone started to ring.

She took it out of her pocket and looked at it, resting her face in one hand, her arm resting on the table, with her phone in the other hand, she was still shaken from the events of what had just happened, before answering.

"I've done something terrible, I'm in a real mess."

"Just hold yourself together, and stick to our plan, ok?" came the reply, before the line disconnected.

She put her phone back into her pocket, before ordering herself another few glasses of wine, by which time, she was starting to feel a little drunk, she hadn't felt that way for some time, and she was starting to feel very relaxed, if a little alone.

Music came on in the pub, so she got up and started to dance and sway to it, raising her glass, in almost a toast to what she had done to Valentino a while ago, with the biggest smile she had given for some time.

The music stopped, and she plonked herself back down in her chair, almost slumping, while carrying on drinking her wine.

Her actions and having to deal with Isobelle and Paul had suddenly all got a bit too much for her, she suddenly burst out crying, but she knew that at least there was one person out of the way, she also knew that she was going to need to speak to Isobelle, to find out what the hell she had been playing at, and also why she had deceived and lied to her about who she was meeting up with, and why?

The time had ticked on, and it was approaching eleven in the evening.

"Come on, I think you've had enough for tonight, time for you to go home, come on, let's be having you," came a voice, the head barman approaching the now very intoxicated Alice, and trying to lift her from her seat.

"I've called you a taxi, and they're nearly here so, come on, on your feet, go and sober up at home."

There was a beep outside, and the taxi service had arrived.

The barman pulled her up from out of her seat and carried her to the back of the taxi.

He bundled her inside before closing the door before he watched the taxi pull off.

"Where are you going love, where do you live?" Where to darling?"

The taxi driver was driving around Lunshill, hoping to get some sense from his drunk passenger.

"Farmhouse," she slurred.

"In Forston Dean, that farmhouse?" he asked, looking through his rear-view mirror, but she looked out for the count, he was never going to get any more sense out of her, he decided to take his chances and drive her there, in the hope that it was the right farmhouse, he wasn't aware of any other one, he also hoped that someone was there to take her in, otherwise he was going to need to practically dump her there.

The taxi pulled up outside the farmhouse, Gabriela came out to see who it was but saw that it was Alice in the back, looking decidedly worse for wear.

She paid the driver, before pulling her out of the taxi, doing her best to carry her inside and making her a black coffee to hopefully sober her up a bit.

"Wow, she has had many drinks by the looks of things," smiled Maria, looking slightly concerned with just how drunk Alice was, but also knowing that she had been going through a lot with both Isobelle and Paul, yet only Gabriela knowing exactly what her intentions were if she had caught up with them, and she had a gut feeling that she had done just that.

"Come, help me take her upstairs to bed, and take her coffee up to her," smiled Maria.

Gabriela grabbed one arm, putting it around her neck, with Maria on the other side, as they struggled to carry her upstairs, but it was where she needed to be.

They just about managed to carry her into the bedroom, before carefully resting her down, turning her on her side, and puffing pillows up behind her back to keep her on her side just in case she was going to be ill.

"Why don't you go and get her coffee, and I will get her a bucket, just in case," smiled Gabriela.

Maria walked downstairs, Gabriela glancing back to make sure she had gone, giving her a chance to look for the knife that she had given Alice.

She saw a bulge in her jeans pocket, that had the knife shape, she looked back to check that Maria wasn't coming, so she reached inside her pocket and pulled the knife out, she could see blood on the handle, and she stood there motionless, just looking at it.

She walked towards the bathroom, opened the knife up, seeing a small splattering of blood, so she ran the hot tap to wash it off, before grabbing some toilet roll and drying the blade and handle, which were both now clean, before she flushed the tissue away down the toilet, putting the knife in her pocket, but concealed from Maria, so she wouldn't ask why she had it.

She then found a bucket and took it into the bedroom, Alice still in the same position that they had left her.

Maria was walking into the bedroom, carrying her coffee and a glass of water and a box of paracetamol.

"Thought she could probably do with the water and tablets for the morning," she smiled.

"Yes, it is probably best we let her sleep this off, maybe let her off helping us on the farm tomorrow, for now, we leave her to rest, maybe we may see Paul and Isobelle, hope they can help us on the farm instead," Gabriela, checking that the knife was well hidden from Maria.

"You ok Gabi, you have an itchy side?" Maria frowned.

"Yes, but it is ok, it will pass," Gabriela smiled.

"Do you wish me to take a look?"

"No, it is ok, let us leave, let her rest," Gabriela was a little annoyed that she had checked for the knife in front of her friend, as they came out of the room, before closing the bedroom door quietly behind them.

"Think it maybe best that we say that Alice is unwell if Paul or Isobelle should ask, yes?" smiled Gabriela.

"Yes, this is probably good Gabi yes," "will stop them from worrying."

Just then, as they get to the bottom of the stairs, Isobelle walked through the door.

Gabriela stood next to Maria, almost gulping, Gabriela knowing that Alice had killed the man who Isobelle had been seeing, but with Maria unaware as to what may have happened.

"You have a good time, Isobelle?" smiled Maria, "we have just put Alice to bed, she is unwell, she is resting upstairs."

"Oh, is she, maybe I should go up and check on her."

"No, she should rest, peace and quiet is what she is needing right now, I'm sure she will feel better tomorrow," "we are making coffee, if you would like this?" smiled Maria.

"Hmmm, no, it's ok, it's been a long day, I think I'll just head up to bed, and I'll see you both tomorrow," smiled Isobelle, clearly looking tired, with whatever it was on her mind, she looked deep in thought.

She slowly trudged up the stairs, Maria giving Gabriela a look of bewilderment, realising that something was up with her.

Isobelle stopped outside Alice's door, putting her hand on the door to open it to check on her, but suddenly thought better of it, instead, walked towards her own bedroom, before closing the door behind her, getting undressed and climbing into bed, she had lots to explain to Alice, and needed advice.

Unbeknown to her, Alice also knew her secret.

The morning arrived, the Spanish girls were once again cooking breakfast, and the smell drifted upstairs, the smells were too much for Isobelle, and she was quickly dressed and about to head downstairs, once again stopping outside Alice's door. This time she opened it slightly, seeing Alice turning over, a bucket by the side of her bed, so she quietly closed the door, before heading down the stairs to eat.

Alice turned over in bed, her head was pounding, as she opened her eyes.

She looked at her watch, and it showed eight in the morning.

'I wonder if she's back yet, she's got some questions to answer' she thought.

She carefully lifted her head off the pillow, it felt like a big beating drum was banging away at her whole body, but she wanted to get up and go down, maybe some strong black coffee was the order of the day.

She pulled on some black shorts and a light blue t-shirt, with speckles of white stars.

She checked her jeans and noticed spots of blood on the back of them, enough for them to be noticeable, but there was no sign of the knife, so she stuffed them in a cupboard in the bedroom, covering them over with towels and sheets, but also thinking that she needed to get them washed, or, better still, dumped somewhere.

She looked around the floor of the bedroom in case the knife had fallen out of her pocket, and looked under the bed and around it, but there was no sign of it.

Did she drop it in the pub last night? Did it fall out in the taxi home?

She felt panicky, because it would have her fingerprints on it, and she would be screwed when Valentino's body was finally found.

She couldn't do anything about it now, she decided to take another look in a while.

She gingerly came out of the bedroom, still feeling rough from the previous night, her head still sore, carrying her empty cup that had the cold coffee in, having poured it down the bathroom sink, only noticing it when she woke, along with the untouched water and the paracetamol, and carefully walked downstairs, the smell of breakfast not making her feel much better.

She saw Gabriela and Isobelle sitting at the breakfast table, Maria in the kitchen cooking, Isobelle gave Alice an awkward stare, before getting up from the table, to go and help Maria in the kitchen.

Alice carefully sat down, opposite Gabriela, still trying to come to terms with yesterday.

Gabriela leant across the table to put her hand on Alice's and whispered.

"I got rid of the knife that was in your pocket, it was stained Alice, what did you do?"

"Ah, that's where it was, phew, I'm relieved, I was looking around the bedroom for it before I came down, and I couldn't see it anywhere, I was worried I'd maybe dropped it in the pub last night, or the taxi even, I don't even remember getting back here but, thank you, at least I know."

"So, what did you do Alice, the knife was stained with

blood, that's what I assume it was," Gabriela continued to whisper.

"I killed him Gabi, that slimy Italian, he was strangling me and I had to do something, he also had a gun in his inside pocket, he'd have killed me, he gave me no choice, please don't breath a word of this to anyone, not even the police, I'll be done for otherwise, sorry, I mean I'll end up going to prison."

Gabriela looked in the direction of the kitchen, and there was still no movement from the door, to check that they were still ok to carry on talking.

"You have done the right thing Alice, you had to defend yourself."

"What have you done with the body, where is he?"

"I've left him down this dark, dingy alley in Lunshill, looks like it's only used by drunks and drug takers, and I've covered him up well so, he won't be found for a while I don't think."

"I have disinfected the knife, wiped it clean so it shouldn't have any fingerprints on it, I've put it back in the box where I got it from to give you, this is between you and me yes," smiled Gabriela, putting her finger to her lips to show that it's going to be their secret.

Gabriela pulled her hand away from Alice's, just as Maria and Isobelle were coming in with breakfast.

"Ah Alice, you're awake, did you sleep well, are you feeling better than yesterday?" she smiled, giving Gabriela a little look and smile, with what they had agreed to say the night before.

Alice holds her head, still banging away from her heavy drinking.

"I know, I had way too mu…"

"This is ok Alice, we understand when you do not feel very well, would you like to eat, with your upset tummy, some toast maybe?" Maria interrupted.

Alice looked silently at Maria and Gabriela, Isobelle looking on, as she started to tuck into her first meal of the day, whilst giving Alice a brief smile.

"Erm yes, I'll erm, manage some toast if that's ok," she smiled.

Breakfast was all finished, Gabriela and Maria started to clear the plates and cutlery, carrying them into the kitchen.

"Alice, I need to speak to you, it's important," Isobelle said, looking slightly worried.

"How was your DATE last night then Isobelle, have a good time did you?" Alice snapped a little, arms crossed in annoyance and anger," "Henry, isn't it?"

"This is what I need to talk to you about," she continued.

"That's good because I need to talk to you too but, not here, not now," we'll find time, for now though, I'm going to rest up, this can wait," Gabriela re-appearing from the kitchen, bringing the toast in for Alice.

There is butter and jam and other spreads on the table Alice, if you would like this?" Gabriela looked awkwardly at the two of them, as they had clearly been chatting.

Just then, the front door opened, it's Paul, re-appearing, having been out all night.

"Ah Paul, we have just had breakfast, but I can make you some if you wish," Gabriela smiled.

"That would be great, please," he smiled, as he headed upstairs to go and wash his hands, giving both Alice and Isobelle a glance as he passed, without even saying a word to them.

Isobelle got her phone out of her pocket and buried her head to send a text, steam almost coming from her thumbs, with her texting so fast.

Alice watched her coldly, knowing that if she was texting Valentino, she wasn't going to get a reply, almost a wry smile coming from her face, her arms angrily crossed.

"Texting your DATE are we Izzy?" Alice sarcastically grinned.

"Erm yes, I've not heard from him, maybe he's busy, I'll text him later."

"Yes, he's probably busy," she smiled.

'...or DEAD,' she thought, still with a wry smile on her face, as she watched Isobelle putting the phone back in her pocket.

"So, we can talk later?" Isobelle asked.

"Oh, you can bank on it!" Alice smiled, looking forward to getting the answers from Isobelle that she was seeking.

"Paul, breakfast," shouted Maria up the stairs, but he was already on his way down.

He walked over to the breakfast table and sat down to eat, just as Isobelle was getting up to go and carry out her farm duties, hers and Alice's eyes locking on her way out, but with little emotion from either of them.

"Going to do some work today are we?" Alice snapped, her arms still crossed, Paul was hardly at the farm these days, doing whatever he was doing with Charlie.

"Yes, I will, but we need to think about getting away from here, maybe we should draw up a plan to get away, we can't stay here forever," he said, tucking into his feast.

"As you've said before, but where do we go Paul?" "Where we're not recognised, at least here we're out of the way, we can talk about it soon but, for now, this is the safest place to be."

"What's got into you?" "You not slept very well?" he murmured, his mouth full of food, lapping it up like he hadn't eaten for weeks.

"Just everything Paul, but you're never here so don't ask what's got into me," she was in no mood to speak to him, especially since he should be helping on the farm, instead of helping Charlie with his drug runs no doubt.

"What of her, your girlfriend?" "she's quiet, she shouldn't even be here, the sooner she's gone, the better."

"You're a fine one to talk, at least she's here, unlike you," "I'm going for a lay down, I'm not doing the farm today, so maybe you can remember what needs to be done," Alice got up from the table, giving him a stern look, before she slowly walked up the stairs to sleep off her headache.

He finished his breakfast, sitting alone, and drinking the coffee that he had poured himself from the pot on the table, before taking his plate, cutlery and coffee cup into the kitchen and placing them on the side, he was unsure as to where they were to go, so he left them where they were, went outside and put some overalls on, to ask the Spanish girls where they wanted him.

Alice meanwhile was laying on her bed, contemplating what she was going to say to Isobelle, and wondered what Isobelle was going to speak to her about, Valentino no doubt!

The day had ticked on, it was lunchtime, it was time to eat.

Alice was still upstairs, so Gabriela went up to check on her, to see if she was ready to have anything to eat.

She saw Alice sitting up on the bed, her pillows puffed up behind her, looking like she was contemplating.

She went to sit on the end of the bed, putting her hand on her foot.

"We're about to do lunch, are you ready to eat?"

"Yes, I'm feeling peckish now, and feeling better too, I've had a few extra hours rest, and starting to feel like my old self, the headache has gone too."

"That's good, come on down when you're ready then, won't be anything too heavy, a few sandwiches, crisps and maybe some cake too, Gabriela smiled.

"Gabi, my jeans from yesterday?" "I've still got some blood on them, on the back, where I knifed him, I've put them in there, under those sheets and towels, what shall I do with them?"

Alice pointed over to the cupboard where they were, Gabriela grabbing them.

"Don't worry, I will wash these, I will make sure the blood is no longer visible yes, do not worry," she grabbed them from where Alice had put them, to take them to her room to hide away, until she had a chance to sort them out.

"Thank you," Alice smiled at her.

She watched her leave the room, giving her a grin as she did.

She got up off the bed, going to the bathroom to wash her hands before she too ventured down.

Paul was sitting at the table, alone, cheeks red, despite his physique and strength, he hadn't worked this hard for some time.

Isobelle was in the kitchen helping Maria prepare lunch, as Alice sat down across the table from him.

"Hard work isn't it!" she smirked, arms crossed, leaning back in her chair, but he just glanced at her, without saying a word.

Lunch was being brought in by the girls, as usual, enough to feed an army, just as Gabriela was coming back down, having concealed the blood-stained jeans of Alice's, before she sat down next to her, ready to gorge on the feast.

They were tucking into the food, Alice glancing over to Isobelle, not taking her eyes off her, but she looked in a world of her own, every so often, checking her mobile phone for any text messages from him, but there was nothing.

Isobelle glanced over to the stone-cold glances of Alice, giving her a grin, Alice smiled back eventually, in a half-hearted way, Isobelle knew that she had to break the news to Alice eventually.

Lunch was finished, Maria and Gabriela started to clear the table, and Paul sat relaxing until he needed to go and finish off his jobs with the others.

"Have you got time for that chat now Alice?"

"Oh, I certainly have," Isobelle nodded her head in the direction of the conservatory, where they could have some privacy.

They were alone, and Alice waited to hear what Isobelle had been playing at.

"Ok so, it's like this…" she frowned, head slightly bowed.

"You can fucking stop right there, I know your FUCKING GAME, you see, I followed you last night, and some things weren't adding up, so, I wanted to see this mystery man for myself and, low and behold, your HENRY, was in fact, and ITALIAN, am I right so far?" she snapped angrily.

"But Alice, you don't understand, he…"

"Oh, I fucking understand alright, you fucking deceived me, you lied, how can I ever trust you again, I'm FUCKING FUMING!"

The shouting could be heard through the farmhouse, the Spanish girls keeping well out of the way, but Paul had got up from the table, so he could listen to the row going on between the two of them a bit better.

Isobelle started to cry uncontrollably, but Alice wasn't having any of it.

"After EVERYTHING he put us through Izzy, and you fucking go behind my back to be with this sleazeball, well, I've got BIG NEWS for you honey… he's fucking DEAD, I killed him so, you won't be seeing him anymore, so you can FUCKING turn your waterworks off now can't you!" Alice turned around to walk out of the room before Isobelle dropped a bombshell.

"I'm carrying his baby… I'M FUCKING PREGNANT!" she screamed and cried at the same time before she crumpled on the floor in despair.

Alice stopped in her tracks, turning round to look at her, a feeling of shock ran through her body, she couldn't quite believe what she had just heard, or even what they were going to do, but Paul, feeling both shocked and angry listening in, had his ideas of what needed to be done.

A FAMILIAR FACE

Alice was still reeling from the shock of Isobelle's bombshell, walking over to her, to get her back on her feet.

"How could you be so stupid Izzy," "what the fuck were you thinking?"

She was still sobbing, as she explained how it happened.

"He contacted me, he must have got hold of my phone while we were trapped in that cellar," "I was out, drunk and he was being all smooth like he was when he charmed us both, and he asked how I was, I wasn't thinking straight, and I told him where I was, like an idiot."

"Go on!" Alice said.

"He met me in Lunshill, he was just, charming, I was very drunk by this point, he wanted to know where we lived, and he was going to kill us both, so I agreed to keep him a secret from you, I was protecting you."

"We chatted over more drinks, he booked this hotel for us and, he fucked me, and now I have a part of him inside me," what am I going to do?" she started to sob uncontrollably.

"So, did he rape you?"

"Yes, no, oh, I don't know," "I kind of wanted to so, oh, I'm not sure."

"How far gone are you?"

"I'm... I'm, not sure, six weeks maybe, what does it matter anyway?" she sobbed.

"We need to think about getting you an abortion, I'll speak to the girls to see who will do it at such short notice around here," Alice heading out of the conservatory, determined that it would sort matters.

"No... no, no abortion, I don't believe in them, I'll work out a way," Alice sighed before leaving the room, it was a tough subject, but Isobelle needed to work this out for herself.

Alice could give her as much support as she could but, at the end of it all, the decision rested with Isobelle and her alone.

Alice felt really hurt by Isobelle, that she couldn't tell her about Valentino, yet on the flip side, kind of understood, especially with the fact that Valentino was going to kill them both if she didn't agree to his demands, but the trust had gone, she wasn't sure she felt the same way about her anymore.

She walked towards the dining room and saw Paul adjusting his trousers.

"So, how much of that did you hear?" she snapped.

"How much of what, I don't know what you mean," still bending down, looking as if he is pulling his socks up, pretending that he hadn't heard the heated row between the two of them.

She looked sternly at him, knowing that he must have been lying, if he had been there all that time.

"Well ok, I heard an argument, but it was quite muffled,

so I didn't hear much so I thought I'd just leave you to it," he said, straight-faced, pulling his trousers down over his socks.

"You ready to come and help out, finish off what we'd done this morning?" he smiled.

Maria and Gabriela came out of the kitchen, after noticing that the rowing had stopped, walking over towards Paul and Alice.

"Is everything ok Alice?" Maria said sorrowfully.

"Where is Isobelle?" Gabriela looked around for her, "is she outside?"

"No, I have left her to get herself together in the conservatory, she'll be out in a minute."

Gabriela and Maria looked at each other, glancing back towards the conservatory, seeing if Isobelle was going to show her face, before heading outside with Paul and Alice to finish off.

They all finished their work and took their workwear and boots off before coming inside.

They found Isobelle sitting at the dining table, in a world of her own.

"Are you ok, do you want to eat with us?" Maria asked.

"If that's ok yes, I will," she had appeared to have pulled herself together after the furious row with Alice, she looked fresh, having had a shower.

Alice's mood with her hadn't changed, and Isobelle decided to go and help Gabriela with dinner.

"Girls, thinking of going out tonight, fancy coming?" Alice smiled at the Spanish helpers, giving Isobelle a sarcastic glance.

"Yes, we would like this very much, the four of us, Isobelle also?" smiled Maria.

"No, it's ok, I'd like to stay here if it's all the same to

you, I have some things to think about," Isobelle nervously grinned, knowing that the atmosphere would only be frosty anyway with Alice being angry with her.

There was a silence between the three of them, as they all sat down to tuck into their meals.

It was an eerie silence at the table, Paul almost entirely engrossed in his phone and Isobelle deep in thought, deciding her next move.

Alice was almost oblivious to how Isobelle was feeling and was more interested in looking forward to going out and not having to worry about what Isobelle was doing, she felt she could now just relax and let her hair down, she was fed up with having to worry about someone else.

The evening food was finished, all wandering off in different directions, the Spanish girls taking all the plates and cutlery through into the kitchen, with Alice and Paul going upstairs.

"Meeting up with your boyfriend tonight, are we?" Alice said to him sharply.

"We may have a few things to discuss yes but I'll be back tonight," he snapped back.

He sat on the bed, scrolling through his phone, watching his wife getting ready to go out.

"When is the last time you fucked me Paul, feels like ages, but you'd rather spend your time with HIM instead," she snapped, "unless you're fucking someone else instead, him maybe?"

"Don't be so FUCKING RIDICULOUS, we need the money, and as soon as this is all done, and we have enough, we can fuck off from here, leave that girlfriend of yours to fend for herself."

"I've got a good idea Paul, you just fucking look after yourself like you have been since you've been here pretty much, no help on the farm, we've done it all, when you should be helping out so, don't you worry about us."

He huffed as he buried his head, as he carried on scrolling through his phone, unaware of just how stunning his wife was, and just how sexy she was looking, ready for her night out with Maria and Gabriela.

She wore a sparkling one-piece grey dress, cut just above the knee and showing off her ample cleavage, before putting on her matching grey shoes, looking every inch the model that he fell in love with.

He took his head out of his phone, he had become slightly aroused at the sight of his wife's sexiness.

She turned around and saw a bulge in his trousers.

She suddenly pulled him up off the bed by his shirt, pushing her up against the wardrobe, wobbling it as he nestled his head on her neck, frantically kissing it all over, her heart began to beat faster, as she pushed his head deeper onto her now slightly sweaty body.

He quickly undid his trousers, pulling down his boxers, as she wrestled her panties down, wanting him inside her, having missed his sexual touch.

She had suddenly become very wet, as she could feel the hardness of his throbbing cock pressing on her thighs, as he continued to kiss her around her neck and ears.

He pulled her dress up around her waist and he lifted her thighs, wrapping them around his waist, as his hard shaft gently slid inside her.

He began to thrust hard up against the wardrobe,

making it rock and hitting the back of the bedroom wall, shuddering downstairs.

Gabriela went up to check that Alice was ok and to also see if she was ready.

"Alice, are you ok, me and Mar…" Gabriela went to go into the bedroom to speak to her, only to pull back, seeing that she and Paul were having sex.

Feeling slightly embarrassed, she stood outside the doorway, smiling, before turning round to walk down the stairs as quietly as she could.

"Is she ok, is she coming?" Maria asked.

Gabriela had a wry smile to herself.

"Not yet, but I'm sure she will be in a minute," she replied, with a slight chuckle.

"Just by hearing the banging noise, was not sure if she had hurt herself, though I suppose he is there also," Maria sighed with relief.

Paul had lifted her up and onto the edge of the bed, thrusting as hard as he could, like he never had before.

"Ah baby, feels so good," Alice moaned, Paul not replying, concentrating on the motions of his thrusting deep inside her.

His pace quickened, he felt himself cumming and almost in an instant, they both came, sliding his now tired body onto her, as she gently wrapped her arms around him, giving themselves time to recover.

"Can I get up to go out now?" she chuckled, going to grab her knickers up from the floor where she had removed them.

Paul lay on top of the quilt, his trousers at the foot of the bed, grinning while he watched her pulling her knickers back up.

"Where did that come from anyway, you've not done that to me for a while now?"

"We've both been so occupied haven't we, with one thing or another anyway, haven't we?"

"You mean YOU have," she frowned.

"Anyway, I'm off, I can't imagine we'll be too late," she walked over to him and planted a kiss on his forehead, as he had gone to the end of the bed and started to pull his boxers and trousers back up.

She made sure that she was back looking her best, adjusting her dress, so she didn't look dishevelled, ready to enjoy herself with the other girls, leaving just Isobelle and Paul at the house, but Alice was sure that he too wouldn't be long in going out to meet back up with Charlie.

"There is plenty of food in the kitchen, help yourselves please," shouted Maria, as they headed out to the waiting taxi that had been booked, while Alice was getting ready upstairs, looking forward to her fun night out.

Alice finally came downstairs, and glanced sorrowfully at Isobelle before she left, thinking how their relationship had disintegrated to nothing, the big wooden farmhouse door was slammed shut, and it was just Isobelle and Paul left alone.

Paul made sure he was completely dressed, adjusting his shirt before he walked out of the bedroom.

Just as he was approaching the stairs, Isobelle walked up, heading towards her bedroom.

"Why the FUCK are you still here, why don't you just fuck off out of all of our lives, that would make life so much easier, I didn't want you with us in the first place," he was in no mood to be around her in the house.

"Huh, you can talk, you are a fucking waste of space, the way you have treated Alice like she's nothing, call yourself a husband!" "A killer yes, but DEFINITELY NOT A HUSBAND!" Isobelle didn't want to be around him anymore, than he did her.

"What are you going on about you bitch, fucking around with my wife, she's mine, not yours!"

"She's not yours, she's her own woman, you're nothing but a fucking control freak, I don't know how she puts up with your shit, she's better off without you!"

He grabbed her around the neck in a fit of anger, pushing her towards the edge of the stairs, Isobelle struggling for breath, whilst trying to wriggle free from his vice-like grip, yet looking over her shoulder, the white of her eyes wide, whilst clinging onto his arm in fear, knowing how close to the edge she was.

"Get off me, you're… you're hurting me, I'm… I'm struggling to breathe," tears were welling up and starting to stream down her face.

"Once a loser, always a loser hey Paul?" she cried.

"How FUCKING DARE YOU talk to me like that, you're better off not HERE," he thrusts at her, Isobelle tumbling down the bottom of the hard wooden staircase, screaming as she fell, lying motionless at the bottom, Paul looked down at her, showing no emotion, giving her body a cold, evil stare.

He casually walks down to her, putting his foot on the side of her waist to see if there is a reaction, but there is no movement, Isobelle is dead!

He realises that he needs to dump her body where he can, as far out of sight as he could, so he calls Charlie.

Ring... ring

Ring... ring

"I'm glad you've called, the boss wants us to do some more drops today, I'll come and pick you up," Charlie was getting ready to give Paul a call before his mobile rang.

"I need to ask a favour of you, I need you to help me move a body, I've got rid of a girl here," Paul had got so used to murder now, that this did not affect him at all.

"Ok, I'll be there soon, moving her will only eat into our time with drug drops, I know of a spot we can dump her, but be ready to go, I'll be there in twenty" Charlie was also cold when it came to murder, and this would just be another dead body to him also.

Paul went into the kitchen to see if he could find any black bin bags to wrap her in, checking drawers, before he came across some heavy-duty black bags.

'These will do,' he thought to himself.

He unravelled some of the bags and tore a few off.

He started to lift her legs to pull one of the bags up before he went up to her head and put the black bin bag over her, she was soon covered head to toe in the bags, making sure they were all tied up, even though it looked like a body.

He checked around for any signs of blood in case he needed to clean it up before he left out.

There was a small pool of blood, so he grabbed an old cloth from the kitchen, and wiped it up, making sure there were no more signs left of it.

He heard a car outside and he peered out of the window, it was Charlie.

"Where is she?" he asked with a cold stare, "the boot is

open ready, we'll put her in there and I'll take it to this old place I know, no-one will find her."

"It's in here," he and Charlie lifted each end, and carried her to the car, putting her in the boot before he slammed it shut, getting in the car, and driving off.

They drove through Lunshill, going another couple of miles, Charlie knowing about an old quarry that was out of use and it was almost in the middle of nowhere.

"This will do, we'll push her over the edge over there, come on, let's get her out and dump her, the boss won't be happy knowing we're fucking around, sorting out your mess."

"Who is your boss anyway, do I get to meet him?"

"No, he's not the type to go socialising, it's just business."

They get her out of the boot of the car and push her down the hill, and into lots more rubbish at the bottom.

"Right, stop fucking about Arnold, let's go," Charlie had two full bags of drugs in the backseat of the car, and they needed to be delivered to his boss' clients by the end of the day, and there were lots of places to go.

Time had ticked on, and the night was starting to draw in, the drugs had been dropped off to their prospective clients and money had been collected, for Charlie to give to his boss.

Meanwhile, at the farmhouse, the girls were back, the house was silent and dark.

"There doesn't seem to be anyone here, I will look for Isobelle," said Gabriela, feeling a little tipsy from her night out.

"We'll definitely have to do this again yes," smiled Maria, almost stumbling into Alice, all three of them very intoxicated, but had a great night out in Lunshill.

"Those men were very hmmm, how you say, hmmm, fit," she continued, almost falling over, such was her intake of alcohol, also being that she was not used to going out drinking, as she and Gabriela were very focused more on their work at the farm, but Alice had felt like a breath of fresh air to them, and it was something that they felt they had been missing out on.

"Isobelle, Paul, are you here?" Gabriela called, but there was a deafening silence.

"There appears that no one is home," she shrugged.

"Isobelle is not here, where the hell can she be, there is no one for her to meet up with now," Alice said.

"How do you mean by this, her date not seeing her now?" Maria was puzzled by Alice saying what she had, Gabriela looked at Alice, knowledgeable with what she knew, but was not willing to let on to Maria, it would only freak her out, and then staying with them may change.

"Oh, no, Isobelle said that it was just going to be a one-off meeting with this guy and that she wasn't going to arrange to see him again, so he just left I guess," Alice felt a little uneasy lying to Maria, but at least Gabriela knew the truth, but also realising that there could not be anything else going on surrounding the farm, it wasn't theirs after all, it belonged to Anne and Steve Greenwood.

"No doubt Paul will be with that scumbag Charlie, but I don't know where Isobelle could be," Alice, albeit slightly drunk, hunting around the house for her.

"Izzy… Izzy… are you around?"

Again, there was silence, and she was fearful of the fact that she had left her with Paul, but she had to wait to see if he knew where she went.

"I'll call her, I'm sure she'll tell me where she is," Alice was now starting to worry about her.

Ring… ring

Ring… ring

'Hey, it's Isobelle, are you ok?"

"Ah Izzy, it's Alice, we cannot find…" she suddenly stopped talking, realising that she hadn't answered, with the rest of the voicemail kicking in.

"… ha-ha, fooled you didn't I, it's just a voicemail… you know what to do…"

"Izzy, it's Alice, where are you, we cannot find you anywhere, let me know if you're ok?" before hanging up.

"Hmmm, no answer there either, and it's starting to get late."

Just then, the front door opened, the girls turning round to wait for Isobelle to walk in, but it was Paul.

"No doubt where you have been I don't want to know," Alice bemoaned.

"Have you seen Izzy, we cannot find her anywhere, she's not in the farmhouse."

"She's gone!" he said, straight-faced, a look of coldness in his eyes.

"Hang on, what do you mean she's gone, what have you said to her?"

"I haven't said anything, she just packed her bags, and left, not even so much as a goodbye."

Alice went to go upstairs to her room and check to see what she had taken out of her wardrobe, Paul realised that, to make his statement to her seem authentic, he had to try and get rid of her clothing, but he had to do it whilst Alice was out of the way.

"Leave it Alice, she's gone, leave her to fend for herself now, she's not worth it."

"What have you done to her, where is she Paul?" Alice was sensing that he was not telling her the truth, he was hiding something, especially knowing just how volatile he could be, and not wanting her in their lives in the first place.

There was suddenly an uneasy atmosphere in the house, and Alice was determined to get to the bottom of where Isobelle was.

"I'm going upstairs to check her room, and if there is something you're hiding from me, I don't know what I'll do."

Alice was frantic with worry, that all was not as it seemed with Paul, so she hurriedly rushed upstairs to check her room.

She almost ran across the landing to her room, and it looked like it had been untouched.

She looked in her wardrobe, just as he was racing upstairs, standing in the doorway, watching his wife rifle through all her drawers, and checking her wardrobe.

Just as he had said, there was nothing left in her room, all her things had gone, her drawers and wardrobe were empty, much to Alice's dismay.

"I will ask you again, where the FUCK is she Paul, seeing that you were so against her being here with us in the first place?"

There was a cold silence from him, he was in no rush to tell her what had happened between the two of them while she was out having a good time.

She sat on the side of Isobelle's bed and wondered what could have happened to her, missing her a little.

"Look, she's gone, she's out of our lives, which is what we wanted wasn't it, now we can think about getting the hell out of here soon, we've got some money coming from me helping Charlie and…"

Alice got up and started to pace the floor in the bedroom, looking over to Paul, looking angrily at him, thinking there was more to what had happened than he was letting on.

"Is that all you care about Paul, those FUCKING DRUGS, helping that low life, getting mixed up in god knows what shit, then actually worrying about Izzy?"

"Just get that FUCKING WOMAN out of your head will you, she had it coming to her the fucking bitch!"

Alice stopped in her tracks, looking at him, with a cold and empty feeling.

"What the FUCK did you just say?" "What have you done to her Paul?"

Alice ran over to him, sobbing and frantically grabbing him by his shirt, shaking him, demanding some answers, but almost knowing what was going to come out of his mouth.

"Get off me you fucking crazy bitch, she's DEAD, ok!"

Alice began to thump his chest violently, whilst letting out an almighty scream, tears streaming down her face, thankfully, the Spanish girls were outside, seeing to the animals, whilst Paul blurted out what had happened.

"She fell down the stairs, I tried to reach out to stop her falling but, I couldn't reach, she was dead at the bottom when I got down to her," he tried to cover his tracks, to soften the blow, Alice continued to cry uncontrollably, sinking her body down his leg, and slumping to the ground.

She felt broken, almost like she had let Isobelle down, that she wasn't there for her, and didn't know what to do for the best.

"Maybe our time is up Paul, maybe I should just get on the phone to the police right now, and tell them everything, because I'm going out of my mind."

"Look Alice, let's just carry on, we'll soon be out of here anyway, let's not let on to the two girls downstairs, or it will certainly be over for us, maybe even them too, they may be dragged in as accessories to murder, that isn't fair on them now, is it?"

Paul tried to remain calm, Alice still in a heap on the floor, at the bottom of his legs, her sobbing starting to calm down, though mascara was dripping down her cheek, still trying to take in what had happened, she was still in a state of shock.

"Hang on, so where the FUCK is she, where have you put her?"

Charlie came and picked me up, and we took her to an old quarry that he knows, just beyond Lunshill, we had to put her somewhere."

"I'm getting a taxi to go and see her for myself," Alice wasn't thinking straight, she was still reeling from the shock of the news and wanted to see if he was telling the truth.

"Alice… Alice… it's late, let's calm down, what's done is done, we'll talk more about this tomorrow but please, not a word to the other two, or they'll freak out and probably go to the police, plus going to see her at the quarry, with everything else there, won't achieve anything will it, plus I'm not sure how to even get down to the bottom of the quarry, it was a long drop down."

Alice burst into tears once again, she was starting to hate him more and more, but she could see the sense of what he was saying, yet at the same time, all she could visualise, was Isobelle's body falling into the quarry, all on her own, amongst all the rubbish and rocks.

"I can't sleep with you tonight, I'm going to sleep in Isobelle's room, maybe she'll come back," Alice still traumatised, hoping that he is lying about her death.

"She's DEAD Alice, do what you want, but I'm going to bed," Paul walked off to the bedroom that he and Alice shared, as she wiped her eyes clear of the now dry mascara, before walking to the bathroom to splash her face with cold water, looking in the mirror and pausing, wondering what the future held from here and wondering if it was all just a bad nightmare, and that she would wake up in a minute.

She dried her face and wandered downstairs to catch up with Maria and Gabriela.

"Are you ok, Alice?" "It looks like you have been crying, is everything ok with the two of you?" "We have just been outside to see to the animals for the night."

"Yes, just a petty argument with him, that's all but I'll be ok," she raised a little smile for them, before sitting down to chat momentarily.

"I'm afraid Izzy, Isobelle, has gone, and she won't be back, she, erm, decided to up and leave, Paul tried to stop her but she just… went," Alice was trying to stop herself from telling them the truth, but realising that it was in all of their best interest not to.

"I'm so sorry Alice, how are you feeling about this?" "And, if there is anything that we can do, of course, we will," both girls were feeling a bit sorry for her, and they would always be there for her when she needed them.

"Anyway, I'm going to bed, I'll say goodnight to you both," Alice sniffled, "I'm going to go and sleep in Izzy's room, just in case she comes back," she smiled, holding back tears.

Gabriela and Maria look at each other, not quite knowing what to say, but with the hope that she would come back, unaware of what has really happened to her.

The next morning, the Spanish girls are preparing breakfast as they normally did, the smells were drifting upstairs to both Paul and Alice, he was up and dressed before there was any sign of Alice.

He walked to Isobelle's room and opened the door, to see his wife laying on top of the bed, her back turned to him, cuddling one of Isobelle's dresses, her eyes wide open, hardly having had a wink of sleep, she was determined to find Isobelle herself, not just taking her evil husbands' word for it, after all, he never really liked her.

She felt a presence by the door and turned round to see him standing there, just looking at her, not saying anything.

She just looks at him, again, without muttering a word, still clutching one of Isobelle's favourite dresses that she wore during one of their nights out, it still smelling of her, as tears started to roll down Alice's cheeks once again.

Paul walked off to walk down the stairs for breakfast, Alice getting up not long after he had gone, wiping the tears from her face, knowing that she had to pull herself together, to head down for breakfast, as she was needing to work on the farm with the others.

She went to the bathroom to splash her face once again

with cold water, and clean her teeth, which was also painful in itself, she would often see Isobelle also using the main bathroom in the house, and she had flashbacks of her using the sink, and smiling at her, during happier times, which brought an immediate smile to Alice's face, she was very fond of her.

She headed downstairs, with an empty feeling in her stomach, not with the smell of food, but that there will be someone missing at the breakfast table.

The Spanish girls look at her, giving her a comforting smile, Paul just looking at her, almost with disdain, as he had just started tucking into his breakfast.

"Are you up to eating Alice?" smiled Maria.

"Yes please, need to get something down me, there's work to be done."

Suddenly, Paul's mobile phone rang once again, almost right on cue, getting up from his chair, and taking the call in the conservatory, it was Charlie once more.

"You do not need to help us on the farm if you are not feeling up to it Alice, it really is ok," Gabriela whispered, "it is seeming that Paul will not be here again, yes?" she continued whispering, gesturing with her head, towards where he had walked.

"Not looking likely is it, no doubt he's arranging another meeting with that nasty man that he meets with, don't trust him as far as I could throw him," she snapped.

"As far as you could throw him?" quizzed Maria, "sorry, I do not know this English word, what is this meaning?"

"Sorry, he's not to be trusted, is what I meant," Alice grinned, looking at the chair where Isobelle would sit, and this again made her feel sad.

"You stay here and rest Alice please, there is no need to help us today if you do not wish," Gabriela could see the sorrowful look on Alice's face and didn't want her to have to do anything that day.

"No, it's ok, I'd sooner get out and do something, take my mind off things, I'd feel worse if I sat inside dwelling on things so, thank you, I'd sooner help you girls out."

Paul was indeed on the phone with Charlie, organising more drug drops.

"Am I going to get to meet the big boss man at some point?" he remarked.

"All in good time Arnold, just relax, you'll get to see him soon, that's a promise," Charlie replied, in an almost sinister voice, "I need you to be ready now, I'm coming to get you," he continued.

Both men then hung up their phones, as Paul came out of the Conservatory and walked into the lounge to get some footwear on, just as the girls were just about to head outside to work on the farm, Alice giving him an angry stare.

"Charlie again, was it?" "Off to do your drug runs?" she angrily whispered across to him, so the other girls wouldn't overhear their conversation.

"You've become a lap dog, he's got you just where he wants you, can you not see that?" but in truth, she was past caring, he had gone some way to killing Isobelle, and maybe he would eventually get his comeuppance, irrespective of him being her husband, she didn't know him anymore, he had changed.

The girls had got into their workwear and their boots to work the farm, just as Charlie was pulling up at the bottom of the farmhouse, away from the eyes of the girls.

Alice spotted him waiting for her husband and went to march down to confront him.

"Just leave it, you don't know what he's capable of, I'll be back later," as he strode off in Charlie's direction.

"Paul, you may need a jacket, they say there is a storm coming," called Maria, but he was oblivious to her call, and just carried on walking down the pathway towards his car, getting in, as the girls watched them pull off.

The girls carried on working the farm, Alice feeling slightly lost, working on her own, without Isobelle, and it felt strange, knowing that she had become a part of her life, but no more, but she was determined to find her eventually.

Meanwhile, back in Lansburton, Detective Buchanan received a call on his works phone from another police headquarters.

"Detective Buchanan, it's Sergeant Miller from Sixth Division."

"Ah, Sergeant Miller, long time no hear, how are you, the wife and kids ok too?"

"Yes, we're good thank you, not as good as you're about to be though," replied the Sergeant.

"Oh, go on," said the Detective, sitting up straight in his chair, getting his feet off his desk.

"You're investigating the Paul Arnold case, aren't you?"

"Yes, I am, what do you know?"

"Are you familiar with a place called Lunshill at all?"

"Yes, it's about an hour away from here."

"Well, there have been sightings of him there, travelling in a car through Lunshill, with someone the force has had dealings with before, a Charlie Grunge, thought you might be interested."

"Sergeant, I could kiss you!" "Just don't tell your wife," he joked, as he slammed his phone down, and moved as quickly out of his chair as he ever had before.

"Are you ok Detective, not seen you move this quick since you realised it was your round at the pub!" joked one of the officers sharing the office.

"It's ok, just got to make a few enquiries, I may be some time," he remarked, grabbing his jacket off the very tall black coat stand, before just about heading out of the office.

"Do you need any backup?" shouted the same officer.

"No no, it's ok, just some enquiries, that's all, I'll call in if I need any backup," his back already turned from the other officers, raising his hand in the air to acknowledge their call down the corridor, and he was soon outside and getting in his car.

'Right, you FUCKING BASTARD, got you now, you're going to FUCKING PAY!' he thought to himself, as he sped off in the direction of Lunshill, knowing that it was going to take him a while to get there, and he still had to find Paul, that's if he was still in the vicinity.

He arrived in Lunshill and parked his car and started to speak to the locals as to the whereabouts of a certain man, having pulled out a picture to show them Paul.

He wandered around, not getting very far, as most of the locals were unfamiliar with him, or are just not wanting to get involved.

'Maybe he's no longer here, DAMN IT, I've probably missed him,' he thought to himself.

'Ah, Lunshill Convenience Store, maybe I'll ask in here,' he mumbled.

He walked in, to be greeted by the shop owner, Jack

Turnbury, flashing a wide smile.

"Hello sir, not seen you in these parts but welcome, feel free to browse around and if I can be of any assistance then please let me know."

"I'm hoping you can, I'm looking for a man; stocky, well-built, around six foot tall, bald head, clean shaven, has he been in here at all?" once again, the detective got the picture of Paul out of his pocket to show Jack, but he wasn't giving the detective any joy either, by giving him a shake of his head, taking the picture from the detective's hand to get a closer look.

The detective had got his badge out of his pocket, to show Jack where he was from.

"I'm Detective Buchanan, there is nothing to worry about, just wanting to ask this man a few questions, that's all," he smiled, so as not to alarm the shop owner.

"No sorry, not familiar with this man, sorry I can't help," said the shop owner.

"Ok, thanks for your time," Neil, dejectedly walking away and close to reaching the exit.

"There was a man come in here though, not him but, another man, not from round here, and there is a farmhouse you could maybe try, it's not far from here, fifteen minutes maybe, in a place called Forston Dean, middle of nowhere but, it's the only place I can think of, he's only been in here the once, he had a bald head come to think of it, but I know that it wasn't that man in the photo."

"Thank you sir, that's been a massive help," Neil smiled.

He quickly hurried out of the door and towards his car, thinking that it may have been Scott that he had been describing.

Finally, he was closing in on Paul.

The girls were still working the farm, Alice in a world of her own, feeding the chickens, as Gabriela and Maria were cleaning out the horse stables.

"Do you wish to come over and work with us, altogether?" called Gabriela, but Alice didn't appear to hear her call.

"Sorry Gabi, did you call me, I was miles away," Alice shouted back over.

"Yes, do you want to come over here to work with us in the stables, apart from being on your own up there?" she smiled, "we can all do the farm together."

"It's ok, I'm fine here, it gives me time to gather my thoughts, but I'll be down to see you in a little while."

"Maria and I will be going into Lunshill in a few moments, we are to get some food for tonight's meal, would you like to come with us?"

Alice walked over to talk, far easier than calling down to each other, chickens had been fed and the pigs were next.

"No, it's ok thanks, I'm going to go inside when you go, I'll just wait for you to come back, I'll be ok."

"Are you sure you wish to stay in the house on your own?" Maria wandered over to join the conversation.

"Honestly, you girls go, I'll just wait in the house, a couple of things I want to sort upstairs anyway but thank you for the offer."

They all go back to where they were working, another 5 minutes had passed, and the Spanish helpers had decided to down tools to go into Lunshill.

"We are going to go now Alice," Maria shouted, "you get yourself inside, there looks like a few angry storm clouds coming, we will take an umbrella with us, just in case we are caught in this, we should not be too long," the girls put their pitch forks down, that they were using to spread the hay out for the horses, go to the back door, removing their overalls and boots before going inside.

Alice wandered over to the farmhouse herself, taking her overalls off, along with her boots, before going inside.

"Help yourself to the kitchen Alice, you don't mind fixing yourself some lunch today do you, we will be back and sort ourselves out when we return," Gabriela said, getting herself ready to venture into Lunshill with Maria.

"No, of course I don't mind sorting myself out, would you like me to prepare you something too for when you get back?"

"Yes, this will be nice, we will be a little while," the girls grabbed their coats and an umbrella before venturing out of the door, not before one of the Spanish helpers called out to Alice once more.

"You sure you will be ok here on your own while we're gone?" Maria was concerned that Alice may be vulnerable on her own, with both Isobelle gone and Paul not there with her.

"Thank you Maria, I will be fine."

The house was deafly quiet, just the faint sound of the animals in the distance making various noises, but she was too busy fixing herself something to eat and getting something ready for the girls too for when they returned.

She had fixed herself up a chicken sandwich, grabbed some crisps and made herself a fresh orange juice and decided to take it upstairs with her, she was still missing Isobelle and wanted to go and sit back in her bedroom, lay on her bed, and carry on smelling the clothes that she remembered her in.

She put her lunch on Isobelle's dressing table, and lay motionless on her bed, wishing she was still in the house and a part of her life, just how she used to be.

Alice didn't know how long she had been laying on the bed when she heard a car pulling up outside.

'The girls must be back, but doesn't seem like they've been gone that long,' she thought, but she continued to lay on the bed.

'I guess I should eat this sandwich I've made for myself, I am peckish, god knows when THAT MAN will be back either, no doubt he'll just stroll in when he feels like it like he normally does,' she thought to herself.

She then heard the downstairs door open before slamming shut.

'That's obviously him, I'm sure the girls would have shouted up to me.'

"Paul, is that you, are you back?"

There was no answer before she heard the door open and close again.

"Paul, Paul, is that you, you could at least answer me when I call out to you!"

'No doubt he's in another one of his moods, I'm sick of it,' she continues to eat her sandwich, but she was curious as to why there had not been any sound from him, so she decided to go downstairs to investigate.

The room had been plunged into darkness, with the storm clouds gathering outside, but she could just about make out three manly figures standing in the lounge, though she couldn't see who they were.

"Who the fuck is there, get out of this house, NOW!" she was feeling a little scared and wondered who these men were, but there was an obvious menace about them.

She could also make out a man sitting in the rocking chair in the room, which was located at the back of the lounge, and he was a larger-built man than the others.

"Is that you Paul, who are you with?" Charlie no doubt!"

She froze, as she could see a cigar being lit by the larger man sitting in the chair, Paul also straining to see who it was.

"Barnes… it's you!" how did you find me?" the lamplight next to the chair being switched on, and there sat the overweight drugs lord from Austin, near Barnwood, with Charlie pointing a gun at Paul's head, whilst standing next to another burly minder of Mr Barnes'.

"We have a lot of catching up to do Arnold, I hope you have been keeping those drugs safe that you stole from me, and tut, tut, you have also killed two of my men but, I'll overlook that, they were a waste of space anyway, but, back to the drugs Arnold… WHERE ARE THEY?" he angrily snapped.

"You DOUBLE-CROSSING BASTARD GRUNGE!" Paul snapped at Charlie.

"Meet the boss Arnold, I know how much he's been looking forward to seeing you again, and you did want to meet him well, now you have," he smirked.

Cigar smoke was drifting through the house, and the stench was making Alice feel sick.

"This the wife Arnold, never met her before, what's your name my dear?" Mr Barnes smirked.

"It's… it's… Alice," she had almost frozen to the spot, not quite sure what to do, with a gun being pointed at Paul.

"Ah, Alice, well Alice, your husband has been a very bad man, and has taken something from me that doesn't belong to him, and, if he doesn't bring the drugs to me now, I'm going to have to kill him you see," the drugs lord was in no mood to be messed about with, "Arnold, I'll tell you what, just to help jog your memory a bit more, why don't we tell you that my other assistant will kill your wife first, how does that sound?" Mr Barnes had decided to ramp up the pressure.

The assistant took his gun out of his inside pocket and pointed it over at Alice, she shook with fear, closing her eyes in fear that the trigger was going to be pulled, she was terrified.

"Keep her out of this, it has nothing to do with her, I'll get your drugs, they're just over here," Paul pointed in the direction of a bureau in the hallway, whilst still keeping his eyes firmly fixed at Charlie's gun, which followed him to the hallway.

Paul put his hand up to semi-protect himself from the gun being pointed at him and continued to watch Charlie, who had followed him into the hallway.

He slowly started to pull a drawer open, and Charlie got suspicious.

"What are you fucking doing?" he snarled.

"I need to reach in for the key, which is in here, so I can get the cupboard open, to get Barnes' drugs out," he snapped, though, in reality, it is where he hid his gun.

He quickly pulled it out and fired it at Charlie, the bullet flying into his arm, making him drop his gun, as Paul dived out of the way and hid behind a pillar in the hallway.

The other guard, hearing the commotion, went to go and help his comrade, and to hunt for Paul.

"He's over there but, careful, he's got a gun," Charlie grunted to his colleague, writhing in agony at the bullet wound.

Meanwhile, after hearing the gun going off, the drug lord flew out of his chair, his cigar flying into the air and catching the thick curtain behind him, setting it alight, the fire was soon starting to catch hold, Alice finding a corner to go and hide in.

Mr Barnes spotted her and ran his overweight body over to her, grabbing her around the neck, as she cowered with fear as to what he was going to do to her.

"You'd better be a good girl and get your husband to get my drugs and you won't get hurt my dear," Mr Barnes grappled with her, trying desperately to free herself from his strong grasp.

Gunshots are still ringing out in the hallway, as Paul managed to peer around the pillar and shoot the other burly bodyguard dead.

He came out from behind the pillar, seeing the man he's just shot sprawled out, Charlie next to him and as he sees Charlie, he shoots Paul in the chest, Paul then manages to shoot Charlie dead with two bullets, one of them to the head, whilst clutching his own chest from the bullet that hit him.

Paul staggered into the lounge, his hand clutching his wound, trying to stop the flow of blood pouring from it, to see that the fire had caught hold, and half of the house is partially ablaze, the fire is spreading.

He then spots the evil drug lord having Alice around the neck, but she was still trying to break free from him, as Paul collapses onto a wall in the room and drops to the floor, but manages to hold the gun in Mr Barnes' direction, but slowly starting to lose consciousness due to his wound.

"Just go get me my drugs Arnold and let us be done with it."

Paul smirks, his eyes starting to close, he was drifting in and out of consciousness, his hand swaying with the gun, still pointing in Mr Barnes' direction.

Alice manages to grab Mr Barnes' arm and bites it, freeing his grip on her, she pulls herself away and over towards the dying Paul.

Paul shoots at the drug lord, with him being a sitting duck, the first bullet hitting him in the chest.

Just as the bullets were flying, the Spanish girls were heading back and saw that the farmhouse was practically ablaze and had also heard the first gunshot.

They dropped the shopping bags and raced up towards the windows, cowering down to see what was happening inside.

"Hay gente muerta adentro," (there are dead people inside) a shocked Maria said to Gabriela, "rapido *necesitamos liberar a los animals,"* (quick we need to release the animals) as they kept low beneath the windows so as not to get spotted.

They manage to open the chicken coop as they all flee from the burning building, followed by the release of the pigs, sheep and horses, the fire now starting to rage, they too decide to run for their lives, leaving whoever was inside to fend for themselves, they were too scared to go and help, they didn't feel there would be anything they could do, the fire was far too intense.

Detective Buchanan suddenly pulled up outside the

farmhouse, having made enquiries in Lunshill as to the possible whereabouts of Paul and races out of his car, just as he hears another gunshot going off, Mr Barnes is also now dead.

The detective races in, and sees Alice snuggling up to Paul, who is now close to death himself.

"Get out Alice, the house is about to burn to the ground…GET OUT…NOW!"

"But, what about Paul and the others?" she cried.

"I'm going to watch Paul die before I get out, he killed my wife Stacey so, do yourself a favour and get the FUCK out of here, before it's too late."

Alice looked at him in shock at what he had just said to her but did as he said and ran out of the house while she could, and towards a waiting car, Charlie's car, the keys were still in the ignition.

She opened the car door, got in and drove away as fast as she could, not being a driver, she drove it as best she could, looking in her rear-view mirror to see if the Detective had managed to escape, before seeing the house finally succumb to the fire, not knowing if the Detective had managed to escape or not, but, she was finally free, but started to cry, realising that Paul was probably dead.

She dried her eyes and drove as quickly as she could towards Barnwood, and to the house that Paul and Sarah shared.

She stopped, left the engine running, and opened the door, to see Sarah sitting waiting for her, suitcase already packed.

"Is he dead? Sarah asked Alice.

"Yes, he is, the plan worked."

"Right, come on, we need to go, get out of here, before anyone finds us, and realises what we have done," Sarah smiled at her, Alice goes to embrace her, she had missed her so much.

"Where are we going to go darling?" Alice was unsure where they could hide.

"I don't know yet, but it will be fun finding out won't it," Sarah smiles, as they head out of the house, leaving the door open and lights on, and get into the waiting car, Sarah decides to drive, as she was a driver herself before the car pulled away and into the darkness, to head into the unknown.

This book is printed on paper from sustainable sources managed under the Forest Stewardship Council (FSC) scheme.

It has been printed in the UK to reduce transportation miles and their impact upon the environment.

For every new title that Troubador publishes, we plant a tree to offset CO_2, partnering with the More Trees scheme.

For more about how Troubador offsets its environmental impact, see www.troubador.co.uk/sustainability-and-community